FIRST ACTION BUREAU

DAMAGED GOODS

Richard Yarrow

FIRST ACTION BUREAU

DAMAGED GOODS

By Richard James

Anderson Entertainment Limited
The Corner House, 2 High Street, Aylesford, Kent, ME20 7BG

Damaged Goods by Richard James

Hardcover edition published
by Anderson Entertainment in 2024.

http://www.gerryanderson.com

ISBN: 978-1-914522-35-2

Editorial director: Jamie Anderson
Cover design: Rob White
Typeset by Rajendra Bisht Singh

Table of Contents

Foreword

I believe it was just before Christmas 2019 when Jamie Anderson and I finally sat down over a gloriously greasy breakfast at my favourite café in Dorset to discuss the ideas we'd been ruminating about, over email and FaceTime, for a brand-new Anderson 'IP'. We wanted it to be a hard-edged adventure range, futuristic but dealing with current themes. Strong characters and a ruthless, complicated female lead – we also hoped that Genevieve Gaunt would play her!

Jamie was (and still is) fascinated with the notion of 'deep fake'. It was very much new territory back then so we talked a lot about it over our bacon, eggs, black pudding, fried bread and incongruously genteel decaffeinated tea. When I finally understood the notion, I suggested we did a kind of spy/assassin story. Spies are cool, aren't they? And I'm not. And surely one of the main reasons for writing is to live out impossible fantasies.

We appropriated the name Nero Jones from a top secret, random source and Jamie started formulating plot ideas about an organisation fighting against an insidious force. Immediately that was the Gerry Anderson stamp, getting the vibe of Spectrum and SHADO (from Captain Scarlet and the Mysterons and UFO, respectively). But there we wanted to comparison to end.

As far as I remember, the organisation's name, First Action Bureau – FAB, came straight from Jamie's head, almost as though he'd been waiting his whole life to say it! We started riffing on the idea of fragile, unreliable memory and ultimately fake realities, and how our characters would discern the minutest of clues to work out what was real and what was not.

Our method for working was simple, Jamie created stuff and I rewrote it. He roughed out a plot, sent it to me, and then I added elements, deleted some, and did some restructuring. My recollection is that Jamie was happy with this process. Mind you, in his version of reality – and let's face it, how will we ever know what's real or fake these days? – he may be railing against my unjust and crass interference. We shall never know as I've personally made sure he's currently engaged on another mission rather than writing his own introduction to this FAB novel.

The scripting proceeded in very much the same way. Jamie wrote what he called a rough (or 'sh*t' as he called it) script and I dived in and retooled it a bit, adding depth, intrigue and character. A lot of the rough was so good that I kept it – and then get confused when reading a scene which began, *'We've got to do something clever and argue a bit here…'* I'd thinking to myself, 'What on earth is he doing? And then I'd realise, 'Of course, this bit hasn't been filled in yet'.

Jamie and I chuckled a lot about all this over numerous FaceTime calls until we finally arrived at a script that we loved.

As this was during the days of lockdown, we recorded remotely with me directing and the cast present in the same session – there was great rapport between everyone. One of my strongest recollections is of Paterson Joseph having an intermittently faulty audio interface, which meant that periodically a growing, hissing sound of white noise would slowly fade in and engulf him. He took it all in his stride and would say, "Oh, hold on, the tide's coming in again!". Then we'd be back to normal and off we'd go. The rest is, well, available as a CD box set or download. I shamelessly suggest you check it out!

But maybe that hissing sound was the resetting of reality – in which case none of this may have happened at all…

Nicholas Briggs, September 2023

RICHARD JAMES

White walls.
Sterile.
Clinical.
A metal chair.
Straps.
A figure, bending. Leaning forwards.
An instrument. A tool.
No, a blade.
Pain.
A harsh light.
Pain.
A scream. Mine?
I scream.
So much pain.
It's done.
My brain is a fog.
A question forms.
From the fog, a question.
Who
am
I?

1

Valentine's Day

The sky was so blue, it looked like a painting. It seemed to hang, suspended behind the London skyline. Familiar landmarks pierced the clear air. Private Hoverjets criss-crossed their way from one horizon to the other, their pilots tasked with delivering their passengers to yet another meeting in the shortest possible time.

Below them, the River Thames snaked its way lazily through the city. It bisected the capital almost perfectly. To the south lay the financial heart of the city. The northern half was home to countless cranes that lifted and spun their heavy loads in a sleepless frenzy. The race was on to rebuild the city after the devastation of recent decades.

'And to your left, you can see New St Paul's Cathedral. It was erected on exactly the same site as the old building in 2038, following the first wave of…'

The boat sped under yet another bridge. Zoe looked around at her fellow travellers. None of them were paying much attention to the recorded commentary. Instead, they stared through the windows at the view or gazed into each other's eyes. Stupidly, she'd forgotten it was Valentine's Day. The boat was almost entirely populated with young lovers, leaning against each other as it sliced silently along the course of the Thames. The water beneath was inky black beneath a bright February sky. Zoe glanced at the young woman by her side. Akari shuffled nervously, unsure where to look.

'Sorry,' Zoe whispered, tugging at her coat sleeve. 'Forgot. I thought we'd have it to ourselves.'

Akari smiled. 'Just so long as you're not expecting champagne and roses.'

'Not on a first date,' Zoe teased. 'But definitely next time.'

She was beginning to love Akari's smile. Her eyes seemed to light up from within. It was early days, but Zoe had a good feeling about this one. If only she could tell Akari the truth.

The boat raced around a bend in the river. As the Tower of London came into view, Zoe's eyes fell on the one man on board who stood apart from everyone else. The only passenger who wasn't part of a couple. She had been watching him ever since the boat had left the jetty. Conspicuously alone, he stood near the aft doors, his arms folded across his chest. He had a square jaw and dark, forbidding eyes. In the twelve minutes duration of the journey so far, Zoe noticed he had barely looked at the view at all. Her suspicions were roused.

'You know,' Akari was saying, 'I never knew London could be so romantic.'

'Mm hmm,' Zoe answered, absently. She was thinking back to when she had first seen the man by the door.

It was in the security queue at the jetty. Concentrating hard, Zoe fought to remember the tiniest of details, certain they would explain just why she was feeling so nervous. There had been lots of couples in the queue, of course. And they had all seemed *really* into each other. She had felt a pang of guilt about her date with Akari and squeezed her hand to make herself feel better. Was she stringing her along? Probably. Any relationship was difficult to maintain in her line of work. Most people just couldn't bear the lies.

She had already surveyed the crowd for potential threats, a habit she could never break even when not on duty. An old couple huddling together against the sharp February wind. A younger pair gazing meaningfully into each other's eyes. A nearby VidScreen flickered into life. Hearts, balloons and kissing couples were played on a loop to get the passengers in the mood. Feeling suddenly awkward, Zoe tried not to meet Akari's gaze. Was this overkill? She wouldn't have blamed Akari if she had made her excuses and left. After all, that's exactly what Zoe had felt like doing.

Each passenger in turn had been directed through the security arch before boarding. It scanned their full length, effectively sniffing for signs of incendiary devices. Intricate sensors looked for the signatures of every known explosive chemical. X-rays were aimed at prospective passengers for signs of suspicious packages. The machine even assessed heart rates and stress hormone levels. Any telltale change in behaviour, a furtive glance or a single bead of sweat, would be enough to set the alarms blaring. Zoe had sighed as she watched the queue snake aboard. The population was repeatedly assured that these measures were necessary for their safety, but she couldn't help thinking they were also required for their control. They had been installed just about everywhere since the Dheghomite Campaign had begun. As a result, the terrorists had been forced to find ever more inventive ways of evading them.

She had watched as the man shuffled along the line, finally reaching the head of the queue in front of the security arch. Zoe had thought there was something suspicious in his lack of reaction as he was waved through by a uniformed attendant. No smile of thanks, no look of anticipation at the journey ahead. It was as if he was devoid of all emotion. A trick to get through, undetected?

Zoe concentrated harder. That wasn't enough to explain her unease. What had she seen? She thought back to the moment the man had passed through the arch. From her position behind him in the queue, Zoe had been able to catch his reflection in a side window in the boat ahead. Focusing his eyes straight ahead of him, the man had walked through, coolly and calmly. Just as the scan had begun, however, Zoe had noticed a movement. It had seemed innocuous enough, but perhaps this was what had caused her disquiet. Pausing briefly for the scan, the man had raised a hand to adjust a button on his coat.

As she remembered this telling detail, Zoe squeezed Akari closer to her, almost instinctively readying herself for action. Turning, Akari gave her a smile, misreading her sudden alertness as a plea for attention.

'This is perfect,' she sighed. 'Thank you.'

Zoe nodded, trying to stay calm. She brushed her Spi-Glasses in a studiedly casual gesture, activating their zoom feature. Something else she hadn't told Akari about.

As the digital image sharpened, Zoe could see the button was subtly different to the others on the coat. Attempts had been made to make it look as near identical as possible, but there were tiny variations in its dimensions and material. It was also giving off a small electronic signature. Zoe blinked to request a readout. A series of numbers scrolled before her eyes. It was a jamming signal. Zoe was suddenly tense. If the man had activated a jamming signal before passing through the scanner, he must have had something to hide.

'Oh, Tower Bridge!' Zoe heard Akari whisper with excitement. 'Come closer to the window and look!'

Zoe followed her to the front of the boat, where they squeezed through the crowd to get a better view. *There must be thirty people in here*, Zoe realised, anxiously. Should she try to convince a few of them to rush him? She quickly dismissed the thought. If, as she suspected, he was carrying something, it would make no difference.

'Emergency stop,' she said absently.

'Huh?'

Zoe looked at Akari. 'The boat's automated, but there must be a way to stop it.'

'Stop it?' Her companion's eyes were wide. 'Why would you want to stop it? Aren't you enjoying yourself?'

Zoe could see she looked hurt. She glanced around quickly for any means of exit. Nothing. The man was standing directly in front of the only escape route. It looked like he knew exactly what he was doing. She scanned the walls for signs of a comms pad. Perhaps she could talk to someone at flight control. Get them to stop the pod.

'Is everything all right, young lady?' An elderly man with an ancient camera slung round his neck was eyeing her, nervously.

'Oh, she's fine,' Akari jumped in, quickly. 'She's just afraid of the water.' She smiled pointedly at Zoe. 'Isn't that right, honey?'

Zoe nodded. She couldn't risk a whole boat full of people panicking. Her gaze fell on the man by the door.

'What's the matter with you, Zoe?' she heard Akari ask. 'You look wired.' Her eyes narrowed, suspiciously. 'Did you take something before the trip?' Akari squeezed her companion playfully round the waist, and Zoe struggled to disentangle herself.

'Okay, babe,' muttered Akari resentfully as she drew away. 'I know when I'm not wanted. Looks like this date was just one big mistake, huh.'

'It's opening!' cried a nearby voice. A short way ahead, Tower Bridge seemed to split in two and throw its arms into the air in greeting.

The man by the door was smiling.

'Everyone come to the window!' Zoe shouted. Her only hope was to put as much distance between the man and the passengers. She hoped desperately that her instincts were wrong. But then, she knew they never had been before. Zoe patted furiously at her coat, only to find her pockets empty.

'What are you doing?' Akari demanded.

Zoe reached up to kiss her new girlfriend, barely able to contain her emotion. 'I'm sorry,' she whispered. Out of the corner of her eye, she could see the man placing his hand in a pocket.

'Sorry?' Akari was confused. 'Sorry for what?'

Zoe stroked her cheek as she spoke, all too aware that these were their final moments together. 'I'm sorry we didn't meet earlier.' She allowed herself a sob. 'And I'm sorry I didn't pack my gun.'

'Gun?' Akari raised her eyebrows. 'Why would you pack a gun?'

The explosion tore through the boat as it passed beneath the bridge. The resulting fireball engulfed almost the entire span of the Thames. The great arms of the bridge groaned in the shockwave before shearing from their moorings and plummeting to the water. The few tourists that had stopped to enjoy the scene from the upper gantry were enveloped in a sheet of flame.

The bulk of the boat sliced into the river, rolling and twisting under the extreme force of the explosion. It lifted a hump of water before it that washed to the sides of the river and spilled over its defences. Passers-by dived for cover behind the thick embankment walls. Still, debris rained down on them. Hot, twisted metal fell on their unprotected heads. Shards of shattered glass caught the bright winter sun, creating incongruous rainbows in the air as they twisted to Earth. The air was full of screams, the water that sloshed over the walls stained with blood.

Soon, everything settled. The city seemed to take a breath. Great plumes of smoke rose from the bridge to stain the blue sky. The river settled back into its lazy pace as debris and body parts were carried downstream. Then, the screams started again. The *crump* of explosions echoed around the city. Smoke rose on the horizon. Buildings tumbled along the skyline. A pall of dust rose into the air, staining everything a sickly grey. From somewhere nearby came the scream of sirens as emergency vehicles resumed their familiar routine. The military police were suddenly out in force, cordoning off roads and marshalling people off the streets. Armoured vehicles patrolled the wide boulevards. It was a well-practised drill, almost unexceptional. Every day this year had seemed to bring a new atrocity, but this had all the makings of being the biggest yet.

2
Break Out

One hundred and twenty-eight kilometres north of the capital stood a low, forbidding building surrounded by sparse woodland. Hexagonal in shape, it rose just two stories high. The perimeter fence that surrounded it was twice as tall, and the steep-sided ditch beyond that was twice as deep. The only road in or out was flanked by two tall towers manned at all times by guards, Tase Pistols at the ready. Built as part of the government's Youth Correction Programme, it was home to six hundred young adults who had been deemed 'at risk' of radicalisation. In many cases, this was simply shorthand for 'difficult to understand' or 'badly behaved'.

Just as she had done for the last two hundred and seventy-eight days, Nero Jones woke to the sound of the morning alarm blaring from the speaker by her cell door. She pulled the pillow over her head as she waited for the alarm to end, then threw it to the floor with a scream. Angling her head, she squinted through the bars of her window to the sky beyond. It was still dark. The strip light above her flickered on and off for a few seconds before settling on an unrelenting glare. Nero squeezed her eyes tight shut. Despite the government's insistence that the Dump *wasn't* a prison, it sure felt like a prison to her. Taking a breath to steel herself, she swung her legs to the floor and sat for a moment, her head hanging almost to her knees. Then, she remembered. Today was the day she would escape.

'Rise and shine!' said Meena cheerily.

Nero groaned. She had heard the same phrase every day for the last nine months, delivered in the same jolly way. But still, she couldn't hate Meena for it. She was in many ways, the perfect cellmate. Chatty, but sensitive enough to know when to shut up. Persistent, but wise enough to know when to back off. Self-sufficient, but clever enough to know when to ask for help. Nero had grown to love her like a sister. Or, at least, how she *imagined* she might have loved a sister.

'It's your turn with the bucket,' Meena was saying as she dangled her legs from the top bunk.

'You try that every morning,' Nero smiled.

Meena jumped to the ground, her long, plaited ponytail swinging behind her. 'One day you might fall for it,' she beamed. Meena had a smile that could get away with murder. Nero never understood how she could look so hot so early in the morning.

'You know you were talking in your sleep?' Meena teased. 'You seemed pretty excited.' She leaned towards Nero with a grin. 'Who is Hudson? And is he worth it?'

Nero reached for her pillow and buried her head in its soft folds for comfort. 'Leave me alone,' she pleaded, but she couldn't hide her smile.

Meena was jabbing at her, playfully. 'Did he break your heart? Or did you break his?' She suddenly pushed Nero back on her bunk and pinched her about the waist. 'He obviously made you feel very happy. You almost woke the whole wing!'

Nero swung her pillow over her head and rammed it into her friend's face with a squeal. Another alarm sounded. Nero could hear the grating sound of every door on her landing springing open. Calming music filled the air.

'Brahms, Symphony Number Three,' she muttered as she stretched her neck with a crack.

'Opium for the masses,' Meena added, standing up to straighten the sheets on her bunk. 'God forbid they ever play anything exciting.'

With a sigh of resolve, Nero reached for her towel and made for the door.

'Don't forget the bucket!' she called over her shoulder.

'Don't *you* forget Hudson!' Meena teased back.

As she stepped into the corridor, Nero felt herself jostled from behind. A small kid with wiry hair turned to snarl at her as he passed.

'Watch where you're going, Jones.'

Nero put her head down and quickened her pace.

There were guards positioned at regular intervals along her route to the showers. As her fellow residents (as the government called them) spilled from their cells, she joined a tide of young men and women who had been similarly rudely awoken. Their tousled hair and crumpled faces bore all the marks of a disturbed sleep. Some had bruises on their necks and faces. At least one had been crying. As they shuffled along the corridor, she was bumped and jostled by those who had already had their showers and were on their way back to their cells. The early shift. They had already been up an hour. After breakfast in the canteen, their day would bring what every other day had brought. Exercise, citizenship lessons, counselling. Every spark of resistance would be pinched out. Only when they were considered model citizens would they be released back to their families. Nero shuddered at the thought.

She kept her head down to avoid eye contact. Except for Meena, Nero had cultivated no friends since being admitted to the programme. It was a deliberate tactic. Friendship led to compromise, intimate knowledge and betrayal. She had learned to keep people at arm's-length. Especially the counsellors. They had poked and probed every corner of her consciousness, determined to root out the green shoots of individuality. As a result, she had retreated back, deeper into the darker recesses. She felt safer there. Only Meena had been let into the dark corners. Nero had trusted her. She had dark corners of her own.

'Step it up, Jones!' Nero felt fingers jab into the small of her back. 'Smells to me like your shower can't come soon enough.'

'Let it go, Tank,' Nero snarled. 'Or I'm gonna shove your soap somewhere it'll never get clean.'

'Fine by me, baby!' Tank jeered as he pulled himself up to his full height. He was almost as wide as he was tall.

'Quiet!' boomed a guard, and the crowd bumped on.

Soon enough, Nero could smell the soap in the air and feel the steam from the showers on her skin. The air became thick and warm, a welcome relief from the bitter cold of the corridor. A shoulder glanced against the side of her head. Nero raised a hand instinctively, dropping her towel to the floor. The Princess stood before her. Even dressed in regulation overalls, she lived up to her nickname. She was tall and willowy with a nose held so high in the air, Nero was sure she would drown in a rainstorm.

'What's up, Princess?' Nero asked, rubbing her cheek. She was sure it was going to bruise. 'Is the air getting thin up there?'

'Oh hello, down there,' The Princess retorted to sniggers from her entourage. They were the most impressionable of the residents. They buzzed around The Princess like wasps round a picnic, eager for whatever crumb she'd throw their way. 'You should be more careful,' she smiled through a row of jewel-encrusted teeth. 'One day you're gonna get stepped on bad. Just like all the other slugs.' The Princess tossed her hair from her shoulders and walked away with her entourage in tow. Nero bent to pick up her towel and shuffled into the shower block. If anyone had been watching, they might just have noticed the faintest of smiles playing on her lips.

As she turned the corner, she was faced with the same, low-ceilinged room that had greeted her every morning. Rows of cubicles lined the walls, flimsy curtains barely concealing those showering inside. A haze of steam hung in the air. Nero looked around as her fellow residents filed into the room and headed for available showers. This was the only place in the entire building not under surveillance, which made it the perfect place to effect her escape. She knew she had only moments.

Finding an empty cubicle, she pulled the curtain behind her. Reaching over the shower tray she punched at the pressure pad, jumping back just as a spray of water fell from the ceiling. To anyone who happened to be interested, it would sound like she was showering with the rest of her wing.

Nero suddenly thought of Meena. Her only friend in the Dump, but even she didn't know Nero's plan. She waved away a sudden pang of guilt at keeping her friend in the dark. It had been necessary, Nero told herself. She'd understand.

Reaching into her trouser pocket, she took out a tiny laser cutter. It had been placed there by the small kid with wiry hair as Nero had stepped from her cell. It had cost her, but it was just what she had ordered. She placed it on the bench before her, then reached to the small of her back. She peeled two MagPads from her skin. Sticky on one side and magnetic on the other, they were used in the workshops to hold tools to the wall. Good old Tank. She knew his work in the metalshop would come in useful. Finally, she reached into the folds of her towel. A plain dinner knife nestled in the middle. Stolen from the canteen kitchen, it had been dropped there by The Princess as the towel had fallen to the ground. Nero sighed. If this didn't work out, she'd be short of funds for months. Contraband costs.

Peering through the curtain, Nero saw everyone was safely out of view. She pulled the bench from her cubicle and carried it carefully to the centre of the room, placing it directly beneath the extractor vent. Standing on the bench, she used the knife to gingerly loosen the screws fixing the cover to the ceiling. It swung down on its hinges. Nero looked up. She could see the fan whirring at speed above her. She swallowed. The vent was just big enough to take her, but it would be tight. Slapping the MagPads on each of her hands, she reached up to make contact with the sides of the chute. The adhesive pulled at her skin as she hauled herself up, but the magnetic pads held fast against the metal. Kicking furiously against the air, she peeled one hand away then planted it again several centimetres further up. Nero's heart was racing. She knew she didn't have long. At last, she felt her feet make contact with metal. Bracing herself against the sides of the shaft, she kicked at the swinging cover to slam it shut behind her. It should hold for long enough. The fan whirled just centimetres from her face. Squinting at her watch, she counted down the seconds to the agreed time. With a splutter, the fan slowed to a stop. She had paid off the janitor with her food rations, but she still wasn't sure she could trust him.

Working fast, Nero pulled the laser cutter from her pocket to free the blades from their fittings. One by one they fell free until just the central spoke remained. She gave it a hefty tug and the entire mechanism was dislodged. It left a gap smaller than the shaft itself, but the smell of fresh air and the glimmer of light beyond gave Nero all the impetus she needed. Slamming her MagPads against the metal and bracing her knees against the walls below her, she made her way slowly through the gap, expelling all the air in her lungs to make her body even smaller.

At last, she reached a kink in the shaft. Wriggling round, she gave a final heave and found herself falling several feet through the open air. She was on the roof. Peeling the MagPads from her palms, she threw them to one side and rolled onto her stomach. Inching painfully across the coarse gravel, she stopped by the corner where the main dormitory block met the gymnasium. From her time in the yard outside, Nero knew this was just about the only section of the building out of sight of surveillance cameras. Reaching down, she untied several lengths of cord that she had fastened together round her waist the night before. She had collected them during a shift at the laundry. Nero allowed herself a smile at the thought of certain inmates seeing their trousers drop to the floor as the bell rang for lights out that evening. But that was hours away. She'd be long gone by then. Tying one end to the guttering, Nero lowered herself slowly from the roof. Finding her makeshift rope hadn't been made quite long enough, she dropped the last few feet and scurried for the shadows. Pressing herself against the outer wall of the gymnasium, she glanced around her. There were no inmates in the yard this early in the morning. And no inmates meant no guards.

A collection of refuse containers stuck out from the building, meaning Nero had somewhere to hide for half the distance to the perimeter fence. Beyond that, she would be in the open. Clutching at the laser cutter, Nero ducked between the containers. Inching her way out into the yard, she glanced again at her watch. Looking up, she could just make out the main entrance, flanked by two watchtowers. The Monday provisions delivery was regular as clockwork. And today, for Nero's sake, it needed to be.

Right on cue, three trucks appeared through the trees. They slowed as they reached the checkpoint, and Nero could hear the drivers engaging in conversation with the guards. The men positioned on the watchtowers leaned over the railings to hear, throwing down remarks of their own.

There was a peal of laughter. Nero knew this was her chance. With the guards distracted, she ran low across the open ground towards the perimeter. Throwing herself to the ground, she raised her laser cutter to the meshed fence. With a flick of a switch, a beam of ultra-heated light began slicing through the wire.

Almost at once, the alarm sounded. Nero froze.

'Okay, Jones,' came a voice from behind her. 'I think that's far enough.'

Her heart pounding, Nero looked back to see two guards with their Tase Pistols raised. She glanced ahead of her. She was almost through the fence, but there was the ditch beyond that. She'd never make it. Letting go her breath, Nero let her face drop to the dirt.

'We tracked you all the way.' One of the guards tapped his goggles. 'Heat sensitive. We had you the moment you got on the roof.'

Nero exhaled. 'Shit.'

A third man pushed his way forward. The governor. 'Don't worry, Jones,' he smiled. 'Things are looking up.' He extended a hand to help her to her feet. 'You're going home.'

'You've lost weight.'

Her mother looked at her with a judgmental gaze. Nero was confused. Why had they released her when they had caught her trying to escape? It was almost impossible to believe she was on her way home. The forest had given way to open countryside. Nero suddenly realised she had no idea where she had spent the last nine months. She smiled at the criticism.

'The food was terrible.'

'As was your behaviour, it seems,' Helene barked back. 'I had weekly reports from the governor.' She leaned forwards in her seat, her mouth thin and cruel. 'I'm not sure you learned anything.'

Nero shrugged. 'I learned how to piss in a bucket.'

Helene snorted with disdain.

'How's Hudson?' Nero asked.

'He's appreciated being looked after properly,' her mother sneered. 'You start college again on Monday. You'll be supervised for the first two weeks.'

'Great.'

'They'll be looking for all the usual signs.'

Nero rolled her eyes. 'Inappropriate activity, disrespect for authority, delinquency.' All the things she excelled at.

'Hopefully, you'll keep a low profile from now on.' Helene sighed. 'Now is not a good time to be put in the spotlight.'

As the driverless car moved onto the hyperway, Nero felt the engine engage its full power. Dampeners kept the forces of acceleration to a minimum in the cabin, but she was aware of the sudden thrust of powerful electric motors.

'And there's another curfew, so that should help you keep out of trouble.'

Helene leaned forward to snap on the VidScreen. The view outside the windscreen dissolved to footage from a rolling news channel. A reporter sat gloomily behind a desk as pictures of destruction played behind him.

"London is on a war footing this morning as the city wakes to the aftermath of several terrorist attacks. While the authorities consider imposing martial law for the third time this year, a video message reported to be from the perpetrators has been released to all news outlets, including this one." The picture changed to show a sinister, artificially generated face. It reminded Nero of a villain from the old animations she had watched as a kid.

"Citizens of the world," came a rumbling, distorted voice, "we have no quarrel with you. Last night's attacks were against your governments and their unfaltering progress towards an unsustainable future. The Earth cries out in anguish, and we must hear her." Images of devastation scrolled across the screen. Glaciers melting, bush fires burning, animations of bacteria multiplying.

"Humankind is a virus." The strange face was replaced with a logo. "We are the vaccine."

Helene punched at the controls and the screen snapped off. The hyperway sped past them.

'What do they want?' Nero asked.

Helene gazed out the window. 'Nobody knows. But it's a dangerous world out there.'

The car slowed to exit the hyperway. Nero could see some London landmarks in the distance. She was amazed by just how much the skyline had changed since she had last seen it. New skyrise blocks pierced the sky. Communication masts stood tall and straight as needles. She noticed, too, that some buildings that she remembered were missing.

Hanging a left at Marble Arch, the car turned into Great Cumberland Place. Nero saw scores of people lining the streets. They held homemade placards with slogans written in garish colours. As the car passed by, she pressed her forehead against the window to read them.

'Kill the Virus!'

'The Earth Cries Out!'

'We are the Vaccine!'

Nero could hear the sound of drums beating and people chanting. Their faces were smeared with colour or made up to represent skulls. Their clothes were ragged and torn. A tall man, clearly the leader of the rabble, blew on a whistle and led the mob in a call and response. Some looked more committed than others, but the overall atmosphere was one of barely contained chaos. Nero could sense that violence was just a provocation away.

'Are they taking sides with the terrorists?' she gasped.

'They're easily led,' Helene spat with disdain. 'Dispossessed and disenfranchised. Empty minds looking for a cause.'

'Are they allowed to protest like that?'

'There's your answer.'

Helene nodded through the windscreen. Nero craned her neck to see a fleet of military response vehicles rumbling towards them. A helicopter kept watch from the skies, its guns plainly visible against the fuselage.

Nero sat back in her seat. Perhaps she had been better off in the Dump after all.

At last, they drew up outside a smart house in Portman Place. The car parked itself on the drive and plugged itself into the charging port. Nero reached back to grab her bag as the gullwing doors swung open.

Hudson was barking from the side gate. Nero smiled. At least someone was pleased to see her. Unhitching the gate, she fell to her knees and held her arms wide. The excitable German Shepherd came bounding towards her, licking her face with enthusiastic yelps as she giggled helplessly.

'Go and unpack your things,' Helene snapped. 'We'll eat soon.'

With that, she walked in the house, leaving the door wide for Nero to follow. Shutting the gate behind her, Nero gave a final wave to Hudson and heaved her bag onto her shoulder.

The house was just as she had left it. Clean and tidy. Everything in its place. It always reminded Nero of one of those show houses used to entice prospective buyers. It had never looked lived in, so it had never felt like a home. Sounds of industry wafted from the kitchen. Helene was already busy cooking. Nine months away, and her mother had barely looked pleased to see her. Nothing changes, Nero thought. As she walked to the back of the house, she heard the soft click of a HooverBot. It whirred from its housing by the door to clean up the dust she had brought in on her shoes. Her presence seemed an annoyance to the house itself.

With a sigh, Nero shuffled her way to her room at the back of the house. It was the room that received the least light in the whole building, yet Helene insisted that she spend untold hours there, slaving over her college work. The air-con snapped on as Nero opened the door.

She gasped.

Silhouetted against the open window, she saw a man sitting on her bed. He smiled broadly as she felt herself caught in a moment of indecision. Should she call for her mother?

'Hello, Nero,' the man said, at last. 'Don't be afraid. I just want to talk.'

3

The Recruit

'Shut the door behind you.'

Nero's heart was pounding. 'Who are you?'

'My name is Nathan Drake,' the man said. 'It won't mean anything to you.'

'Why shouldn't I scream right now?'

Drake nodded. 'You could. And the police would be called and I would be taken away. And you'd never know.'

'Know what?'

'What I was offering.'

Nero was thinking hard.

'If I meant any harm, wouldn't you know by now?'

Drake was a squat, middle-aged man with a bald dome of a head and dark, piercing eyes. Nero calculated she could use his size against him if he tried to rush her. And he seemed unarmed. Finally making up her mind, she closed the door behind her with a soft click.

'Good,' soothed Drake, approvingly. 'Now, shall we talk?'

Nero flicked her eyes to the open window. 'Does my mother know you're here?'

Drake shook his head. 'No one knows I'm here.'

'How did you get past Hudson?'

'Pheromone spray.' Drake held up a small, plastic bottle. 'He loves me now.'

'What do you want?'

'Why don't you sit down?'

Nero raised an eyebrow. 'You think I should sit on my bed with a strange man twice my age?'

Drake nodded. 'Sorry. Didn't think it through.'

'What do you want?' Nero repeated, swinging her bag to the floor and doing her best to look defiant.

'That's easy,' Drake said. 'You. Or, at least, your expertise.'

Expertise? Had this guy even come to the right place? Nero had no expertise in anything, except perhaps in knowing how to get out of trouble. But then, she was also an expert at getting *into* trouble in the first place.

'Go on,' she said.

Drake cleared his throat. 'I guess you've seen the news?'

'The bombs?' Nero nodded. 'I saw it in the car. Protestors, too.'

'The world has changed since you've been away, Nero. The old certainties are no longer quite so certain.'

'I was never too keen on the old certainties anyway,' Nero huffed. Just where was this heading?

'Everything we take for granted is at risk. The modern world itself.'

'The terrorists?' Nero's interest was piqued.

'Dheghomites. They're a cult-like terrorist group with a death wish. Trouble is, they want to take the rest of us with them.'

'What do they want?'

'To kill you.'

Nero's blood ran cold.

'And me,' Drake continued, 'and ninety per cent of the world's population. Everyone, in fact, except members of their own sect.'

Nero swallowed. 'How?'

'Anyway they can.'

Drake let the silence hang in the air, giving time for Nero to think.

'What can I do about it?' she asked, plaintively.

Drake rose from the bed and walked to close the window. He gestured through the glass, a subtle nod to someone outside that all was okay.

'Recently, they've upped their game. Over the last few months they've sabotaged the energy grid, tried to hack our defence mainframe and even attempted an assassination on the Prime Minister.'

Nero's eyes were wide. She'd been away a *long* time.

'And now the bombing campaign. They're calling it a new St Valentine's Day Massacre. A series of explosions on or near landmarks around the world. We lost one of our best agents at Tower Bridge.'

'Why?' Nero was still at a loss to explain what this man was doing in her bedroom.

'They want to bomb us into the Stone Age.'

Another silence.

'The Dheghomites look on the human race as a virus. Literally, a virus on the face of the Earth. Propagating, multiplying.'

'We are the vaccine,' Nero said, almost to herself.

Drake nodded. 'They believe technology has enabled humankind to outgrow themselves. That we, as a species, should have been self-limiting, like fish in a pond. But tech has allowed us to proliferate. To overreach ourselves. And the planet is suffering.'

'The Earth cries out.' Nero remembered the slogans on the protestors' placards.

'If a virus proliferates, the host dies,' Drake continued. 'That's what they believe we're doing to the Earth.'

Nero couldn't hide her sympathies. 'That's a good cause to die for.'

'Maybe,' Drake agreed. 'But not to kill for.'

'Remind me,' Nero said suddenly. 'Just why are you here?'

Drake turned to look her in the eye. 'We need you. And people like you.'

'We?'

Drake took a breath. 'I'm from the First Action Bureau. You won't have heard of us.'

'A man I don't know from something I won't have heard of.' Nero scoffed. 'You might want to look at your recruitment technique.'

'We specialise in predicting criminal activity before it occurs.'

'How?'

'Big data collected over decades. Internet chatter and behavioural analytics tied to quantum artificial intelligence.'

'Neat. But none of that helped you yesterday.'

'We were a sleeper agency until last night. Operating in the shadows. Now, following the attacks, we've been given the green light.'

'By who?'

Drake puffed out his cheeks. 'I'm impressed, Nero. You're asking all the right questions.

'So, answer them.'

Drake sat back down on the corner of the bed. 'We're global. Funded by international agencies with branches all over the world. All going online as we speak.'

'And why me?'

'To put it simply, you've got what it takes.' Drake looked suddenly apologetic. 'We've been watching you.'

'The Dump?'

Drake nodded. 'It's full of the sort of people we need. And you're the best of them. Resourceful, courageous, careful.'

'Careful enough to get caught escaping,' Nero scoffed. Drake smiled. 'But clever enough to try.'

Suddenly it all made sense. Nero had been wondering why she had been released after being caught attempting to escape. It should have cost her a week in solitary. Instead, she'd found herself homeward bound.

Drake pulled an electronic slate from an inside jacket pocket and jabbed at the screen. 'You've had a busy few months.' He pulled up a list. 'A total of fourteen days in solitary for organising multiple wing rebellions. Various punishments for questioning authority, sanctions for critical thinking.' He slipped the slate back into his jacket. 'In short, you're just what I need. You were taken to the Dump to make you a model citizen. Turns out, they made you into the perfect spy.'

'Spy?' Nero was enthralled.

Drake shrugged. 'To all intents and purposes. Working with our intel, you'll intercept the Dheghomites' schemes before they happen. You'll be given the training and the means. Join us, and you'll have all the protections and privileges the Bureau can give you.'

Nero blinked. She was so enrapt that she'd failed to notice she was sitting on the bed after all.

Drake raised his eyebrows. 'What do you say, Nero? Will you help us?'

'My mother – '

'You could tell her the truth.' Drake interrupted. 'Or we could say you've been sent for further behavioural correction.'

Nero rolled her eyes. 'Yeah. She'd buy that.' Drake smiled in sympathy.

'And if I say no?'

Drake shifted uncomfortably before getting to his feet. He walked again to the window. 'You'll spend your whole life behind bars. First, you'll be sent back to the Dump. When you come of age, you'll be moved to a maximum security prison. You'll be in the system indefinitely.'

Nero's eyes blazed. 'You bastard,' she hissed. 'What if I tell the world? Go to the authorities and tell them you threatened me?'

'It won't get you anywhere. The government will deny the Bureau's very existence. And this conversation will never have happened.'

Never have happened? What did he mean by that? How could it have never happened? Before she had a chance to respond, Drake was facing her again.

'Think about it, Nero. We'll give you a few days. Go about your business. Go back to college. But think about it.'

Drake smiled again. It was the same smile, Nero noticed, only now it didn't seem so friendly. He walked to the window and punched at the button on the wall. The glass pane slid up. Before he stepped through, he seemed to have a final thought and turned back into the room.

'Think carefully, Nero. After all, what is it they say? Today is the first day of the rest of your life? It's up to you exactly *which* life.'

Gesturing again to his unseen companion outside, Drake stepped through the window. Shifting her weight, Nero watched as he made his way to the garden gate, patting Hudson playfully on the head as he passed. Nero shook her head to clear it and looked around. The only evidence of the strange man ever having been in her room was a slight depression where he had sat on her bed. As the gate snapped shut behind him, she ran to the window.

'How will you know?' she shouted after him, not caring if her mother heard from the kitchen or not. 'How will you know what I decide?'

She listened carefully for a reply, but all she heard was the whirring of an approaching helicopter, coming to take Nathan Drake back to whatever godforsaken secret agency he worked for.

4

Off the Rails

The next morning, it was like it had never happened. Nero's alarm sounded in the darkness. It took her a while to orientate. She was home, but it didn't feel like it. Half remembered posters on the wall. A wardrobe full of clothes that didn't fit. With a start, she realised this wasn't home at all. It was just somewhere she lived. She missed Meena. What she wouldn't give to hear her now.

'Rise and shine,' she said to herself.

Three loud bangs on the door.

'I hope you're awake?' came Helene's muffled voice.

Nero pulled the covers over her face. 'I'm awake, Mum.'

'You've got thirty minutes,' was the terse reply.

'And good morning to you, too,' Nero murmured.

It felt odd to shower in privacy. After she had dried herself, she found a box of new clothes on her bed. She didn't like any of them. Reaching into her bag, Nero pulled out her regulation issue t-shirt and sweatpants. They smelt of her cell.

As she sat down to eat her breakfast, she heard the front door slam.

'Okay. Bye, then.'

Alone in the house, Nero ate her cereal in silence. She never thought she would miss the mayhem of the Dump. Another alarm sounded from the clock on the wall. Looking up, Nero saw a simple command was displayed on its small screen. LEAVE.

Nero shook her head. 'It's like she's here with me.'

As she collected her things for college, she paused by the stairs. It was almost as if she could hear his voice.

'*Come on up, Nero! The game's set up and ready to go.*' A memory flashed before her eyes. A dice. Some playing pieces. The smell of aftershave. '*Loser cooks for a week!*'

She shook her head as she felt Hudson nuzzling at her hand.

'Good boy,' she soothed. If it wasn't for Hudson, she'd be glad to leave the house. It was full of ghosts. After a quick cuddle with the dog, she clicked the door shut behind her and made her way to the rail stop.

The monorail ran the length of the main roads and across the river to Southwark, rising high over Trafalgar Square. Cars were suspended from a central rail strung between pylons six metres in the air. While the roads below were often gridlocked, the monorail kept the population of London moving with smooth efficiency.

Fastening her coat against the cold wind, Nero climbed the steps to the rail stop and scanned her ID at the gate. It swung open to admit her and she joined the other commuters on the platform. Looking down at the street below, Nero saw that not much had changed. There were new animated billboards at the roadside but, apart from that, it seemed just as it had nine months ago. Nero could barely believe it had been that long since her last journey on the monorail. She still couldn't get used to the feeling of freedom. She knew it was an illusion, of course. She was no more free here than at the Dump. It was just a different sort of prison. She was going back to college, destined to a life of drudgery with no hope of escape. If she was lucky, she'd find a mundane job in some office somewhere. Perhaps her mother would put in a good word for her at the labs. Nero huffed. She doubted it.

Looking up, she saw the pod rounding the corner from Edgware Road. She wasn't looking forward to her first day back at college. How was she expected to catch up on nearly a year's work? Would her education at the Dump count for anything? In truth, she had learned more there than all her previous experiences at school. It just wasn't the sort of thing you'd get certificates for.

The pod came to a stop beside the platform, swinging almost imperceptibly on its connecting arm as the doors hissed open. Stepping aboard, Nero saw it was already packed with commuters.

'Push me again and you'll get my stick in your balls,' she heard an old lady say. Nothing changes, thought Nero. She moved along the length of the pod until she found a space towards the back. She leaned against the curved windows as the doors slid shut and, after a moment, the motors whirred into life. Nero felt the gentle nudge of movement. The pod gained speed quickly, cruising from pylon to pylon with a hum. Nero had twenty minutes to fill until her destination. Putting her buds in her ears, she jabbed at her watch to select some music. A pounding bass rhythm seemed the perfect accompaniment to the unfolding cityscape. Soon she was gazing through the window, but lost in a world of her own.

Just as she turned back from the window, she felt the pod give a lurch. Several of the passengers gasped. Nero snatched her buds from her ears.

'Something's happened,' said the old lady with the stick. 'Up ahead.'

Peering between the heads in front of her, Nero could see a smudge of smoke rising in the air.

'Looks serious,' she heard someone else say. 'We'd better get off at the next stop.'

As they approached the next platform, several of the passengers bent to collect their belongings. The crush of commuters began to shuffle to the door in anticipation of their arrival. But the pod showed no sign of slowing.

'What's going on?'

'Why aren't we stopping?'

Nero's eyes narrowed. This didn't seem right at all. She could see passengers waiting on the raised platform ahead. As the pod approached, they jumped back in surprise. She just had time to catch the looks of astonishment on their faces as they sped past. Several threw up their hands in exasperation.

'Oh, my.' A wiry looking man with long hair was looking straight ahead. The monorail had turned a corner to run parallel with Regent Street, giving everyone aboard a clear view of the crossing over Trafalgar Square. Or, at least, the space where the crossing used to be.

'It's gone,' gasped the old lady.

Nero leaned forward for a better view. Where the monorail had once risen into the air to clear the square, there was now a twisted mass of steaming metal hanging fifty metres above the ground. Any pod attempting to cross it now would plummet to the ground. Nero doubted there would be any survivors.

'Another bomb!' The man sounded as scared as he looked.

'What are we going to do?' shrieked a panicked passenger. 'Why didn't it stop?'

Nero thought fast. 'This line runs in a circle.' She looked up. 'Communications must be sent via the rail. The circuit's been broken, so the pod's receiving no guidance.'

The man with the long hair was standing now, his dark eyes full of fear. 'Well, wh-what do we do?'

'Get the doors open!' screamed a man in a suit.

'And what?' sneered a woman next to him. 'Jump? That's a long way down.'

'Can't we call for help?' offered the old woman, grappling with her phone in her arthritic hands.

'No time,' breathed Nero. 'Before anyone got to us, we'd be making pretty patterns on the pavement.' She noticed the man with the long hair raising a hand to his mouth. 'Sorry,' she whispered.

'How long do you think we've got, young lady?' the old woman asked.

Nero bit her lip as she thought. 'Maybe…' A sudden thought came to her. 'Can you walk without that?' She pointed at the woman's stick.

'Uh, a little,' came the reply.

'Great.' Nero snatched the stick away and turned to face a group of passengers by the rear window. 'Punch that window out. Use whatever you can.'

RICHARD JAMES

'Hey!' wailed the old lady. 'She's got my stick.'

'If you don't let me use this for a few minutes, none of us will be walking out of here anyway. Stick or no stick.'

The woman nodded, but Nero couldn't help notice her reluctance. Some people. Hearing a crack behind her, she turned to see the glass falling from the rear window. Three men had battered it loose with their shoulders.

'Okay,' called Nero above the noise of the rushing air, 'Now give me a hand up.'

'Up?' whimpered the long-haired man. 'You're going… out there?'

Nero looked around. 'Don't see anyone else volunteering.'

The pod was lurching left and right as its speed increased. Some of the passengers screamed.

Nero grabbed at a strap handle to steady herself, then staggered to the rear of the pod.

'I need to get on the roof,' she rasped, ramming the old lady's stick through a belt loop. 'And I need to get there quick.'

Two of the men bent their knees to provide a step up, while other passengers crowded round the window to help Nero up and out. Hands grabbed at her clothes to steady her.

With the wind whipping about her face, Nero looked down to see the ground racing away beneath her. Startled pedestrians screamed as they struggled to make sense of the spectacle. People stepped from their stationary cars to stare in astonishment.

'Get me up!' Nero ordered. 'Push!'

With an effort, the two men gave a heave and Nero struggled for purchase against the smooth metal. Her hands flailing against empty air, she felt herself tipping back and falling from the pod. Hands grabbed at her to stop her descent.

'Try again!' she called, hanging precariously from the window. 'I think I saw a hold!'

She felt herself being swung back and forth until, with another heave, she was launched upwards and towards the roof. Squinting against the rushing air, Nero saw a guard rail running the length of the pod. Stretching forward, she scrambled to get a hold. At last, feeling cold metal beneath her fingers, she grabbed at the rail. Sensing she had a tight enough grip she pulled herself up, kicking her legs behind her to give her some traction against the wind.

Finally, she was crouched on the roof of the pod, keeping a hold of the guard rail as she twisted to see ahead of her. The end of the line was moments away. She could hear screaming from the street below. Crowds were running to Trafalgar Square, eager to see how the drama would end. The pod was rising on its monorail now, lifting up above the surrounding rooftops at a dizzying speed.

Nero grit her teeth and spun round to the connecting arm, almost losing her footing as she did so. Clutching at the wide pole, she looked up to where it connected to the monorail. A box-like contraption housed the motor unit. Nero swallowed hard. She was going to have to climb.

Bracing her knees against the pole, she stretched hand over hand to inch slowly up towards the rail. The metal was smooth and slippery, and Nero grimaced as her fingers took the entire weight of her body. Using the soles of her regulation issue pumps to grip the pole beneath her, she reached down to free the old woman's stick from her belt loops.

'Sorry lady,' she breathed, 'but this need is greater.'

Looking directly up, Nero could see an opening at the front and rear of the motor's housing. Inside, she guessed, a series of wheels gripped the monorail above, turning furiously as the pod sped ever faster. Even with the wind rushing in her ears, she could hear the whine of the motors. Swinging the stick above her head and keeping a tight hold of the pole with her other hand, Nero jabbed at the opening. The end of the stick glanced against metal. *Shit. Missed.* She lunged again. This time, the tip of the stick made contact with the wheels inside. With a scream, Nero leaned her weight against it. She could feel the stick bumping against the monorail. Suddenly, it made its way between the rail and the wheels. It juddered violently in Nero's hand. She kept a tight hold and pushed all the harder. The end of the stick began to split and shatter as the spinning wheels chewed it up. Jammed with wooden splinters, the wheels were finally dislodged. Nero could hear the rasp of metal upon metal. A shower of sparks spat into the air. With a look of grim determination, she jammed the stick home. It was wrenched from her hand with such ferocity that she was sure she must have lost some fingers, but the job was done. As the stick went spinning through the air, the remnant chips of wood made their way deeper into the mechanism, completely dislocating the wheels along one side of the monorail. With a jerk, the pod began to slow. Nero heard another scream of panic from the passengers inside. Holding tight to the arm, she turned around to see their progress towards the shattered rail was slowing. Metre by metre, it came nearer but, centimetre by centimetre, the pod slowed. With a final shudder, it came to a swinging halt, a hand's width from the end of the rail. There was silence.

Suddenly, it became clear to those on the ground that disaster had been averted. The assembled crowd broke into spontaneous applause. Nero screamed with relief, dropped from the pole and banged her foot on the roof of the pod.

'Now, old lady!' she shrieked. 'Now you can call for help.'

She dropped to her knees with relief. Just a few feet away on the statue of Lord Horatio Nelson, a pigeon sat, nonplussed, on his hat. Nero couldn't help laughing at its quizzical expression. Then, her gaze fell to the square beneath. Just by one of the fountains, she was sure she saw someone she recognised; a squat, officious looking man with a bald head watching the unfolding scene. Just as she was about to shout out to him, the man turned his collar up and walked calmly away.

5

Home Sweet Home

'Well, who was he? What did he want?'
Helene didn't look too pleased to be called home from the labs.

'Mum!' Nero wailed. 'I just saved a whole pod full of people!'

Helene's eyes narrowed. 'And why didn't you tell me there was a strange man in our house?'

Nero shrugged. 'I trusted him.'

'You obviously learned nothing at that correctional facility.'

'They said to respect our elders. He was older than me.'

'And now you're some sort of hero.' Exasperated, Helene gestured at the VidScreen in the corner. It was streaming footage of the monorail pod screaming towards Trafalgar Square.

'Sure,' Nero smirked. 'Why not?' The picture changed to Nero hanging onto the pod having brought it to a halt. 'That's not a very flattering angle.'

'Normal people don't get themselves into that kind of mess.'

'It wasn't exactly my fault, Mum. Tell me what I should have done?'

Helene stabbed at the remote and the picture disappeared. She shook her head. 'And now we're part of some sort of investigation.' She had reluctantly picked Nero up from the local military police station near Leicester Square. They had been impressed with her daughter, but cautioned them they would need to ask them some questions in the next few days. 'Why can't you just keep your head down?'

Nero knew what was coming.

'You've been completely out of control since your father left.'

There it was. The reason for everything, at least as far as Helene was concerned.

'You used to be such a compliant child.'

Nero was aghast. 'Since when did children have to be compliant?'

'Since the world changed, Nero.' Her mother rounded on her, her expression somewhere between disappointment and rage. 'We all have to watch our step now. Stay in the shadows and stay out of trouble.' She pointed at the VidScreen. 'You've just got your face on every newscast around the world.'

'So what if they need to ask us a few questions? What do you think they'll find?'

'Whatever they want to find. Before you know it, you'll be blamed for that bomb.'

'Christ, Mum.' Nero puffed out her cheeks. 'When did you get so… *nervy*?'

There was silence as Helene played awkwardly with her fingers. 'It hasn't been easy, Nero,' she said at last.

Her daughter knew what was required of her. These were just like the arguments they'd had before she was sent away. 'I know,' Nero said quietly. She took a breath. 'Perhaps it's best if I move on somewhere else.'

'With that man?' Helene spat.

'No,' Nero said calmly. 'But he's offered me a post.'

'In his fantasy agency?' Helene was at a loss. 'What does he want from you?'

'I don't know,' Nero admitted. 'But I think he sees something in me. Something special.'

'Special is *dangerous*,' her mother cautioned.

'No one's ever wanted me before.'

'Oh Nero, listen to yourself. Try thinking of others for a change. Think of me. Would you really leave me on my own after everything I've been through?'

'I went through it, too,' Nero snapped back. 'Besides, you'll have Hudson.' Nero reached down to scratch the dog behind his ears. He gave an appreciative whimper.

Helene rolled her eyes. 'How do you know you can believe this man?'

'How do you know I can't?'

'He broke into our house!' Helene threw up her arms in exasperation.

'He's offered me a future!' Nero was surprised by the passion in her own voice. She remembered her glimpse of Nathan Drake at Trafalgar Square. He said he would know when Nero had made her decision, but what happened next?

The silence was so thick, Nero thought she could touch it.

When her mother spoke at last, it was with a simmering rage. 'I see. Then it seems you have a choice to make.' Helene walked to the front door and clicked it open. 'Leave this house and walk into God knows whatever danger awaits, or stay with me and keep in the shadows.'

Put like that, thought Nero, *it wasn't even a choice.*

The sky had burst. The rain fell in fat drops, spattering against the pavement as Nero walked the streets. The military police had set up roadblocks ahead of the curfew. If Nero was still walking in a couple of hours' time, she'd be sent straight back home or held in a cell overnight. She pulled her coat around her. Her feet were wet. She had no idea where she was going. She looked around the rain-soaked street and up to the glistening roofs. Was Drake watching her now? Did he know she'd made her decision? Was he even for real? She didn't relish the thought of going back home if he wasn't. She'd never live it down.

A drunk man barged passed her, slamming against her arm as he staggered into the road.

'Hey!' Nero called after him. 'Watch where you're walking!' As she cradled her arm, she noticed a leaflet fluttering to the pavement. Looking around her first, she bent to pick it up.

'Worship at St Bride's,' the leaflet read, 'I am the way, the truth and the life.'

An address was printed beneath a picture of a striking looking church. Fleet Street. An easy walk. She glanced behind her to see the 'drunk' walking in a perfectly straight line on the pavement.

'Message received and understood,' Nero muttered.

The streets were emptier than she remembered them. The last time she had walked through Covent Garden, it had been teeming with people. Now, it was practically deserted. Dropping down to Fleet Street via Bow Street, Nero was glad to avoid Trafalgar Square. The rescue was long over, but she didn't relish the prospect of being presented with just how close she'd come to dying a horrible death that morning. Some things just didn't bear thinking about.

As she turned the corner onto Aldwych, Nero noticed people hurrying home from work, their heads down so as to avoid any eye contact. The pubs and bars were already lowering their shutters in anticipation of the curfew. A theatre displayed notices of cancellation. This was clearly not the city that Nero had once known.

At last, St Bride's Church stood before her in the rain. It was an impressive building with a tiered conical spire that reminded Nero of a wedding cake. The main door stood ajar. Stepping gingerly inside, Nero found herself walking on a crazily-patterned tile floor. Its geometric shapes led the eye to an ornate wooden altar. As her footsteps echoed round the cavernous space, she realised she was alone. She wasn't quite sure what she had been expecting, but it certainly wasn't this. Perhaps Helene had been right. Maybe Drake wasn't to be trusted after all.

A movement out the corner of her eye caused her to turn. A half-glimpsed figure ducked through a door marked 'Crypt and Charnel House'.

'This just gets better,' Nero muttered. 'What even is a charnel house?'

The answer to that question surprised her. Nero found herself in a poky, low ceilinged room with crumbling brick walls. The cracked plaster seemed to be hanging on for dear life. A single electric lamp lit the room. It was just bright enough that Nero could make out a jumble of shapes on the floor. Peering nearer, she gasped. Skeletons. Some complete, others missing limbs or heads. Nero shivered, suddenly feeling the intense cold in the air. They were gathered into piles along the edges of the room. A shelf held a row of skulls, brown and waxy from the passage of time.

'They were discovered after the Second World War.'

Nero almost jumped out of her skin. Amplified by the small space, it was impossible to tell how close the voice was.

'When the bomb damage was repaired,' it continued, 'the workers discovered a room full of over two hundred skeletons. Casualties of the various plagues that have visited the city.'

'Do I have to tip the guide?' Nero asked drily, sounding braver than she felt.

There was a sardonic chuckle and Nero noticed the lights grow dim. All except one. Looking down a stone corridor that led from the room, she could see an illuminated tomb, lit by an overhead lamp. She walked carefully along the uneven floor, conscious of her breath hanging in the air like a cold mist. She stopped at a carving of an angel crouched over an open book. On its stone pages, Nero could make out some words in Latin, some dates and a name. Nathan Drake.

'My condolences,' she called out. No reply. Looking closer through the gloom, she noticed the two initial letters were raised slightly higher than the rest of the name. *There must be a reason for that.* Reaching out, she planted a hand over each of the letters and leaned her weight against the stone. As she felt the buttons sink into the stone, the plinth on which she stood began to revolve. In just a few seconds, the whole statue had turned through a hole in the wall, delivering Nero into a brightly lit corridor with smooth, metallic walls.

Stepping off the plinth as the statue began spinning again, Nero was surprised to see a small, box-like bot racing towards her. It whistled in greeting, then turned and raced away.

'I guess that's bot for *follow me*.'

Nero followed the speeding bot through a corridor lined with offices and laboratories. Peering through open doors as she passed, she saw technicians at work in front of banks of quantum computer units that whirred and clicked.

Finally, the bot stopped before an office door and whistled. With a soft click, the door opened and the bot wheeled way, its job done. Nero stepped inside, already convinced she would know who was waiting inside.

And she was right.

'Come in, Nero.'

Nathan Drake sat behind a seemingly empty desk. As Nero approached, she saw a touch screen embedded in the desktop. He was surrounded by huge, high-resolution screens, each displaying views of different global landmarks.

'I have to show my ID every time I take an Uber. How come you just let me walk right in?'

With the faintest of smiles, Drake pressed a button on his desk. A screen directly behind him played recorded footage of Nero walking the streets of London, as if from the perspective of another pedestrian. The camera shuddered as the Nero on the screen looked up in alarm.

'Hey!' came her voice from a speaker, tinny and thin. 'Watch where you're walking!' The image froze. A grid appeared over the screen, folding itself to the contours of her face. Text scrolled along the top of the display. 'Facial recognition,' it read. 'Nero Jones.'

A waveform appeared as she heard her voice again. 'Hey! Watch where you're walking!'

'Vocal recognition, Nero Jones.'

Now, the angle switched to a surveillance camera fixed on a nearby roof. It zoomed in as Nero bent down to pick up the leaflet. As she fingered the paper, the image froze where her thumb had been. A bar scrolled down the length of the screen, highlighting a whorled pattern as it passed.

'Fingerprint recognition,' announced the text. 'Nero Jones.'

Next, footage of Nero entering the church. As she slipped gingerly through the door, the image froze again. It was bathed in a spectrum of colour from infrared to ultraviolet.

The text flashed again. 'Unarmed'.

Drake punched a button and the screen went blank. 'As you can see, we're nothing if not thorough.'

Nero ground her teeth. 'You get a kick out of spying on young women?'

'We have to be cautious,' Drake replied. 'These days, not everyone is who they seem.'

'Including you?' Nero thought back to the name on the tomb. 'Is Nathan Drake even your real name?'

'Does it matter?'

'If you want my trust.'

Drake folded his arms. 'As it happens,' he smiled, 'it is. The tomb is just my private joke.'

'You don't think it's tempting fate a little?'

'I don't believe in fate, Nero. That's what makes my job so difficult.'

'Well,' Nero sighed, 'I've given up everything I have to get here. So you'd better start talking.'

Drake rose and leaned against his desk. 'You'll be part of our elite Pre-emptive Force. You'll be fully trained, fully equipped and fully – '

'Did you plant that bomb?' Nero interrupted.

Drake looked blank. 'Bomb?'

'In Trafalgar Square. I saw you by the fountain. You know, just after I'd saved all those lives.'

'Why would I have planted the bomb?'

Nero noticed he was trying hard to maintain eye contact. She ploughed on. 'If I was looking to recruit someone into some top-secret pre-emptive force, I'd probably want to engineer a situation to test them. To see if they had what it takes.'

'But that would involve putting innocent lives at risk,' Drake said, coolly.

'Yes,' said Nero, meeting his gaze. 'It would.'

Drake didn't even flinch. Nero wasn't sure just how far she could trust him.

'So, what's next?' she asked at last.

Drake reached behind him to punch a button on his desk. 'Psych test,' he said with a smile.

6

The Mind's Eye

Nero fought to relax. She had been placed in a dark room, lying down on a padded lounger suspended in the middle of the room. Her arms and feet had been secured, she was assured, for her own safety. Probes and sensors had been attached to her head and body. Through an observation window several feet away, she saw Drake standing expectantly as a technician busied themselves at a computer console.

'Comfortable?' Drake smiled, leaning into a microphone on the desk. His voice echoed round the room.

Nero gave a non-committal shrug.

'It's quite simple,' Drake continued, 'You'll be asked a series of questions and presented with a few scenarios. Answer honestly. The equipment will be monitoring your responses anyway, so honesty is always the best policy.'

Nero smirked at the irony.

'Ready?' asked the technician.

'Born ready,' Nero replied drily.

A lighting rig above her snapped on and she was bathed in different coloured light. It cycled from red and blue to yellow and green but was never bright enough to cause any discomfort. Soothing, ambient music accompanied the strange display. Nero had to admit, it was relaxing.

A low, sonorous voice interrupted her thoughts.

'Subject, Nero Jones. Psych evaluation. Beginning now. Hello, Nero.'

'Er, hello.'

Glancing through the window, Nero could see Drake and the technician gazing down at their monitors. Had the test begun already?

'Which three words describe you best?'

Nero laughed. 'What?'

'Which three words describe you best?' asked the voice again, with exactly the same intonation.

'Bored, bored, bored,' Nero replied, mischievously.

'What is something that you could do tomorrow that will make your day better?'

'Walk out of here.'

'What do you think about when you wake up?'

'Going back to bed.'

'If you could make one rule, what would it be?'

'That there should be no rules.' In spite of herself, Nero was beginning to enjoy herself.

'What is the nicest thing a friend has ever done for you?'

Her mind flicked back to the Dump. Meena stood by the window in their cell, her eyes sparkling.

'What is the nicest thing a friend – '

'Given me her chocolate,' Nero interrupted.

'What is something that you want, but don't want to ask for?'

'Chocolate.'

'If you could choose a new name for yourself, what would it be?'

'Mistress of the Universe.' Nero was getting bored again.

'Who would you save in an emergency, your dog or a friend?'

'What?'

The voice began again. 'Who would you save – '

'I heard,' Nero snapped. 'My dog.'

'Who would you save, your dog or your father?'

Nero had had enough. 'What kind of bullshit is this?'

'Who would you save, your dog or your father?'

Nero looked through the glass. The technician was peering back at her, awaiting her reply.

'You must reply, Nero,' came Drake's voice in the darkness. Nero maintained a stony silence. Drake gave a nod to the technician, instructing him to continue.

'Who would you save,' the disembodied voice continued, 'your mother or your father?'

Nero was aghast. 'This is sick.'

'Who would you kill, your dog or a friend?'

'What the – '

'Please study the following images. Tell me what you see.' A series of pictures were displayed on the ceiling above her.

'Sun, rain, chocolate, Moon,' Nero thought she might as well play along if it meant the process would be over quicker. A picture of Hudson appeared. Nero tried not to give anything away. 'Dog,' she said, as neutral as possible. Then, a picture of a middle-aged woman at her work in a laboratory. 'Mother,' Nero said, trying to keep the emotion from her voice. A picture of a kindly looking man, jet black hair and a wide smile. His arms were outstretched, as if reaching for a small child.

Nero swallowed.

'Father,' she whispered.

'Louder, please,' came the technician's voice from the speaker.

Nero cleared her throat. 'Father,' she repeated. She knew they had no doubt she recognised him. It was her physical responses that interested them. She imagined whatever reading they were looking at would be going crazy. Her heart was pounding.

The picture disappeared and she was left in the dark.

'Nero,' came a new voice. A voice she recognised.

'Nero,' it said again. 'I forgive you.'

'You're sick!' Nero exclaimed, squirming in her chair.

'I forgive you,' her father said again. The music grew louder. Its tempo increased.

Nero stopped struggling and, quite suddenly, laughed.

'You're pathetic, Drake,' she called, lifting her head to see through the glass. 'Not everyone has father issues. I don't need his forgiveness. He loved me.' The coloured lights flashed again and Nero felt a sudden chill. An image flashed into her mind. A bright room. A chair. A blade. The music was growing more frenetic.

'What are you doing?' She shook her head. 'I don't know that place.' The blade drew nearer and Nero felt a sudden pain behind her ear. 'Get out of my head!' She shrieked. The images played again in her mind. Her mother, her father, her dog. This time, there was another. Meena. And the pain grew sharper.

'Which would you kill?' the low voice asked, calmly.

The images seemed to rotate above her. *Could Drake see all this?* Nero twisted against her restraints.

'Which would you kill?'

'Which one, Nero?' Drake's voice added to the cacophony.

'You!' Nero screamed. 'I'd kill *you* before any of them!'

With that, the pictures disappeared and the music stopped. Nero squinted as the lights snapped on and the room was bathed in a bright, phosphorescent glare.

There was a moment of silence.

A door clicked open and the technician walked in. Without saying a word, they removed the sensors and undid the restraints holding Nero to the chair.

'What the hell was that?' Nero demanded. The technician declined to answer, instead tipping the chair so Nero could step off. It was as if nothing had happened.

Nero rubbed at her wrists where the straps had held her. 'You're sick,' she spat as she passed Drake. He was standing in the doorway, his arms folded. He winked at the technician as they resumed their place by the monitors.

'I think she passed,' he smiled.

Nero sat in the canteen. It was almost impossible to imagine this entire complex lay sprawling beneath the streets of London. She looked around at the assembled diners. They were mostly young, she noticed. Were they all members of the 'Pre-emptive Force' that Drake had mentioned? Just how big was this Bureau, anyway? She guessed that she must have already seen some of them working on the banks of computers as she had entered. But to what end? What could possibly need all that computer power? She bit down on her rather uninspiring sandwich.

'You should've gone for the salad.'

She almost choked on her stodgy mouthful. Turning round, she saw a wiry young man walking towards her with a tray of food. He flicked his long hair from his eyes as he sat opposite her.

'And you should really drink some water.'

'You!' She recognised him at once.

'Uh, it's Benjamin,' the man stuttered, almost apologetically. 'Benjamin Saal.'

'What the hell – ?' Nero's day was getting weirder. 'You were on the monorail.'

Benjamin nodded. 'I found you at the Dump.' He picked at his food with a fork. 'I recommended Drake keep an eye on you.'

Nero sighed. 'You sneaky bastard.'

'You can thank me later.' He looked down. 'And you *should* have some water with your lunch.'

'Thanks for your concern.' Nero leaned across the table. 'I guess you reported back on my performance on the monorail, too?'

Benjamin looked away. 'Just the highlights,' he muttered.

'So, he *did* plant that bomb. As a test.' Nero slapped her hand against the table. 'I knew it.'

'Er, no actually.' Benjamin leaned in, his voice low. 'But we *did* know it was going to happen.'

Nero didn't believe him for a moment. 'How?'

Benjamin smiled. 'It's what we do,' he shrugged.

'Wait.' Nero was thinking hard. 'If you knew that monorail was going to be bombed, *why did you get on?*'

'Oh, that's easy.' Benjamin stabbed at his food. 'Because I knew you'd stop it.'

'What? That's ridiculous.'

Benjamin winked. 'It's what we do,' he repeated.

'You wink at me again,' Nero warned him, 'and you'll have to reach down your throat to get that fork back.'

Benjamin blinked.

'This place gives me the creeps. Do you know what they just did to me?'

'Psych test, I guess.' Benjamin took a mouthful. 'I wouldn't worry about it.'

'It was torture.'

'I remember mine.' Benjamin shivered involuntarily. 'You in?'

'In?'

'The Bureau. Are you joining us?'

Nero sat back, pushing her plate away from her. 'Do I have a choice?'

'Depends what other options you have.'

Nero scoffed. That was it, in a nutshell. She *had* no other options.

'What do you do here?' she asked, changing the subject.

Benjamin gulped down his mouthful and reached for a glass of water. 'Big data,' he said between sips. Nero stared at him. 'I collate data. Mine it, crunch it. It's fascinating.'

Nero rolled her eyes. 'Whatever floats your boat.'

'It's actually at the heart of what we do. It's what First Action Bureau is all about.' He waved his fork in front of him. 'The clue's in the name.'

'Enlighten me, oh wise one.'

'On a quantum level, everything is predictable.' Benjamin seemed suddenly in his element. 'Look close enough and there are patterns everywhere, leading to an inevitable fixed point.'

Nero pretended to understand. 'Okay…'

'It's just a matter of getting enough data. The beauty of the twenty-first century is that data proliferates. People give it away! Geographical, political, behavioural. Big data.'

'Wow. So like normal data, but big.'

Benjamin could tell he was being teased. 'You might have trouble predicting the outcome of a race if you didn't know the runners. But what if I was able to feed you real time data on the state of their health, their emotions, past performances, average times. Then you could make a prediction.'

Nero understood at last. 'So you're doing the same with the Dheghomites?'

'Exactly. Tracking known operatives where we can, logging their behavioural data, their internet chatter and feeding it through our super-fast artificial intelligence. Using their past behaviour to predict the future.'

'The computers I saw.'

Benjamin resisted the urge to wink again.

'And this shit *works*?' Nero was agog.

'We're getting there.'

Everything was falling into place. 'So, the Pre-emptive Force...'

'Stops crime before it happens. The clue's –'

'In the name,' Nero interrupted. 'Yeah, I get it. Drake called it an *elite* force.'

Benjamin smiled. 'Don't let it go to your head.' He cleared his plate and looked suddenly sheepish. 'Um,' he stuttered. 'I don't suppose – '

Nero frowned. 'What are you doing?'

Benjamin took a breath. 'I don't suppose you'd like dinner tonight? I mean, with me. And on me. My treat.'

The silence was painful.

'Christ, you just ruined a perfectly normal conversation. And when I say *normal*, I mean *weird*. But you just made it weirder.'

'So that's a no, then?' Benjamin blushed.

Nero scraped her chair noisily against the floor as she stood up. Benjamin was sure it was to get the whole room's attention.

'It's more than a no,' Nero began, enraged. 'It's a *you can stick your dinner where the sun don't shine*.' There were chuckles all around, mostly, Nero noticed, from the young women in the room. She smiled sweetly. 'But be sure to drink enough water with it.'

She turned smartly away and headed for the door, a wicked smile playing across her face.

'Ah, Nero.'

Drake intercepted her in the corridor outside.

'You'll be glad to hear the rest of the day is your own. So, we'll see you in the morning for your first day's training.'

He held out his hand. As Nero returned the gesture, he clapped his other hand over the top of hers.

'Ow!' Nero protested, drawing back. Looking down, she saw a barcode imprinted on the back of her hand. Slowly, it sunk beneath her skin.

'Subcutaneous code,' Drake smiled.

'Don't you need to ask consent before you do stuff like that?'

'You'll need it to get in.'

Nero rubbed the back of her hand to relieve the pain. 'In where?'

'Well, you've got to stay somewhere,' Drake smiled. 'The car waiting outside will take you straight there.' He looked her up and down. 'You'll find some fresh clothes in the wardrobe. For God's sake, put them on.'

The car drove Nero eastwards. Through the window, she saw a heavy military police presence in the more rebellious areas. In New Cross, two groups of rival protesters were separated with water cannons and carted away into waiting armoured vehicles. Nero wondered when they would see the light of day again.

The great, glittering skyscrapers rose high into the sky, reminders of an age when money ruled. Nowadays if you had it, you certainly wouldn't show it. Ostentatious displays of wealth were so turn of the century.

'We have arrived at your destination,' a robotic voice chimed. The gull wing door swung open and Nero stepped out onto the wet pavement. A tall apartment block stood before her.

'Sorry,' she said, turning. 'Which one – ?'

But the door had hissed shut behind her and the car drove away with a hum.

'Great. Thanks.'

Nero lifted a hand to shield her eyes from the rain and sighed. She noticed a camera mounted by the smart door ahead of her. Nero remembered Drake's awkward hand shake as she had left the Bureau. Rolling up her sleeve, she angled the back of her hand so it faced the screen.

'Let's hope it's a warm welcome,' she muttered.

'Welcome, Nero Jones,' said a computer voice that Nero recognised. Just a few hours ago it had been asking her who she would rather kill.

The door clicked open.

As Nero stepped into the hallway, a light strip directed her up the stairs to a top floor. Another door swung open as she presented the back of her hand, and Nero found herself in a smart, minimalist apartment.

'Welcome, Nero Jones,' came the computer voice again. 'I am Home.'

A *housemate*, Nero sighed. *Great.*

'Your apartment includes smart defence technology. You will be safe here.'

'Good to know,' Nero breathed.

'Your heartbeat is elevated. Shall I play you soothing music?'

'Coffee will be fine.' Nero threw her bag on the sofa and wandered into a bedroom.

'Your caffeine intake will be monitored,' continued the voice as Nero sat on the bed.

'Hey!' she complained. 'Can't a girl get any privacy?'

The computer seemed to think for a while. 'I am Home,' it replied at last.

'Sure,' Nero sighed as she fell back on the plush pillows.

She heard a ping from the kitchen. 'Your coffee is ready.'

Nero raised her eyebrows. 'I could get used to this.'

As she walked to the kitchen, a light shone on a table in the corner. 'Your computer hub is operational,' came the computer voice. A touchscreen was embedded in the desktop. 'You may access all Bureau databases, schematics and agent logs for which you are authorised from here.'

Nero nodded. 'I'm guessing I won't be authorised for much.'

'You may contact the Bureau, or anyone else, from here. All calls are encrypted.' The voice sounded almost pleased with itself. 'I have taken the liberty of copying your contacts from your phone.'

Nero looked surprised. 'Do you think you could ask next time?'

The computer sounded apologetic. 'Noted,' it said.

Collecting her coffee from a beverage station, Nero stood at the window, cradling the cup in her hands. She let her gaze wander across the London rooftops.

'Okay, Home,' she said, thoughtfully. 'Call *home*.'

'Calling home,' the computer obliged.

Nero heard a ring tone sounding. She wasn't entirely sure what she was going to say, but felt she should at least check in. Surely her mother would want to know where she was? That she was okay?

There was a click and the line went dead. 'Would you like me to try again?'

'No,' Nero replied after a pause. Sipping her coffee, she wandered over to the computer hub. 'I can call anyone, anywhere, huh?' she said aloud.

'Anyone,' the computer confirmed.

A smile played over Nero's face as she thought of the one thing that would improve her life immensely.

'Call Sublight Pizza,' she said. 'I want a nine-inch pan, stuffed crust Hawaiian. With extra pineapple.'

7

Boot Camp

The alarm sounded early. Too early.

'It is six, a.m.'

Nero buried her head under her pillow.

'Incoming call,' the voice continued. 'Nathan Drake, First Action Bureau.'

Nero groaned. 'Can't I at least have breakfast first?'

'Good morning, Nero,' came a cheery voice.

'Don't you ever sleep?' Nero mumbled. She looked up to see a projection of Drake's face hovering above her bedside table.

'Woh! Nero cried, pulling her covers up to her chin.

'You have half an hour to get yourself ready,' Drake continued, oblivious. 'A car will be standing by outside.'

'For what?' Nero blinked in the morning light.

'Training.'

The streets were still wet. As the car drove noiselessly through the streets to Fleet Street, Nero wolfed down her nutrient bar. Tomorrow, she promised herself, she'd have a proper breakfast. That would please the stupid computer.

Just as she had done the day before, Nero descended the stairs into the crypt beneath St Bride's. It was too early for any visitors, or even for any staff to be on duty. Nero wondered how many of them knew there was a secret intergovernmental agency beneath their feet. At each doorway, she held her hand up to a screen to gain access. She noticed the security cameras flashed green at every access point, no doubt confirming that she was indeed Nero Jones.

'You're late!' The voice echoed down the corridor.

Turning, Nero saw a middle-aged man in a tracksuit tapping his foot, impatiently.

'For what?'

The man shook his head and puffed out his cheeks in exasperation. Gesturing to Nero that she should follow him, he turned down the corridor and opened a door she hadn't noticed yesterday. She found herself going deeper still, following the man down yet more flights of stone steps. *Just how far down did this place go?* She could practically *feel* the irritation radiating from the figure in front.

At last, they turned into a large exercise hall lined with ropes and bars. Punch bags hung in a corner near a full-size boxing ring. A variety of exercise machines stood in another, hooked up to myriad screens and monitors. Most surprising of all, however, was the line of young men and women facing her, all about her age, and all looking nervous as hell.

'Okay, Jones,' the man said, 'my name is Gunther but you can call me whatever you want. In another life I'd be your personal trainer and you'd pay me thirty grand a year to make you feel good about yourself. But in this life I exist only to give you pain.'

Nero looked around. From the looks on the assembled faces, she had a feeling he'd already made this speech this morning. And it wasn't funny then.

'Perhaps you think you can afford to be late because you know it all already.'

'No,' Nero replied with care, 'I was late because my bed wouldn't let me go.'

Someone sniggered.

Gunther nodded and put his hands on his hips. 'Cute. Why don't you join the line and make yourself at home?'

Nero shuffled over to her fellow recruits. This felt too much like the Dump for comfort. 'You should know that I have a problem with authority,' she smirked.

Another snigger.

'That's okay,' the man smiled. 'I have a problem with skinny little runts acting up in front of the class. So, how we gonna settle this?' He unzipped his tracksuit top and threw it to one side. Nero could see his stomach muscles flexing beneath his white vest. 'Wanna come at me?'

Nero frowned. 'Huh?'

Gunther spread his arms wide. 'Sure! Come at me!' He slapped his chest dramatically. 'You put me on the floor, you get to come in an hour later every day. I put you down, you get here an hour before everyone else.'

Nero smiled. Seemed like a fair deal. She paused, quietly assessing her best line of attack. Then, turning to face her new colleagues, she slipped out of her shoes to feel the floor beneath her bare feet.

'Left deltoid,' she whispered with a wink. Her companions stared back, uncomprehending. With that, she turned, took a breath and launched herself at the man in the vest. She went in low, her bowed head barrelling into his stomach.

Gunther was waiting for her. As her head connected, he tensed his core, wrapped his arms around Nero's waist and lifted her legs clean off the floor. Thinking fast, Nero kicked her feet into the air, trying desperately to make contact with his head. Gunther let her go and she fell to the floor, steadying herself with outstretched arms as she landed.

'Try again,' Gunther growled. 'This time, act like you mean it.'

This time, Nero went for his feet. Wrapping a leg around his, she put a shoulder to his chest in an effort to throw him off balance. Gunther staggered back and managed to get a leg free. Planting a foot behind himself, he leaned into her weight, forcing her to push all the harder. Then, he simply stepped aside.

Nero felt herself falling forwards through the air as she struggled to swing her legs forward to take her weight. At last she felt a foot flat on the ground. Thinking fast, she shifted her body to place the maximum weight over it, then reached down with outstretched fingers to steady herself. Another step forward and she was able to stand, straight and steady.

'Let's make this quick, shall we?' Gunther scoffed. 'I feel cruel playing with you like this.'

'Quick as you like,' Nero smiled back. Settling herself on her haunches, she raised her hands, claw-like, in front of her. It was a stance she'd seen in old movies.

Gunther almost danced towards her, swinging his fists in the air. Ducking and feinting to avoid the blows, Nero seized her moment. Stepping deftly to one side, she delivered a swift jab to Gunther's shoulder. The effect was instant. With wide eyes of disbelief, he grabbed his arm in pain. An involuntary howl escaped his lips as he fell first to his knees, then to the floor.

'Left deltoid,' Nero nodded to her captive audience. She pointed down at Gunther's writhing form. 'I guessed he'd just had his Provax jab. He looks about the right age. Leaves a subcutaneous bruise that hurts like hell, apparently. Anyone else notice the telltale red mark?' The assembled crew shook their heads in wonder. 'Just me, then.'

As Gunther struggled to his feet, the picture of embarrassment, Nero bent down to retrieve her shoes.

'Now we know where we stand,' she grinned, 'I'm heading to the canteen to catch myself a proper breakfast.' She leaned in close to the sheepish Gunther. 'I hear it's the most important meal of the day.'

As she headed to the door, Nero turned for a final potshot. 'I'll see you in the morning, Gunther. An hour later than everyone else.'

Gunther was no trouble the next morning. In fact, Nero took pity on him and came in on time anyway.

'He was a walkover for the rest of the day yesterday,' said Harrison in the canteen afterwards. 'You must have softened him up for us.'

Harrison was a tall young man with bright red hair and pale skin.

'Glad to hear it,' Nero smiled as she slurped on her shake. She wouldn't tell the computer about that. 'So, how did you get here?'

Harrison took a mouthful of his chicken salad. 'My dad was secret service, so it was kinda inevitable.'

'Was?' Nero asked, carefully.

'We only found out after he died.' He corrected himself. 'When he was killed.'

Nero dropped her eyes. 'I'm sorry. I lost my dad, too. So I know what that's like.'

'Sure,' Harrison nodded, 'but I bet you didn't get handed a whole heap of surprises when he died. Turns out we didn't know him at all. He kept a whole side of his life secret.'

'I guess he had to.'

'That didn't make it any easier.'

Nero drained her glass. 'So why are you here? Isn't it a little like history repeating?'

Harrison leaned over the table. 'Because, tough as it was, I also discovered my dad was a hero. They couldn't tell us much, but it seems he was almost solely responsible for thwarting a terrorist attack. He saved hundreds of lives. Took a couple of bad guys with him when he went, too.' He cleaned his plate. 'I want a piece of that action.'

There was a glint in his eye that Nero almost found frightening.

'How about *your* dad?'

Nero nodded. 'Plane crash.'

Harrison was thoughtful. 'I think I would've preferred that,' he said.

Nero looked around at her fellow recruits. Did everyone in the room have similar stories to tell? Were they all damaged? Is that what the Bureau saw in them? Before she had time to think any further, the double doors to the canteen flew open.

'Okay,' called Gunther from the doorway. 'I hope you enjoyed your calories, because you're going to need them.'

The treadmills were hooked up and ready to go.

'One each,' Gunther bellowed. 'Choose your poison.'

Nero walked straight to a machine in the corner. As she jumped aboard, Gunther pulled a large transparent dome from its mooring in the ceiling and placed it over her head.

'Take a hold of this,' he snapped, and Nero felt him strap a glove onto her right hand. 'Today we're measuring your strength, speed, skill and stamina so we know which areas to work on.' He walked along the line, fixing the head pieces around each recruit and fastening the gloves onto their hands. 'These sensor gloves will measure your heart rate, sweat rate and just about every other rate you can think of.' He stopped at the end of the line. 'As you breathe in and out, those helmets will be monitoring your oxygen intake, lung capacity and expiration rate. The treadmill will be measuring your balance, weight distribution, stride length and asymmetry. By the end of today, we'll know more about you. At least, you when you're running. And, yes, it's going to be a long day. Once you're up to speed, the treadmills will respond to your pace. Slow down and they'll slow down with you. Speed up, and they'll keep pace.'

Nero noticed he was enjoying himself.

'But, of course, we want to know how you operate under pressure, so expect a few surprises, too.'

Nero didn't like the sound of that. The technician stood behind a computer console and, at a nod from Gunther, jabbed at a button. The treadmills began to roll with a jerk, slowly at first but gaining in speed as the recruits got used to their momentum.

Nero settled her breathing into a manageable rhythm, timed with her running strides. As the treadmill stabilised, she found the easy, fluid movement that she had used during exercise sessions at the Dump. Looking through the transparent helmet device, she noticed the technician was monitoring each recruit's progress on a bank of holographic screens projected into the air in front of him. She could see graph lines and scrolling text indicating how each of them was performing. Nero was determined to beat them all. Once she'd found her stride, she could run for hours.

A sudden discomfort in her right hand distracted her. Reaching across to scratch at the glove, she felt the pain grow as she slowed. A sharp, tingling feeling. Nero looked around at the other runners to see they were obviously experiencing a similar sensation. She could see their looks of confusion through their transparent headpieces.

'Expect a few surprises,' Gunther had said. She looked across to where their coach was standing next to the technician. Both had their eyes on the holographic read outs. Nero had the impression they were avoiding her gaze deliberately.

As she slowed to look down at her glove, she felt the pain increasing. A stinging, burning sensation was travelling up her whole arm. She heard gasps of pain from the other recruits. She scratched at the glove's straps to release it, but it was tied fast. She dropped her pace further and felt the pain increase in her shoulder. Was it getting worse as she slowed down? Nero dipped her head and leaned forwards on her treadmill, increasing her pace as she did so. The pain subsided. She dropped her speed and the burning, stabbing sensation returned.

'Electric shock,' Nero panted to herself. 'The bastards.'

She could see a couple of the recruits were clutching at their arms as they slowed, clearly only moments from giving up. She caught Harrison's eye through his headpiece. He had figured it out, too. He nodded at her.

'We got this,' he mouthed, before dropping his head and increasing his speed.

Nero did the same, channelling all her energy into her tired legs. They would have to outrun the pain. The burning subsided as she ran on. Not daring to drop her speed, she settled into a sustainable rhythm, licking her lips as her mouth began to dry.

At least two of her colleagues had given up. A young woman sat on her motionless treadmill, a look of relief on her face as Gunther removed her glove. A flustered looking man rubbed his shoulder as he waited in turn, a look of frustration on his sweaty face.

Nero was determined to run on, the occasional stab of pain reminding her to keep the pace up. Then, she heard a noise. It sounded so out of place, it took a moment for her to realise what it was. Dogs barking. They sounded fierce, and there was a whole pack of them. Another of Gunther's surprises? She felt the stabbing pain in her arm again as she inadvertently slowed to look around. Quickening her pace, she saw three dogs running straight for her, their eyes blazing. She swerved as one lunged for her legs. How could this be possible? The others followed, drooling and snarling as they threw themselves upon her. The pain shot up her arm as she slowed. Sweat pricked at her forehead. The muscles in her legs burned with the exertion. Then she realised. None of the dogs had actually made contact. They jumped at her, snarled at her, but never hurt her. They couldn't. They were nothing more than phantoms, images projected onto her headset. They couldn't hurt her. And, with that realisation, they disappeared. Nero pushed on.

Looking to her side, she could see that Harrison had foundered. He had stepped off his treadmill, looking around in terrified confusion for any sign of the dogs. As Gunther released him, Harrison realised what had happened and threw his glove to the floor in frustration.

Only Nero remained.

Suddenly, it was dark. Nero became conscious of her own breathing, the regular in and out between strides. She was tiring now, but she did not dare drop her speed. In the darkness, she heard another sound, faint at first but growing in strength. A buzzing, humming sound that seemed to be coming from inside her head.

It's an illusion, she told herself. *Like the dogs. Just keep on running.*

The darkness was disconcerting, as was the fact that Nero was sure she was being watched by all her fellow recruits somewhere beyond it. The buzzing grew louder. It seemed to swoop all around her, growing with intensity as it filled her head. Wasps. It sounded like a swarm of wasps. Nero felt the cold steel of adrenaline as it coursed through her veins. Concentrating on maintaining her speed, she tried to ignore the dreadful noise. Then, she felt the first sting.

'What the hell – ?' she heard herself scream, and she thought of the other recruits in the room. Were they watching her? Were they laughing? Another sting, sharp and painful, struck her cheek. She tried to wave the swarm away with her arms, aware at the same time that none of this was real. The headset had somehow affected her eyesight, plunging her into darkness. The glove had accessed her nervous system, delivering little shocks all over her body

RICHARD JAMES

that *felt* like wasp stings. She had to remember that *none of this was real...* and keep running.

The swarm swooped all at once. Her whole body became a vessel of pain. Each individual sting seemed to coalesce with its neighbour so that soon, she knew nothing but the sharp agony of poison just beneath her skin. Images formed in her mind.

A blade.
A bright light.
A question.
Who
am
I?

But still, she kept on running. A doorway appeared before her and Nero couldn't tell if it was real or not. She seemed to have been running for hours. Her legs were slowing beneath her. The pain of the electric shocks mingled with the agony of the wasp stings, growing in intensity with every stride. She knew she had to make it to the door, but she feared whatever might be on the other side.

All she knew was pain.

She raised her hands before her to push the door open. Just as she thought she could take no more, it swung open at her touch and –

The pain stopped. At once. The lights seemed to flick on, and Nero looked around, sweat stinging her eyes. Her chest heaved as she fought for air. She dared to slow her pace and then stop. The recruits stood around her, applauding. Even Gunther looked impressed. He lifted the headset away and set about undoing Nero's glove.

'That's a first,' he said as he helped her off the treadmill. 'No one's ever made it through the door.'

Nero wiped the sweat from her face and caught her breath. She couldn't decide whether she wanted to hug him or throw him to the floor.

'Congratulations on your balanced breakfast,' droned the computer voice the next morning,

Nero rolled her eyes. 'You're great company, Home,' she sighed, 'but do you have to be so patronising?'

Her legs ached after the previous day's exertions and she swore she could still feel a tingling in her right hand. She was in no mood to be cajoled by an over-enthusiastic computer.

'I shall adjust my presets accordingly,' the disembodied voice intoned. 'In the meantime, you have thirty minutes until your car arrives.'

Nero wolfed down the last of her poached egg and avocado, snatching a handful of nuts as she headed to the bathroom.

'Make the bath a hot one please, Home,' she called over her shoulder. 'I need a soak.'

Nero noticed a change in the way people looked at her at the Bureau. It was something she had never seen before. A wide-eyed glance as she entered a room. A slight dipping of the gaze before she was spoken to.

'What's going on, Harrison?' she asked her friend as they walked down the stairs. 'Why is everyone looking at me funny?'

Harrison laughed as he nudged her playfully with his elbow. 'Doofus!' he roared. 'It's called *respect*.'

Nero nodded. No wonder she hadn't seen it before. As they rounded the corner, Nero slowed her pace. Benjamin Saal stood in the doorway to a lab.

'You're with me this morning,' he smiled nervously. 'Tech talk.'

Nero rolled her eyes as the other recruits filed past her.

'Whoop-de-doo,' she sighed.

The lights flicked on as the little group took their seats, Nero next to Harrison. The glass desks in front of them contained embedded touch screen keyboards. On top of them were placed delicate lenses joined by a thin, transparent frame. Benjamin cleared his throat.

'Ladies and gentlemen,' he began, 'first things first.' He held up his own pair of high-tech spectacles.

'Spi-Glasses,' he said. 'Stands for sensory projection and investigation.'

Nero rolled her eyes.

'They're connected to our central computer. I'll introduce you to that in a moment, but first, try them on for size.'

The recruits did as they were instructed and looked around the room. '

You'll see no difference yet, but try a series of three rapid blinks.'

There was laughter in the room as the students watched each other blinking feverishly.

'Just three!' cautioned Benjamin. 'That should bring up a text menu that only you can see on the inside of the lens.'

Nero followed suit. Sure enough, a menu appeared to hang in the air before her.

'Okay,' Benjamin continued. 'Now play around. See what you can find. You can use tiny eye movements to navigate.'

There was a snigger from the back of the room.

'Looks like someone's found the X-ray application,' Benjamin grinned, suddenly embarrassed as he caught Nero's eye. 'Anyway,' he stuttered, 'that's standard Bureau issue, so they're yours now. They've been developed in tandem with the security forces so they're undetectable by most scanners. You can investigate further in your own time.' He slipped the glasses from his nose. 'But now, allow me to introduce the brains of the Bureau.'

With a swipe on his desktop, Benjamin activated holographic screens above the recruits' desks. On them were displayed six letters that spun in the air.

'B.R.A.I.N.S.' he smiled. 'Bureau rapid artificial intelligence neural server.'

Nero groaned. This guy loved his acronyms.

'I thought of it myself,' said Benjamin. Clearly not getting quite the response he'd hoped for, he ploughed on. 'It's the framework behind everything at the Bureau. It continually monitors the building and everything in it. And that includes you.' Another swipe and the images changed. Each screen displayed what seemed to be a real time picture of whoever was seated before it. Nero gazed at her image, watching it move left and right as she tried to duck away from its all-seeing eye. Text and numbers scrolled across the screen, detailing her vital signs and current position. Benjamin stroked his computer interface with a mischievous chuckle and the image peeled away to show Nero's inner organs, pumping and pulsating with life.

'Gross,' she breathed as she looked around her. Her colleagues were looking at their own images in various states of wonder or disgust.

'Hey,' laughed Harrison, 'I'm even better looking on the inside!'

Sharing a smile with her companion, Nero caught a look in Benjamin's eye. Was that *jealousy*?

Benjamin adjusted his glasses. 'BRAINS is also connected to our predictive systems, constantly monitoring data and communications to pinpoint Dheghomite activity. Aside from that, it's the repository of all knowledge.'

'*All* knowledge?' Nero was sceptical.

'We have access to every government's security files and schematics.' Benjamin was looking smug. 'Coupled with the system's generative AI, BRAINS is able to search pretty much any database in the world for information, thinking for itself.'

Another swipe across Benjamin's desktop brought up an image of a spinning Earth. Seemingly hundreds of red lines linked a series of pulsating points situated around the world. 'This shows just how deep our network goes, but it's constantly seeking more connections. The more connections, the more powerful the system becomes.'

'And we have access to all this data?' Harrison asked.

Benjamin hesitated. 'Agents have access to the data they need.'

'Who decides what we need?'

'BRAINS itself,' Benjamin replied, a note of pride in his voice. 'You can access the system via any computer interface in the building, or even in your apartments. Just hold your hand up to the screen for an ID verification, then simply ask for what you need.' He looked around the room. 'Any questions?'

'Yes,' came a voice from the back of the room. 'Just one.'

Nero spun round to see Nathan Drake standing in the doorway. He caught her eye. 'Could Nero Jones please come with me?'

As Nero followed Drake from the room, she noticed Harrison looking after her, a questioning look on his face.

Beats me, Nero shrugged.

As they rounded the corner to Drake's office, she felt a sharp, stabbing pain in her temples. She gasped.

'Are you okay?' Drake asked, noticing the break in her stride.

'I think so,' Nero replied, though she wasn't sure. Her vision was blurred and her own voice seemed distant somehow. Muffled. She shook her head. The pain subsided.

'Nero, I have some news for you.'

Drake gestured that she should follow him into his office. The door hummed shut behind them. Nero noticed the glass wall that separated them from the corridor outside had darkened. Drake clearly didn't want anyone to see.

'It's classified Top Secret, naturally.' He looked more serious than ever. 'But I think you're both ready.'

Nero raised an eyebrow. 'Both?'

'Hi, Nero.'

Nero spun round to see someone she recognised at once.

'Meena!' She struggled to understand. 'What are you doing here? Are you Bureau, too?'

Meena looked to Drake for his permission to speak. He nodded.

'Drake recruited me from the Dump. I think we've been on parallel training courses.'

Nero was aghast. Just how many recruits were there?

'Are you based here?'

Meena shook her head. 'New St Paul's.'

So, the Bureau had other facilities.

'Well, I hope you're more ready for this than I am.' Nero gazed at Drake to make her point. 'Sounds like this is going to be a baptism of fire.' She turned to Meena. 'What do you know?'

'Only what I have told her,' Drake interrupted, 'and what I'm about to tell you.'

Meena looked suddenly excited. 'He's got an assignment for us.'

'Your first for the Bureau's Pre-emptive Force.' Drake looked almost proud.

Nero blinked. 'I've literally had three days' training.'

'You're ready,' Drake smiled as he walked round his desk. 'You're sharp. You're fit.' He tapped the computer console on his desk. 'Your stats are impressive. And you won't be alone. You'll have Meena and we'll have your back.'

'What's the assignment?'

'Why don't you sit down and I'll fill you in?'

Nero sat quietly in the chair opposite Drake's desk as he called up the details on his computer. Meena looked on, her arms folded, impassive. A tall, snake-like structure was projected before them.

Nero's eyes narrowed. 'The Clarke Elevator.'

'It's been shipping goods and materials into low orbit for ten years. A hundred thousand kilometres of toughened steel, held up by nothing more than centrifugal force.' Drake jabbed at his desk and the image disappeared. 'And it's in their sights.'

Nero caught her breath. 'The Dheghomites?'

'Who else? It's the perfect symbol of humankind's hubris. We're literally overreaching ourselves.'

'How do you know?' Nero sat forward in her chair as Drake pulled up reams of figures on his desktop. They scrolled in the air between them.

'We've seen a spike in the data. All the probability points indicate an attack on the elevator. Explosives planted somewhere along its length.'

'*Somewhere*? If your system's so good, why can't you be more precise?'

Drake sighed. 'The bigger the event, the greater the variables. This is huge, so the predictions are in flux. The nearest we can get is that there will be a strike on the elevator sometime in the next three days.'

The image of the elevator appeared again. It was tethered to a large, artificial island in the Pacific Ocean and stretched up into the Earth's atmosphere and beyond.

'As you can imagine,' Drake continued, 'the results would be catastrophic.' There was a flash of light at the base of the shaft. 'If the blast occurred where the elevator is tethered,' he explained, 'the entire structure would lift into space. Along with anything, or *anyone* currently on board.'

The simulation showed exactly as Drake had said. The elevator shaft was cut adrift from its moorings and began to rise remorselessly through the atmosphere. The simulation reset itself for the next demonstration.

'If a break occurred somewhere around the twenty-five thousand kilometre mark, the lower part would fall to Earth, reaching two thirds of the way around the world.' A flash of light appeared along the elevator's length and the two parts separated. 'A half-kilometre wide tube of toughened steel falling at the speed of sound would crush everything in its path. Bogota, Singapore, Kinshasa all lay in its projected path. Millions would die.'

Nero watched as the simulation unfolded before her. As the elevator fell, it crashed into various population centres. A series of numbers displayed the projected fatalities.

'Meanwhile, the upper portion would rise to a higher orbit, unstable and beyond hope of immediate rescue.'

Again, the image was reset.

'Which are they planning?' Meena asked, agog.

Drake snapped the simulation off and the image disappeared. 'We don't know,' he shrugged. 'All we know is that *something* is planned.'

'An inside job?' Meena was chewing her lip in thought.

'That's for you to find out.'

Nero was thinking fast. 'Benjamin Saal told me you knew I'd be successful in halting the monorail.' She swallowed. 'Will we stop this?'

Drake sighed and shook his head. 'If I knew I would tell you. But the data's too vague on the eventual outcome for now.'

'Great!' Nero hissed in exasperation. She looked at Meena. 'Are you happy with this?'

'This is what we do, Jones,' Drake interrupted before Meena could respond. 'And you're ready for it.' He reached into his desk. 'Two young women barely out of childhood travelling alone will undoubtedly raise suspicions,' he said, pulling two computer pads from a drawer. 'Your cover stories are on these slates. Only you have access via your ID stamps.' He gestured to the back of Nero's hand. 'Learn them. Stick to them. You'll also find the elevator's history and schematics in the relevant folders. Memorise what you can on the journey. We'll be in touch every step of the way.'

Meena could sense Nero's disquiet. 'Hey,' she soothed. 'You and me against the world. It'll be just like the old days.'

8

Baptism of Fire

The security was almost stifling. It seemed to Nero that they had to show their ID at every step. Every time they hopped aboard a new mode of transport, there would be scanners to negotiate. People stared at one another with suspicion. There were armed military police everywhere and makeshift checkpoints on the busier roads. At last, the two Bureau agents found themselves at the final hurdle. The officious looking woman at the airport security point had clearly had a long day.

'Next!' she barked.

Meena stepped forward and looked into the camera.

'Passport.'

She handed over her ID.

The woman glared at Meena and then at the image on her screen. Satisfied at last, she waved her through.

'Have a nice day,' she sneered, none too convincingly. 'Next!'

Nero stepped forward.

'Look into the camera,' the woman commanded with impressive disinterest.

Nero looked into the camera.

'Passport,' the woman drawled, holding out her hand. 'Where are you going, Ms…'

'Pike,' Nero lied. 'Like the fish.' Next time she was going to choose her own alias. 'San Francisco, then Kiribati.'

The woman blinked.

'Pacific island,' Nero explained, obligingly. 'I'm travelling as part of the Bright and Bold Initiative.'

The woman looked blank again.

'Schools' programme. Apparently, I'm the best of the best.' Nero tried not to laugh as she caught Meena's eye behind the barrier. Her interrogator looked her up and down.

'I know, right?' Nero shrugged. 'What can I say?'

A light on the camera flashed green. The woman passed Nero's passport back and waved her on. 'Enjoy your flight,' she yawned.

'Once more with feeling,' Nero muttered under her breath. Secretly, she was impressed. Their fake IDs had proven sufficiently convincing at every stage of her journey, though Nero noticed that she was always the one who was questioned further. Perhaps, having spent a lifetime getting into trouble, she just had that look about her. Thankfully, the scanners had even missed the tiny earpiece embedded in the bones of her inner ear. The Bureau security team clearly knew what they were doing.

'You through, Ms Pike?' came Drake's voice.

'Just about,' Nero reported back. 'We're making our way to the gate.'

'We'll send you more intel once you're on board.'

The flight took off on time. Nero stared through the window as the suburbs of London grew small beneath her, then settled back in her chair. Flying executive class gave each of the young women their own small, self-contained pod. It comprised a computer terminal, entertainment screen, food tray, magazine pocket and extendible seat. Blankets, pillows and an eye mask were placed in her overhead locker. Swinging the whole unit to face the window gave her enough privacy to browse her Bureau computer slate undisturbed. To be honest, she relished the prospect of spending a little time alone. Her personal computer pad beeped into life as she held the back of her hand to the screen. Navigating away from the homepage, Nero settled first on the biography files.

'*Nicole Pike*,' the text read, '*Date of Birth, 28.01.39. Mother, Daphne Colman, chemist. Father, Sebastian Pike, teacher. Education, Latymer College, Hammersmith, London.*

Awarded Bright and Bold status, 2055. Purpose of visit, engineering placement, Clarke Elevator.'

So much for the headlines. Nero knew there were other files that went into more details of the fictitious Ms Pike's life; her hobbies, aptitudes, exam results, likes and dislikes, boyfriends. She was the model of perfection. Nero hated her and envied her all at once. Perhaps she would enjoy being her.

Nero pinched the bridge of her nose. Supersonic flight always played hell with her sinuses. Even at full speed, it would be another five hours before the Overture landed at Schwarzenegger Airport, San Francisco. Swiping her slate's screen, she opened the files relating to the Clarke Elevator. It wouldn't hurt to brush up on her history. At the wave of a finger, text and images scrolled before her. She tapped the *connect* button to hear the text via her earpiece.

'The idea of a space elevator entered popular consciousness thanks to twentieth century science fiction writer, Arthur C. Clarke. Clarke postulated an elevator shaft moored on the Earth's equator and stretching up to a launch platform in orbit. The tether would enable the lifting of machinery and vehicle parts for launch from the orbiting platform, thus negating the need for expensive, inefficient and wasteful rocket launches. As technology progressed throughout the early twenty-first century, sufficient advances were made to produce the materials necessary to maintain integrity in such challenging conditions. The Clarke Elevator was built over a twenty-three year period, eventually opening to commercial and private customers in 2047.' A picture of a bustling concourse filled the screen.

'To maximise profit,' the accompanying voice reported, 'hotels, retail outlets and recreation centres are incorporated into the lower reaches of the elevator, with the central elevator cars able to carry loads in excess of a thousand tons.'

A promotional video played of cranes loading equipment into the central elevator, while happy tourists sat to eat their dinner at the swanky restaurants. They waved enthusiastically as the car began to rise in the elevator shaft and the camera swooped to follow its progress. Another camera caught the moment of arrival on the space platform, a hundred thousand kilometres above the Earth's surface. 'The more adventurous holiday maker,' the voice continued, 'can even enjoy time in space, courtesy of the many hotels stationed on the platform.' The picture cut to a space liner lifting from a launch pad. More text scrolled across the screen, listing the daily schedule of flights to the Moon and Mars and its satellites. Without the burden of launching rockets from the Earth, space travel had become almost commonplace in the last decade, no longer the preserve of the rich elite.

Nero yawned. As an attendant arrived with a lunch that looked almost edible, she turned her chair away from the window to eat. Her mind was full of questions. She was terrified that, within the next three days, one way or another, they would all be answered.

Her dinner finished, Nero idly clicked her slate back on. She wondered just how far her computer authorisation would get her. Waving her hand across the screen, she called up a menu of Bureau personnel and clicked on Nathan Drake.

'*Educated at Cambridge, three years in Military Intelligence, seconded to First Action Bureau. Decorated for services to the government, black belt in karate, vegetarian.*'

Nero thought for a moment. If she had to come up with the blandest biography ever, that would be it. She gave a half smile and searched for the name Lucien Harrison. A picture of her newest friend flashed before her, his red hair and pale skin recognisable at once.

'*Educated at Belmont Academy, expelled, Foster Wood High School, suspended, George Traynor College, expelled.*'

Naughty boy, Nero smirked.

'*Royal Electrical and Mechanical Engineers, tours of duty, Oman and Dubai, decorated. Commonwealth medal, kickboxing.*'

Impressive.

Benjamin Saal had told her that the Bureau computer was able to search pretty much any database in the world. A deep impulse took over. Her heart pounding, Nero entered the name *Jonathan Aurelius Jones, Doctor*.

The result was almost instantaneous, and it stopped her breath.

ACCESS: DENIED.

Nero tried again using every combination of his name and adding pertinent details to the search request. Education, spouse, name of daughter. Still, the result was the same.

ACCESS: DENIED.

Benjamin had mentioned that the computer would give Bureau agents *the information they needed*. Why would she not have the authorisation to search for information on her own father?

The connecting flight was not so comfortable. The old, reconditioned 737 rattled through the cloud layer as it swooped over the Pacific. Nero was glad she had done all her reading during the earlier, much smoother flight. She wasn't quite so glad she had eaten so much. Peering through the window into the morning sun, Nero gasped at the view. Meena leaned over to gaze out of the window in awe. Punching its way through the clouds and reaching up as far as they could see, the space elevator was incongruous against the perfect blue sky. Angling her head against the glass, Nero strained to see the end of the huge shaft. She knew it was unlikely. Improbable though it might seem, the elevator's end was still several tens of thousands of metres above her. Nero shook her head to clear it. She could barely take it in. Even at this distance, the elevator's half-kilometre width looked substantial and solid. It was almost impossible to believe that an explosion of any sort could affect it.

She heard a beep in her ear. 'How are you both?' Drake's voice was as clear as if he had been sitting next to her.

'We're twenty minutes out from Kiribati,' Nero heard Meena answer. The cabin shook. 'If we make it in one piece.'

'Excellent. There'll be a boat waiting for you. It's a busy port so you'll have to be sharp to find it.'

'Oh, we're sharp,' Nero smirked.

'When you get to the elevator, there's a reservation for you at the hotel Utopia.'

'The Utopia,' Nero sighed. 'Got it.'

'And we've got some more intel for you. I'm passing you over.'

Nero heard a click and another familiar voice chimed in her ear.

'Hello, Nero. Miss me?'

Nero rolled her eyes. 'Like I miss my appendix. Hello, Benji.'

She could tell he was disappointed by her response.

'And hello, Meena,' he continued as if suddenly aware he had a wider audience. 'We've had a spike in the data. It suggests the attack will be tomorrow. And it's going to be big.'

'That makes me feel a whole lot better, thanks,' Meena muttered.

'Hopefully, we'll have more by the time you arrive.'

'Hopefully?' Nero repeated. 'Is *hope* all we've got left?'

'Just – be careful.' The note of concern in his voice was almost touching. 'And Nero?'

'Yeah?'

'It's Benjamin. I hate Benji.'

The line clicked and he was gone. With a smile at Meena, Nero settled back in her seat for the remainder of the flight. Just as she felt herself dozing off, her thoughts were interrupted by the sound of the pilot announcing their descent. Once again, Meena leaned towards the window as the plane rattled its way through the clouds.

Kiribati was a series of drowned islands. Rising sea levels had eaten away at their shores and infiltrated their jungles. Ironically for many of the islanders, they had been saved by the pinnacle of Western technology, the coming of the Clarke Elevator. It had been constructed some fifteen kilometres away on its own artificial island, but the islands of Kiribati had become the jumping off point for tourists and commercial interests who had their space in the elevator booked. The nearest and the biggest was Kiritimati, previously known as Christmas Island. It had a notorious history. The site of American nuclear tests in the 1960s, Kiritimati had spent the next seven decades living with its atomic legacy. The building of the space elevator had lifted it from poverty and given it a prominent position in local geopolitics. Money had poured in as quickly as the rising tides. Shore defences were strengthened, infrastructure rebuilt. The population saw their island transformed. Now it was a bustling transport hub, the only transport connection to the elevator. A huge port had been built on the island's north side, big enough to provide almost all the inhabitants with a job.

Nero found her boat easily enough. A gruff looking man with a sign reading *Nicole Pike and Hazeema Ahmed* leaned against the mooring, a cigarette dangling from his lips. Nero hadn't seen anyone smoke for years.

Once aboard, the two young women sat with their backs to the engine. The little craft buzzed around the harbour before heading for the open seas of the Pacific, giving Nero the chance to marvel at the hulking ships docked there. Many were loaded with rocket parts, ready for their transport to the elevator. She recognised the fuselage of an X23 space liner resting on the deck of a huge carrier. The people bustling around to secure it looked like ants. Behind it, a tourist ship had let go its anchor to slip from the harbour, a band playing on its sundeck.

The little boat skipped across the waves, into the shadow cast by the vast construction ahead. Shielding her eyes with a hand, Nero traced the elevator up as high as she could see. The clouds had cleared by now, but still its very top was invisible.

'Look as closely as you like,' the captain growled from the wheel, 'you'll never see the top. Some people just can't look at it.'

Nero could understand. The sight seemed to play with her concept of reality itself. *How can something be so tall?*

'You okay?' Meena asked.

Nero smiled weakly. Surprised to feel a pang of vertigo, she looked down to the horizon to steady herself.

'Is it always so humid?' Nero asked, trying to take her mind off the towering monstrosity in front.

The captain laughed. 'Gotta love this sea air! I'm a Utah boy. It's so dry there, you can feel your skin crack like baked mud.'

At last, the boat docked on Clarke Island, an expanse of sand, concrete and steel sunk down through the sea to the atoll beneath. Nero shuddered to think just how deep such a tall construction would need its foundations. The captain seemed to sense her unease as she stepped onto the quayside.

'Try not to think about it,' he winked. 'It's not going to fall. It's physics!'

'Thanks,' she replied. If he had known what she knew, perhaps he wouldn't be so certain.

Nero and Meena slung their bags over their shoulders and walked the short distance to the entrance.

Nero was glad to get into the shade of the atrium. The walls were lined with tall palm trees and cascading water features that helped to cool the air. It was busy with tourists and workers, some lounging in the various restaurants and bars that seemed to run around the entire perimeter, others hurrying towards the loading bays in the huge central shaft that would occasionally open to admit them. For the first few hundred metres, the elevator shaft was made of toughened glass so it was possible to see each huge car as it lifted into the air. The elevator itself operated on a counterweight principle. As one car rose, so another fell, passing each other at the midway point and arriving at their destinations at the same time.

'It's physics,' Meena reminded her, playfully. Nero couldn't help an involuntary shudder.

Looking around, she saw a sign for the Utopia Hotel, its balconies opening out among the fronds of various trees planted in the atrium.

'That's us.'

The reception was wide and spacious with low sofas and loungers placed tastefully around glass tables. Large works of modern art hung from the walls. A grand sculpture dominated the room, though Nero couldn't tell exactly what it was a sculpture of.

The receptionist looked up as she approached.

'Ms Pike,' he smiled as he scanned their passport. 'Like the fish.'

Nero gave him a steely stare. Meena had teased her on the plane that her alias, Hazeema, meant *beautiful woman* in her native Urdu. Next time, Nero vowed, she would pick something to match it.

'And Ms Ahmed. You are very welcome.' He tapped a keyboard on his desktop. 'You are in room three-seventy,' he said as he read from the screen. He looked disparagingly at their backpacks as he continued. 'Would you like us to take your, er, *bags*, up to your room?'

'We can manage, thanks.' Meena flashed him a smile. 'But we've come a long way. Could you send up a pitcher of iced tea? Then I think we'd like to be left alone.' She gave him a wink. 'You know, to catch up on our sleep?'

Meena turned from the desk and walked towards the lifts. Nero gave the receptionist an apologetic smile then, catching her reflection in the mirror behind him, she noticed she was blushing with embarrassment.

9

The Space Elevator

The room was plush, opulent even, a far cry from the Dump.

'If they could see us now,' Meena beamed, her dark eyes shining.

Nero studied her friend intently as Meena waved the back of her hand in front of her screen. She looked somehow different to when they'd last seen each other. It was barely a week ago, but she seemed older, more controlled somehow. Perhaps that's how Nero appeared, too. Maybe the Bureau's training was rubbing off on her after all.

'First things first,' Meena said. 'I'm going to do a little digging through the Bureau's mainframe.'

'You mean BRAINS,' Nero smirked.

'Oh God, did he tell you that, too?' Meena rolled her eyes. 'The guy's an embarrassment.'

A series of numbers and letters scrolled in the air before them.

'You've logged in just in time,' came Drake's voice in Nero's earpiece. She guessed Meena could hear him too. 'We've managed to pinpoint the exact time of the incident.'

Nero swallowed, suddenly aware of the seriousness of the situation. The numbers resolved themselves into a coherent sequence. *One, one, three, zero.*

'That gives us three hours,' Meena gasped, meeting Nero's gaze.

'That's the *when*,' Nero said. 'What about the *where*?'

'We've narrowed it down,' came Drake's voice, 'but it's not precise.'

The scrolling numbers were replaced by a projection of the Clarke Elevator, snaking up into space. A red line was drawn around its circumference, several thousand metres up.

'That's the twenty-five thousand kilometre mark,' Drake continued. 'The worst-case scenario. An explosion at that height would sever the elevator and send the bottom portion crashing to Earth.'

'That all you got?' Nero asked.

'We'll have more intel the closer we get to the event. That's when all the probability points conjoin.' Nero noticed a note of doubt in his voice. 'At least, that's what they tell me.'

By *they*, Nero knew he meant Benjamin Saal. She wasn't exactly thrilled that her life was in his hands.

'Do we know *who*?' Meena was walking to the window.

'Again, not yet.' Drake sounded apologetic. 'But – '

'We'll know when we get there,' Nero interrupted.

'Or, at least we'll know who it *isn't*.'

Nero sighed. 'I suppose that's some comfort.'

'We'll keep you in the loop as we know more,' Drake concluded. Nero felt the comms click off, though she wasn't sure Drake wouldn't still be listening.

'What do we do now?'

Meena smiled back. 'Our job.'

She leaned toward the projection, pinching her fingers and opening them again to zoom in closer on the image.

'The Bureau computer has obviously hacked into the elevator's schematics,' she muttered almost to herself. 'So, let's see what it's found.' A single section of the elevator, labelled Epsilon Three Five, came into focus and Meena began to interpret what she saw.

As she continued, Nero pulled out her computer pad. 'Two heads are better than one,' she smiled, holding the back of her hand up to the slate's sensor. 'Computer,' she said quietly, 'let me see the current customer manifest. Give me everyone who's visited, stayed at or even eaten at Clarke Island in the last twenty-four hours.'

An inventory of names scrolled through the air.

'There must be hundreds of people here.' Nero peered closer at the list. Column by column, their security status flashed green. 'And they all registered clear on the security scans.' She knew that everyone landing on Clarke Island would have been subject to intense scanning. The whole world seemed scared. And not without good reason.

'I think I've got a lead on the *where*,' Meena reported. Nero turned to see a smaller section of the projection flashing red. 'The elevator was constructed in sections half a kilometre high, then lifted inside the tube to be assembled. So, every five hundred metres, there's a point of weakness.' She was reading from a text box in the corner of the image. 'Not enough to cause any problems to the elevator, but enough to be exploited.' She pointed at the spinning display. 'If I were to plant a bomb, I'd plant it there.'

'Why not at any other point?' Nero asked. 'If there's a weak spot every five hundred metres, you could be out by half a kilometre either way.'

Meena smiled. 'Exhaust ports.' The revolving image showed ducts opening out onto the elevator's smooth surface at intervals around its circumference. 'At high altitude, internal pressure is maintained in the tube by the introduction of argon. It's an inert gas,' Meena read, 'but needs to be regulated as the elevator flexes with the turn of the Earth. As it expands, some of it is vented into the atmosphere to maintain equilibrium.' She pointed to where a plume of gas was being ejected into space. 'A ventilation duct on a weak spot, twenty-five thousand kilometres up.' She turned to Nero with a conspiratorial smile. '*That's* where I'd plant my bomb.'

Nero was impressed. 'Okay,' she muttered. 'So we're looking for someone who'd have access to the vents.' She turned back to her slate. 'Computer, show me the maintenance schedule for the Clarke Elevator for the next three hours. And give me the names of the service teams.'

The list of names disappeared, to be replaced with a timetable. Date and times down one side, names down another, duties highlighted underneath. '0900,' Nero read. 'Vent inspection, deck Epsilon three zero one.'

Pictures of a man and a woman appeared on the projection.

'Hernandes and Kapoor,' Nero read.

Meena leaned over her shoulder. 'How would they get through the elevator security with the explosives they needed?'

Nero had a thought. 'Computer, show me information about argon.' Nero read the text aloud as it scrolled before her.

'Noble gas… chemical symbol, AR… atomic number, 18… third most abundant gas in Earth's atmosphere… does not burn, but may react explosively with liquid nitrogen.'

'Hold it there,' Meena snapped. 'Liquid nitrogen?' Her fingers danced across her own slate. 'Nitrogen is standard issue in atmospheric engineering. It's used to cool superheated components for repair.' A text box flashed before her. 'That's an inventory of current maintenance stores.'

Nero saw something interesting in the list. 'Liquid nitrogen,' she read aloud. 'Two thousand five hundred litres.'

Meena whistled. 'Put a hundred litres of that in an argon atmosphere next to a timer and an ignition circuit,' she said gravely, 'and you wouldn't need a bomb.'

Nero waved her hand and her display disappeared. 'Then it looks like we have the *where*, the *when*, the *who* and the *how*.'

Meena nodded. 'And we didn't need a supercomputer to work it out.'

'So,' Nero wondered aloud. 'Now what?'

Meena nodded to her display. 'Well, we've got access to their security systems and we know where they keep their supplies.' She turned to Nero, a broad grin spreading across her face. 'Let's go take a ride!'

10

The Big Bang

It was almost too easy. With their ID codes synchronised to the elevator's security systems, it was a simple matter of holding up their hands to gain access. The maintenance store was a large warehouse of a room lined with shelves and cupboards. With the maintenance shift already underway, Nero and Meena found themselves alone with the chemicals, tools and equipment used in the day to day running of the elevator.

'Take your pick,' Meena grinned as she shrugged into the nearest service suit. It was a one piece overall with pockets and a utility belt for hanging tools. Heavy boots and gloves completed the look. As Nero chose a uniform for herself, Meena roamed the shelves for appropriate tools.

'If the Bureau won't give us weapons,' she mused, tossing Nero a heavy laser torch, 'we'll have to find our own.'

In a matter of minutes, they were fully equipped and making their way across the bustling concourse to the elevator entrance. It was busier now than it had been just a few hours earlier. Nero noticed whole families browsing the shops and restaurants.

'Shouldn't we do something?' she gasped. 'Warn everyone?'

Meena threw her a look. 'Do you think they'd believe us?'

'We could sound an alarm,' Nero countered. 'Get everyone evacuated.'

'There would be panic,' Meena replied reasonably. 'And not enough transport for everyone. The best thing we can do is our job.'

They were waved through the elevator entrance by a surly looking attendant.

'You're running late.'

'We missed the start of the shift,' Nero snapped back. 'So, report us.'

The attendant sneered as the doors closed behind them.

The elevator car took up half the tube's interior. If this one was on the ground, Nero knew, the other must be docked at the space platform, a hundred thousand kilometres above her. It was a dizzying thought.

The passenger compartment was spacious enough, but only took up a fraction of the elevator car. They were joined by a dozen or so fellow passengers for the journey up into the Earth's atmosphere, a couple of whom were dressed in smart pilot's uniforms. Beside them, were families and couples dressed in expensive clothes, with trolleys of luggage secured beside them. Nero wondered where they were headed. Some of them, no doubt, to Mars or the Moon, where smart new holiday habitats had just been opened. Others were perhaps bound for hotels on the space platform itself. They had become increasingly popular with wealthy holidaymakers, affording the opportunity to dine in zero gravity while gazing down at breathtaking views of the revolving Earth.

Above them, on a loading bay supported by the roof, Nero knew there would be engine components and supplies for delivery to the space platform. There, they would be transferred into orbit then assembled or delivered to waiting ships for their onward journeys.

'So, where are you getting off?' The attendant looked annoyed at the interruption to his morning's schedule.

'Epsilon Three Five,' Nero replied as she eased herself onto one of the seats.

The attendant punched the information into a computer console.

'Hold very tight, please.'

Nero felt barely anything as the ground dropped away. Screens in the wall showed the external view as the elevator shot into the air. Clarke Island receded beneath them, the Pacific Ocean widening as they rose.

'I got a spaceman.'

Nero looked down to see a small child had jumped from his seat.

'He's coming with me to Mars.' He held a small stuffed toy in front of Nero's face. It was a comical astronaut with a child's face.

Nero read the legend emblazoned across his T-shirt; 'MY PARENTS TOOK ME TO THE CLARKE ELEVATOR AND ALL THEY GOT ME WAS THIS LOUSY T-SHIRT.' She couldn't help smiling in spite of the seriousness of the situation. She'd had trouble processing the sheer numbers involved in the projected catastrophe, but somehow this one child had brought it home. Suddenly, it seemed all the more imperative that their mission should succeed. She looked at her friend as the elevator rose through the atmosphere.

Meena was clenching her jaw, clearly focussed on the magnitude of their mission. Again, Nero was struck by how much she had changed since their time at the Dump. Controlled, methodical, mature. Thankfully, Nero felt Meena's calm rubbing off on her. She took deep breaths and felt her racing heart settle.

'You have ninety minutes,' Drake's voice buzzed in her ear. Nero had apprised him of their plan before they had left the hotel room. 'The Bureau computer has confirmed your conclusions.' There was a pause. 'And we have a probability score for your success.'

Nero eyed Meena carefully. 'Tell us,' she whispered, already dreading the answer.

'The computer puts your chances at forty per cent.'

Nero nodded as Meena caught her gaze. 'We'll take that,' she replied, a note of steely determination in her voice.

'The people look like ants!' The child squealed as the screens continued to show the scene outside. Nero looked across to see Clarke Island could barely be seen now. They must be five thousand metres high already.

She glanced at the attendant to see him looking at his fingernails, clearly bored. Nero wondered how he hadn't yet been replaced by a holographic interface. If his vintage attendant's uniform and pillbox hat were meant to convey to the passengers a feeling of exotic adventure, it was completely undermined by his surly attitude.

The minutes passed. Nero swung her bag from her shoulder and reached for her Spi-Glasses. She had paired them to the Bureau computer to receive real time telemetry. As the elevator slowed, she slipped them on and tapped the frames to activate them.

'Epsilon Three Five,' drawled the attendant. He jabbed at the control panel and a door in the elevator wall slid to one side. He stabbed at the button again and another door hissed open to reveal the interior of the shaft wall.

Before leaving, Nero bent to the kid with the spaceman toy. 'Look after him,' she whispered, conspiratorially.

'I will,' the child nodded.

'I was talking to your spaceman.' Nero tousled the child's hair, then followed her friend through the doors and into the elevator shaft's superstructure.

She heard, or rather *felt*, the elevator depart behind them. The accelerated movement of air produced an audible *whump*, followed by an eerie whistling sound. The walls of the elevator were two hundred metres thick, a honeycomb of maintenance gantries, walkways and vents.

'Drake,' Nero barked, activating her comms, 'do you know where we're headed?'

'Sector seven,' came the brusque reply. 'Sending it to you now.'

Nero's Spi-Glasses displayed a yellow line along the floor of the corridor.

'The vent is two metres ahead.'

'Do we know when the next argon ejection is scheduled?' Meena walked carefully ahead, following the line projected onto her Spi-Glasses lenses.

'Running it now. The closer we get, the more precise we can be.'

'That's helpful,' Nero smirked.

'Eleven minutes,' Drake replied at last.

'Okay,' Nero breathed. 'Then we've got no time to stand around talking.'

The corridor ahead curved to their left. Pressing her hand to the metal wall as she walked, Nero was sure she could sense the cold of space leaching through. It was an impossibility, she told herself. According to the schematics she had poured over in the hotel room, the wall was tens of metres thick.

'Wait,' came Meena's voice, suddenly tense. 'You hear that?'

Pressing themselves to the inner wall, they both strained to listen in the silence. For a while, all Nero could hear was her own heart beating against her chest and her rapid breathing. Then, almost imperceptibly at first, came a new sound. Voices.

'I hear them,' Nero whispered. She tapped the frames of her Spi-Glasses and flicked her eyes across the systems menu that appeared before her.

APPLICATIONS>VIEW>RADIOGRAPHY
>LOW
>MEDIUM
>HIGH

With a series of rapid eye movements, Nero selected the *HIGH* setting. She gasped as the ground beneath her seemed to drop away.

'What can you see?' Meena reached out to steady her. Nero clasped her hand tightly, as if her life depended on it. In truth, she felt like it did.

She found herself hanging in space, twenty-five thousand kilometres above the Earth. Almost the entire face of the planet was laid out beneath her. She could see cloud systems swathing whole continents and the ice cap of the North Pole reflecting the harsh glare of the sun. The great oceans glistened and sparkled. Breathe, she thought to herself. I must remember to breathe. She looked directly ahead, through the inner walls of the elevator shaft, and saw two figures crouching low. Their attention was fixed on a large cylinder on the ground by their feet.

'Got them,' Nero panted. 'A man and a woman just ahead.'

'Hernandes and Kapoor? The maintenance shift?' Meena tried to peer round the curve of the corridor. 'I assumed they'd be long gone.'

'I guess they didn't want to risk the device being discovered,' hissed Nero. 'So they're setting it at the last moment and going up with it.'

'A suicide mission,' Meena nodded. 'Martyrs to the Dheghomite cause.'

'At least we've got the element of surprise,' Nero whispered as she slipped her Spi-Glasses from her nose. 'For now.'

'Reckon we can take them?' Meena was shrugging her bag from her back.

'Do we have a choice?' Nero took a deep breath and inched further along the corridor.

Meena followed carefully, a heavy metal wrench from the maintenance stores balanced carefully in her hands. They stopped as they rounded the corner, and saw the two maintenance crew leaning over their work. They squatted beside the vent that ran through an enclosed tube from the interior shaft to the exterior wall. A hatch had been opened in the top of the tube, ready to receive the explosives as the argon discharge began.

Nero turned to Meena and gestured wordlessly. *You take the guy on the right, I'll take Kapoor on the left.*

Meena nodded in understanding as Nero flicked a button on her laser torch. A short, powerful beam flickered and spat in front of them.

Just as they were preparing themselves for a mad dash towards their quarry, Nero felt a sharp pain in her temple. It was enough to make her gasp aloud in agony and drop the torch to the floor with a clatter.

The terrorists turned at once as the two young women ducked back out of sight. Meena shot a questioning look at Nero who was slowly recovering.

'What was that?' she hissed.

Nero didn't dare look at her. Instead, she took a breath and rushed forwards. As she rounded the corner, she slammed into Hernandes. Hearing the noise, he had clearly elected to investigate. Nero caught him off guard just as he was bending for the discarded laser torch. She barrelled into his shoulder and sent him flailing to the floor with a cry of surprise.

Kapoor responded at once, leaping to her feet and reaching for a side pocket. As Meena ran round the corner, she found herself confronted with the barrel of a snub-nosed laser pistol. She raised her hand instinctively in front of her face in a vain attempt to protect herself and ducked to the floor. Just as Kapoor released her shot, Nero launched herself at the startled woman, sending her reeling. A sizzling bolt of superheated light glanced off the elevator shaft with a *ching*! as the gun flew from Kapoor's hand.

Hernandes, meanwhile, had struggled to his feet. As the gun clattered down the corridor, he sprinted towards it in an effort to retrieve the smoking firearm.

Nero had recovered her balance and threw herself at Hernandes's outstretched arm. She was sure she heard the snap of bone as she landed with her full weight on his elbow. Hernandes gave an almost animal-like cry of pain.

'The device!' yelled Meena, as her eye fell upon the menacing looking cylinder by the vent. A small box had been connected to the deadly payload. Nero guessed it was an improvised detonator.

Just as she dashed for the cylinder, she heard a roar from behind. Kapoor grabbed her by the shoulders and swung her into the wall. Nero winced with pain as her head made contact with metal, then turned to face her opponent. Kapoor held her by the neck with one hand and clawed at her face with the other. Her eyes burned with a fierce belligerence. Just as Nero was sure she was about to lose consciousness, she saw Meena rising up behind her assailant, her heavy metal wrench raised high in the air before her.

With an audible *clang*, Meena brought the tool crashing down on Kapoor's head. She sunk to the floor with a dazed expression, leaving Nero to mouth a quick *thank you* to her friend.

Turning back to attend to the device, they saw Hernandes standing before them. Sweat ran down his face from his forehead and the neck of his overall was soaked. His useless hand hung limp at his side but, in his other, he held Kapoor's discarded laser pistol. He had them both clearly in his sight.

Just as Nero and Meena considered their options, Hernandes opened fire.

But not at them.

A barrage of laser fire strafed the ceiling and inner walls of the corridor. The two young women threw themselves to the floor and shielded their eyes against the glare. The metal buckled and warped in the intense heat. As Nero squinted through her fingers, she saw an entire section of the ceiling give way. Supporting struts and ducts crashed to the floor, glowing white hot as huge panels of steaming metal lodged themselves against the walls.

'He's cut us off!' Meena cried above the noise of rending metal. 'We'll never get through!'

Nero dusted herself down as she stood up. 'Drake? How long do we have?'

'Six minutes,' came the tense reply. 'How's it going up there?'

Nero glanced at the wall of glowing metal in front of her. 'Could be better,' she sighed. 'The elevator is five hundred metres wide.'

'So?' Meena blinked.

'If we can't go forward,' Nero continued, nodding at the obstacle ahead, 'we gotta go back.'

Meena frowned.

'*Pi r squared.*' Nero was smiling. 'Whoever thought that would come in handy?'

'Nero,' Meena cautioned, 'we don't have long...'

'Yeah, but we've got long enough.' Nero spun round to face the way they had come. 'A cylinder with a diameter of five hundred metres will have a circumference of a kilometre and a half.' She looked at Meena. 'I've got a little under six minutes to run fifteen hundred metres.'

Meena's eyes were wide. 'Reckon you can do it?'

Nero was almost hurt that her old friend would doubt her. 'Just watch me,' she smirked.

She settled herself for a moment then tensed every muscle in her body, ready to run. If she could defeat Gunther's barking dogs and stinging bees, then she could sure as hell run the circumference of a space elevator in six minutes or less.

'I'll be right behind you,' Meena said softly. 'Or at least, as near as I can be.'

Taking off at speed, Nero fought the urge to pace herself. Meena's footsteps soon disappeared behind her as she lowered her head and fell into a punishing rhythm. Soon, her lungs burned and her legs complained of the pain. The lactic acid in her muscles conspired with her relentless motion to induce cramp in her thighs, but still she pressed on. Soon, the distance covered and the distance yet to run became a blur. The corridor looked the same at every turn. Sparse, functional and bathed in a harsh artificial light, it confused the senses. Nero felt like she had been running for hours.

At last, she slowed. Hugging the interior wall, she tried her best to regulate her breathing so as not to give herself away. Hernandes and the device were just around the corner. Dropping low, Nero saw that he was almost heedless of his damaged arm, working at speed to complete his task, one handed. Dropping her gaze, her eye fell on something more welcome. Her laser torch, discarded in the tussle with Hernandes.

Thinking fast, Nero dropped to the floor and rolled. Grabbing the torch as she passed it, she sprang to her feet before Hernandes had time to react. Raising it high, and pressing the button to activate its fizzing blade of light, Nero plunged the laser into the terrorist's shoulder and sliced downwards. Hernandes let go a scream of agony and fell backwards, his good hand rising to his shoulder in a futile attempt to relieve the pain.

'You've got thirty seconds,' came Drake's voice in her ear. Nero didn't bother to respond. Instead, she leaped over to the cylinder. It lay on top of the ventilation tube, resting by the open hatch in readiness. Her first instinct was to grab at the detonation device and pull it free, but she guessed that wouldn't end well for anybody. Instead, she pulled the laser torch from Hernandes' inert body and leaned forward over the cylinder. The detonator had been soldered onto its outer casing. It would have to be removed carefully.

'Ten seconds,' came Drake's voice.

'Nero!' Meena shouted from the corridor as she sprinted to join her friend. 'Dump it now! Before the argon ejection!'

'It's on a timer! It'll blow!'

'But it'll blow outside the elevator!'

Meena was right. Dropping the laser torch and prising the vent hatch open, Nero carefully angled the cylinder down into the hole. It rested at the bottom of the tube, its detonation box blinking steadily in the dark.

I've got to get in there with it, reasoned Nero. *I've got to push it out into the atmosphere.* She clambered on top of the tube. The hatch was just big enough to take her.

Meena screamed as she drew alongside the vent. With no time to even acknowledge her arrival, Nero's head disappeared through the hatch.

Looking into the void, Nero could see the outer door was opening in readiness for the ejection. She reached up to close the hatch above her as the air was sucked from the compartment. Nero felt the sudden cold freezing her veins. Her lips felt numb. She gasped for breath. If she could just wait long enough...

Guessing she had only moments until the chamber was flooded with argon, Nero braced her legs against the cylinder and pushed. It slid closer to the outside hatch. Summoning her strength, Nero pushed again. This time, the outrush of air carried the cylinder with it and Nero watched as it spun out into the atmosphere, the blue-green globe revolving slowly beneath it.

The thin air suddenly turned thick. Fighting unconsciousness, Nero tasted a metallic tang at the back of her throat. Argon. The ejection had begun. Her sight fading, Nero looked past her feet to see the cylinder falling to Earth. As the argon gas hissed all around her, she saw it explode away from the elevator, its tiny fragments dissipating in the atmosphere.

The elevator was safe.

Nero's lungs felt fit to burst. Her whole body was numb from the cold. She had been braced against the chamber's sides to prevent her slipping away through the door but now, with her energy fading, she relaxed her muscles and began to slip. At last the argon ejection stopped and the hatch above her sprang open.

'I told you I'd be right behind you.'

Nero looked up to see a friendly face. Meena reached down to grab at her friend but Nero, almost unconscious now, felt her body slip away through the tube and into the atmosphere, the life finally draining from her as she fell from the elevator.

11

Aftermath

The alarm sounded.

'It is six, a.m.'

She snapped her eyes open and sat bolt upright in her bed, breathing fast. Sweat pricked at her forehead. The sheets were wet. For a moment she couldn't tell where she was. She was both here and not here. *Cognitive dissonance*, she thought. *The ability to hold two opposing views at the same time.* Here and not here. Now and not now. She was held in a moment out of time, not sure even who she was.

Who
am
I?

'It is six, a.m.,' the expressionless voice repeated. A voice she both recognised and didn't recognise. She looked around the room. The bed, a table, a desk, a door to the bathroom, another to the living room. It was beginning to feel familiar, like a shape materialising from the fog.

'Home,' she heard herself say, 'where am I?'

'Your apartment,' came the calm reply. 'Thirty-three, Silk Street, Barbican, London.' There was a pause. 'Are you quite well?'

Nero shivered, suddenly cold. 'You tell me.'

'Your heartbeat and core temperature are unusually high. As are your blood pressure and cortisol level. And you have been grinding your teeth.'

Nero nodded. That would explain the headache. 'You appear to have been under enormous stress.'

'But I've been in bed.'

'Correct.'

Nero was scared. What the hell had just happened? It had all felt so real. It was real. Had to be. 'How long was I asleep?'

'Seven hours, eighteen minutes and twenty-three seconds.'

'And I was right here, a*ll the time*?'

There was a pause.

'Are you quite – '

'Yes, I'm fine,' Nero snapped. She wasn't fine, though. She was frightened. There was a question she didn't dare ask. She was afraid of the answer. 'I need a coffee,' she said, swinging her legs from the bed. 'And I need it so caffeinated you could stand your spoon in it.'

'That is inadvisable,' the voice droned as she walked to the kitchen. 'Caffeine is a stimulant. My diagnosis suggests it would prove detrimental to your current well-being.'

Nero turned. 'Diagnosis?' she countered. 'What diagnosis?'

The computer seemed to weigh up whether she should be told or not. 'Your symptoms are consistent with patients exhibiting panic disorder.'

'A panic attack?' Nero shook her head. 'You think I'm having a panic attack?'

'It is the most reasonable supposition. And easily treated with medication and therapy.'

Nero put one hand on the kitchen worktop as her coffee was prepared. 'How do I get a second opinion?' she drawled.

'I am happy to run a full psych evaluation.'

'No,' she barked. 'That's not necessary.' In truth, she was scared of what it might find.

'Coffee will do.'

She sipped from her cup in silence. 'Home,' she said at last, 'The Bureau monitors my location at all times.'

'That is correct.'

'And you're hooked up to the Bureau computer?' She felt stupid even saying it.

'I am.'

She gnawed at her lip and swallowed. 'Have I been abroad since joining the Bureau?'

'You have not,'

'Have I been anywhere except my apartment and the Bureau facility in Fleet Street?'

'You have not.'

Nero fought to steady her breathing. She refused to believe none of it had happened. The elevator, Meena. It was real. She *remembered* it. But if it *had* happened, how had she survived? She wanted to scream.

'Incoming call,' the voice announced, suddenly. 'Nathan Drake, First Action Bureau.'

Shit. Bad timing. Should she tell him? Nero downed the last of her coffee. What was there to tell?

'Incoming call,' the voice repeated, emotionless as ever.

'Okay, okay,' sighed Nero as she walked into the living room. 'I'll take it.'

Drake's disembodied head appeared in the space above Nero's computer hub.

'Good morning, Nero,' he said in his usual officious tone. 'I'm sorry to bother you so early.'

'It's fine,' Nero shrugged. 'I had a restless night.' He didn't need to know any more than that, she decided.

'I have some news.' Drake seemed hesitant. 'It's about your mother. She's disappeared.'

A rumble of thunder rolled across the steel grey sky. The car dropped Nero right outside the front door. She had noticed on the journey that the demonstrations had increased. There was a palpable sense of fear in the air. She had seen protestors manhandled by the security forces and even bundled away into unmarked vans. It was getting more difficult to see just who the enemy was.

Hudson jumped at the garden gate as Nero approached.

'Good boy!' she cooed as she rubbed him behind the ears. 'It's okay, Hudson. You're coming home with me.' Satisfied that the dog was calm, she pushed open the front door. For the second time in just a few days, she found Nathan Drake in her living room.

'I'm sorry, Nero.' He sounded sincere.

Nero looked around the room. Everything was just as she had last seen it, except it seemed infused with her mother's absence. Nero felt like a stranger in her own home. It was difficult to believe she'd come back so soon.

'What happened?' she whispered, suddenly aware of how strange her voice sounded in the silence of the room.

Drake shrugged. 'We don't know. We intercepted a missing person's report submitted to the police from Albion Laboratories.'

'It's where she works,' Nero confirmed.

'They've had no contact from her for three days.'

'That long?' Nero felt a sudden pang of guilt.

'We stood the military police down so we could investigate ourselves.'

Nero raised an eyebrow.

'If the mother of one of our agents disappears,' Drake explained, 'we need to get to the bottom of it. Our guys were here all night.'

'What did they find?'

Drake shuffled his feet, suddenly uncomfortable. 'Aside from a hungry dog, not much.'

Another pang of guilt. *Poor Hudson.*

'Who took her?'

'We can't be sure anyone *has* taken her,' Drake assured her. 'But your association with the Bureau might well have made her a target. That's why we've secured the property and taken over the investigation.'

Nero looked around her. She had never felt so alone. 'Security?'

'All devices were deactivated on the day she disappeared.'

'What about local surveillance? London is the most watched city on Earth right now.'

'Nothing.'

Nero found that difficult to believe.

'Then, whatever happened,' she said, 'it was planned.'

Drake nodded. 'Possibly.'

Nero stood for a while, trying to take in the full implications. Had her joining the Bureau put her mother in danger? If so, she wasn't sure she could live with herself. 'Can I have some time alone?' she asked at last.

Drake stood aside. 'Of course.' He moved to the door as he spoke. 'You'll need some time to process all this. I'll check in with you tomorrow.'

'Thank you.'

As the door closed behind him, Nero took a breath to steady her nerves. She was still unnerved by her vivid dream, if dream it was. If she concentrated hard enough, she could still taste the acrid tang of argon gas at the back of her throat. She could still feel the numbing cold of the thinning air. Nero gave an involuntary shiver.

Waving her hand over a side table, she scrolled through a series of family photos as they were projected on a wall from a photocube. Her mother and father on a wedding anniversary. Nero with an early birthday cake. Her father, fishing. Hudson as a puppy. Pictures from a simpler time. Before the divorce. Each one brought a smile to her face. The final picture in the sequence made her pause. It was the last picture taken of her father before he left. He was dressed in a smart suit and tie, his tanned skin and full head of hair giving him the air of an old-fashioned movie star.

Nero remembered being told of his death. Luckily, Meena had been next to her in the visitor's suite. Helene had made a surprise appearance between her usual monthly visits. She had sat opposite Nero and delivered the facts in an unnervingly cool manner. Grief, Meena had told her afterwards, affected different people in different ways. At the end of the conversation, Helene had said a simple *goodbye* and left. 'Is that it?' Nero had shouted after her. She winced at the memory.

She waved her hand to close the program and, for a while, stood staring into empty space. If both her parents were gone, would that make her an orphan? She frowned. Perhaps fortune had given her an opportunity to find the truth. With the full weight of the Bureau behind her, maybe she was able, at last, to get to the bottom of her father's death. The trouble was, it would mean swallowing her pride and taking someone up on their invitation.

Benjamin Saal couldn't help looking like the cat who had got the cream.

'Not eating your fish?' he asked, reaching over the table with his fork.

'It's overcooked,' Nero replied, toying with it with her knife. 'If I was eating alone, I'd send it back.' Frankly, she wished she *was* eating alone. 'I'll wait for dessert.'

Benjamin frowned. 'So, what caused this change of heart? Did I win you over with my tech talk? I hear some girls like that stuff.'

Nero almost choked on her drink. 'Sure, Benji. How could I resist?' She saw Benjamin wince.

'Could you... *not* call me Benji?' he whined.

Nero relented. 'Okay,' she nodded. Perhaps she needed to keep on his good side. 'Maybe I need a friend right now.'

Benjamin clearly wasn't satisfied with her answer. 'What about Harrison?' he asked, trying to sound blasé. 'You two seem to be getting pretty close.'

So, he *was* feeling jealous.

'Well,' Nero teased. 'You know. Birds of a feather.'

Benjamin looked confused. 'No, I don't know.'

'Troubled childhood. Issues with authority. I think we have a lot in common.'

'I see.' Benjamin seemed relieved.

'Oh, and he's pretty hot, too.'

Benjamin pushed his plate away, trying to hide his disappointment with a weak smile. 'So, why did you take me up on my offer if it wasn't for my scintillating conversation or lack of a six pack?'

Nero smiled. 'Oh, come on Benji – sorry, *Benjamin* – does there have to be an ulterior motive? Perhaps I just wanted someone to talk down to.'

'You know, I could just get the bill.' Benjamin made to gesture to a waitress.

'I'm sorry,' Nero said quickly. 'I didn't mean to be rude.'

Benjamin scrutinised her with his dark eyes.

Actually, he *is* quite handsome, Nero thought, against her better judgement.

'Well,' he beamed sweetly, 'if I can't take a bit of heat from our best new recruit, who can I take it from?'

'Best new recruit?' Nero replied. 'Do I get a badge for that?'

'No,' Benjamin replied, lifting his hand to a passing waiter. 'You get dessert.'

'Good enough for me. I'll have the chocolate brownie.'

With the order taken, Nero leaned back in her chair to eye the small man opposite her. She guessed he could be trusted. But how could she be sure?

'In your talk yesterday, which was actually fascinating by the way, you mentioned that each agent had access to the Bureau computer?'

'BRAINS,' Benjamin corrected her. 'To some degree, yes.'

'Well done on the name by the way,' Nero soothed. 'Acronyms are so sexy, don't you think?' Leaning forward, she gave her dinner companion a lascivious wink.

Feeling suddenly flustered, Benjamin ploughed on. 'There are various levels of authorisation to protect any information of a sensitive nature.'

'A sensitive nature?' Nero repeated softly, maintaining eye contact.

Benjamin cleared his throat. 'Er, yes. Only those at senior level have complete access.'

'I see.' Nero played with her fork. 'And just how senior are you? No wait,' she said before Benjamin could reply. 'Let me guess. I think you're very senior.'

Benjamin swallowed. 'Fairly senior, yes.'

'Impressive.' Nero maintained eye contact for just a little longer than was necessary. Benjamin watched as Nero's dessert was placed before her. She attacked the brownie with gusto.

'Chocolate is a girl's best friend,' she said, mischievously.

'Why did you ask about my computer access?'

'Oh, you know,' Nero said through a mouthful of chocolate. 'Just curious.'

'What about?'

This was too easy.

'*You.*'

The silence was palpable. It seemed to last for hours. Benjamin swallowed hard. He watched just a little too closely as Nero licked the last of the chocolate from her lips.

Poor Benji, she thought. She almost felt guilty.

'Maybe,' Benjamin began, nervously, 'we could continue this… somewhere else?'

He had never looked so ridiculous, thought Nero. Or so sweet.

'Good idea,' she agreed, lowering her voice half an octave. Then she asked a question she never thought she'd ask of Benjamin Saal. 'Can we go back to yours?'

It was a quick walk to Benjamin's apartment. In the chill of the February evening, Nero pulled her hood over her head. It also shielded her from the ubiquitous security cameras that she was sure would be following their every move. Benjamin took her a longer route, away from the demonstrations that raged on the main streets. They seemed almost non-stop. She could hear opposing chants in favour of or against the Dheghomites' aims. They didn't seem to care that their petty politics had cost lives. It made her feel sick.

At last, Benjamin stopped before a smart town house in Holborn and raised the back of his hand to the scanner.

'Welcome home, darling,' purred a sultry female voice. 'Come on in.'

Benjamin looked embarrassed. Nero was aghast. 'You chose that voice?' she squealed.

'I get lonely,' was all Benjamin would say. Nero noticed that he couldn't meet her eye. She was suddenly regretting her decision to accompany him home.

The apartment was smart and clean, but not at all homely. Neutral walls and functional furniture. Nothing controversial, nothing outside the bounds of normal taste. In short, it was boring.

'How long have you been here?' she asked.

Benjamin thought. 'Three years.'

'And you haven't thought to put any pictures up?'

'Why would I put pictures up?' Benjamin looked confused. 'Coffee?'

Nero nodded. 'Strong and black.' She flopped onto the sofa.

'Home?' Benjamin called. 'Two espressos, please.'

'Of course, darling,' came the response.

Nero rolled her eyes. 'That is *so* weird.'

Benjamin ignored her and slid next to her on the sofa, hooking a stray strand of hair behind his ear and gazing deep into Nero's eyes.

'So,' he breathed, 'wanna tell me the *real* reason you came back to my apartment?'

Was he trying to be alluring?

'I'm guessing it wasn't just for the coffee…'

Nero sprang to her feet as Benjamin rested a hand on her shoulder. 'I need access to the Bureau computer,' she said, suddenly serious.

Benjamin was crestfallen. 'Why?'

Nero took a breath. What she was about to ask would make her sound mad. Perhaps she was. 'Benji?' She saw him wince. 'What did we do yesterday? At the Bureau, I mean.'

'Yesterday?' Benjamin narrowed his eyes. 'You feeling okay?'

'Humour me.'

'My talk, remember?'

'That was yesterday? You're sure?'

'Of course.' Benjamin looked suspiciously at her. 'And then Drake called you out. I didn't see you for the rest of the day. I guess you went home.'

Nero was thinking fast. Would she really have had the time to fly to a mid Pacific island, prevent a terrorist attack, then wake up in her own bed? Maybe. But that wouldn't have explained how she had survived the fall. If there *was* a fall. 'Is there any way I can access my own location records? I didn't have authorisation on my slate.'

'You want to find out where you were yesterday?'

Nero nodded.

Benjamin blinked in confusion. 'You don't know?'

'I'm just asking you to do one thing for me.' Nero batted her eyelids. '*Benjamin*.'

Benjamin sighed. 'It's strictly against protocol.'

'Sure it is. But you're *senior*.' Nero winked again, just as she had in the restaurant. 'You can work it out.'

'My clearance is greater than yours, but I don't have access to everything.'

'I just need to know where the Bureau thinks I was after your talk yesterday.'

Benjamin seemed to give up. 'Okay, sure. I could use a Ghost Profile, I guess.'

'Ghost Profile?'

Benjamin was moving to the computer hub in the corner of the room. He waved the back of his hand over the screen and a password prompt appeared in the air. His fingers danced across the desktop keyboard.

'Password, zero, zero, zero,' he said quietly.

'*That's* your password?'

'It's keyed to my voice anyway,' Benjamin explained patiently. 'So I might as well keep it simple.'

Nero shook her head. 'Okay. But what's a Ghost Profile?'

Benjamin's fingers were typing on a virtual keyboard projected in the air before him. 'I can piggyback on another profile that's currently active.'

'Won't they know?'

'Nope. And neither will BRAINS.'

'So, as long as they're logged in, so are you?'

'Exactly.'

An alarm chimed.

'And we're in. Our tracks will be covered.'

Nero got the impression he'd done this before.

'I'm arranging for a temporary clearance upgrade,' Benjamin muttered as his fingers danced across the screen. 'Should get us to where we need to be.'

Another alarm.

'Woah!' Benjamin cried. 'That was close.' He turned to Nero. 'They just logged out, but I've jumped onto another user.' His attention was back on the screen. 'I'd better be quick.'

A series of numbers and symbols scrolled in the air.

'Here we go. Location tracking. Nero Jones. Let me input yesterday's date and we'll see.' Benjamin suddenly turned to Nero, the penny dropping. 'This is why you wanted to meet for dinner,' he said quietly.

Nero shrugged and met his gaze. 'Sorry,' she said. And she was.

Benjamin dropped his head for a moment. Another alarm brought him back to the task at hand. 'Here we are.' He was quieter now. Nero felt sorry for him. 'According to BRAINS, you went straight home after your meeting with Drake. And you stayed there.'

If that was right, it was exactly as Nero had feared. Perhaps she *was* going mad. She turned away to hide her confusion from Benjamin. The whole experience aboard the Clarke Elevator had felt so *real*.

'Could you do me just one more favour?' she asked, suddenly. 'Search for Doctor Jonathan Aurelius Jones.'

Benjamin raised an eyebrow. 'Your father?'

Nero nodded. 'Just see what you can find.'

'Okay.' Benjamin turned back to the screen, manipulating a series of symbols with his fingers as if they were putty. 'I'm doing a simple Net Search first. Let's see where that gets us.'

A ream of text scrolled through the air, beside a three-dimensional projection of the man that Nero knew as her father. It brought a tear to her eye.

'Distinguished physics professor,' Benjamin read, 'Nobel prize nominee, author of papers and books, father to one – ' He paused. 'Died in a plane crash, twenty-fourth of December, 2056.' He looked at Nero with pity. 'Must've been a hell of a Christmas. I'm sorry.' He tapped at the display. 'This is all publicly available. Nothing new there, I guess.'

'I tried to search Bureau records for him,' Nero said quietly. 'It wouldn't give me access.'

Benjamin nodded. 'Which would suggest there's more to this than meets the eye.' Another alarm sounded. 'Logged out again. Give me a second.'

'Could Drake catch us snooping?' Nero asked suddenly. 'Surely these searches would appear in the records?'

Benjamin smiled. 'Not when you're as clever as me. I'm employing a cleaner program as the user logs off. It literally cleans up after itself.'

Nero was impressed. 'You're quite the catch,' she said, generously. 'For the Bureau, I mean.'

Benjamin huffed. 'And one day, maybe that'll be reflected in my pay packet.' Another alarm. 'Okay, I'm in again. Searching.'

A familiar phrase flashed before Nero's eyes.

ACCESS: DENIED.

'Hmm.' Benjamin swept the hair from his eyes. 'Okay, let's try another way.' His fingers danced over the stream of letters and numbers and, suddenly, the screen flashed green. 'I've got him,' Benjamin announced. Nero leaned in close to see. 'Everything that's publicly available, but government records, too.'

'They're not publicly available?'

'Not since we started to worry about ID cloning. I've got his birth and marriage certificates, tax and medical records, death certificate. All seems to be in order.'

Nero took a breath. 'Let's take a look at his death certificate,' she said, her voice thick with emotion.

Benjamin called up a digital certificate containing details of the death of Doctor Jonathan Aurelius Jones. The date of death was listed alongside the cause; ACCIDENT. Means of injury, PLANE CRASH. Immediate cause of death, FRACTURE OF SKULL, FRACTURE OF ENTIRE BODY, THIRD DEGREE BURNS.

Nero looked away, a lump in her throat.

'Let's take a look here.' Benjamin called up details of the plane crash. 'Twenty-fourth of December, 2056...' News footage of a crash site flickered before him. 'Yup, there it is. It crashed just after take-off from Delta Municipal Airport.'

Nero couldn't bear to look.

'That's odd.' There was something in Benjamin's voice that made her turn back to the screen. 'The digital signature is dated the day before the accident.'

'Huh?' Nero frowned. 'What does that mean?'

'Benjamin was thinking it through. 'It means,' he began, cautiously, 'that the death certificate was uploaded *the day before the accident.*'

Nero's eyes were wide. 'But that's impossible! How could they possibly know?'

Benjamin shook his head. 'Could be a simple user error. These things are sometimes rushed.'

Nero tried to make sense of the information. 'Can you call up the passenger manifest for that flight?'

'I guess so,' Benjamin muttered as his fingers went back to work. 'We've got everything we need. Flight number, airline, time.' Again, the screen flashed green. 'Got it!' A representation of the interior of an aircraft appeared on the screen. Each seat, seen from above, was numbered and labelled with a link. 'It was pretty full,' Benjamin noted, sadly. 'Tragic.'

Methodically, he made his way through each link, checking the names of the passengers on that fateful flight. Nero watched as each name appeared briefly on the screen. By the end, it was clear her father had not been on that plane.

Benjamin held Nero's gaze in silence.

'But...' Nero wasn't sure what to say. 'He's buried in Mortlake Cemetery. I went to his funeral.' She remembered her mother at the graveside, stern as ever, as the coffin was lowered. Nero had been grateful that Meena had been allowed to accompany her. She was the only person to offer Nero any comfort. Almost as soon as the coffin was in the ground, they had both been bundled back into a security van and taken back to the Dump. She didn't remember her mother even saying goodbye.

'He may well be dead,' Benjamin whispered, 'but he didn't die on that plane.'

'Where would he have bought his ticket?' Nero blurted, trying hard to control her emotions. 'Is there even any record that he *intended* to be on it?'

'Hmm.' Benji thought for a moment then, once again, his fingers were a blur. 'I need to access historic ticket sales for all the major airlines and agents operating out of Delta Municipal.' He muttered to himself as he worked, his hair hanging down in front of his face. Finally, he sat back as another alarm sounded.

'Kicked out again?' Nero was desperate for news.

Benjamin ran his fingers through his hair. 'Yeah, but I got what I needed.' He closed down the screen with a wave of his hand. 'Not only was your father not on that flight, he never even bought a ticket for it.'

Nero was aghast. She had woken up in the middle of one mystery, and now found herself right in the heart of another.

12
Déjà Vu

A bright light.
A betrayal.
Pain.

What have you done?
What do you want?
Who are you?
Why?
Who
am
I?

For the second morning in a row, Nero woke in a frenzy. For a while, she wondered just how much of her meeting with Benjamin had actually happened. She was learning not to trust her own senses. Groping for her clothes in the darkness, she dug into her pocket for a tissue and felt something hard between her fingers. The photocube from her house. So that, at least, was real. Funny, she didn't remember taking it.

'Home,' she called. 'What time is it?'

'Four thirty, a.m.' came the response in a flat monotone.

Nero groaned. 'Give me some light,' she yawned. 'Not too bright.'

As the light faded up, Nero swung her legs from the bed and made her way to the kitchen, the bed covers slung over her shoulders.

'Black coffee please, Home.'

She took a square of chocolate from the work top as her drink was poured, then threw herself on the sofa, wrapping herself in her bed clothes against the cold of the night.

She reached forward to the coffee table and slid the photocube into a port. A series of colourful images appeared before her, formed in mid-air by a soft, pulsating light. She scrolled through the pictures with her hand, taking comforting sips of her coffee as the memories came flooding back.

She paused at images of her father. He looked as handsome as ever at whatever age. Pictures of him with her as a child brought tears to Nero's eyes. Multiple images showed her riding on his shoulders, paddling in the sea or walking through the countryside. She zoomed in on one image to see her father looking at her as she climbed a tree. There was a look on his face that she longed to see again. Pride.

In contrast, the pictures featuring her mother showed a woman one step removed from family life. Helene was always stood to one side, or even behind Nero and her father. There were very few pictures of all three of them standing together as a family. It was like she was an observer, thought Nero. Detached.

'Incoming call,' the voice announced. 'Nathan Drake, First Action Bureau.'

The noise startled her. It was still early. What did Drake want at this hour?

'I'll take it,' she snapped, and Drake's sombre face appeared above the computer hub in the corner.

'Nero, I'm sorry it's so early,' he said.

'That's okay,' Nero sighed. 'Do you have news of my mother?'

'I'm afraid not. It's an assignment. I'm assembling my team right now, and I want you on it.'

Nero looked around the briefing room. She was pleased to see Harrison sitting next to her, along with two women she didn't recognise.

'They from the other Bureau facilities?' she asked Harrison as they sat waiting for their briefing.

He looked at her, blank. 'What other facilities?'

Wow. The Bureau liked to play their cards close to their chest.

'Doesn't matter,' she said. 'Just something I heard somewhere.'

'Good morning, everyone.' Nathan Drake strode to the front of the room, Benjamin Saal at his side. Nero inadvertently exchanged glances with Benjamin. She looked away at once, remembering the night before.

'I hope you managed to grab some food on the way in.' Drake stood with his arms folded across his chest. 'And I apologise for the early start, but time is very definitely not on our side.'

Nero looked around to see her fellow agents were all leaning forwards in their seats, primed to receive the details of their latest assignment.

'You've all been picked because you're the best of the best, and this assignment requires nothing less. You're a mix of old hands and new blood and I expect you to watch and learn from each other.'

Was that a warning? Nero noticed the older agents narrowing their eyes in her direction.

'Jones and Harrison are new recruits,' Drake continued, gesturing to where they sat in the room. 'But they're top of their class.'

The two rookie agents squirmed in their seats.

'Kahu and Chang have been with us since the beginning. Chang will be your leader in the field.'

Chang waved idly at the rest of the room, nodding at Nero and Harrison.

'Kahu is our explosives expert,' Drake said, gesturing to a woman in the corner. 'Listen to her.'

Kahu refused to even acknowledge the rest of the room, choosing instead to focus all her attention on her shoes.

'She's also chosen the weapons for her and Chang.'

'What do we get?' asked Harrison, perhaps not unreasonably.

'Our junior agents have to live by their wits,' Drake replied. 'But you'll – '

'I know,' interrupted Harrison. 'We'll be supported all the way.'

'You need to work together,' Drake continued in measured tones. 'As ever, you'll have full backup and support from the Bureau and its computer.'

Nero almost laughed at how no one else called it BRAINS.

'Your cover stories are on your slates. You'll have time to learn them on the plane but not much, so I hope you're quick studies.'

Nero frowned. So far, this was sounding like the briefing she'd received before her phantom assignment on the Clarke Elevator. Almost word for word. Did that make it any more real?

'I'm going to hand you over to Benjamin Saal who many of you know.' Drake gestured to the wiry young man. 'He'll give you everything we've discovered so far.'

Drake stood aside to let Benjamin take the floor. He looked the most tired of everyone. He cleared his throat, awkwardly.

'We have been monitoring recent probability and causation spikes surrounding the Dheghomite movement.' He shook his hair from his face. In his white lab coat and glasses, Nero thought he looked almost professional.

'We've fed the results through our quantum computer, BRAINS,' he looked pleased with himself again, 'and have been decoding the results. It looks like there's going to be a massive terrorist strike in a little over two days' time. Here.'

He waved his hand over the desktop screen and an image of a tall building appeared, glistening in the sun. A row of flags fluttered in the breeze. A river rolled past, casting gleams of reflected light on the whole scene. Nero wondered if it was a real-time image.

'This is the United Nations building in New York,' Benjamin explained. 'All indications are that this is the target.'

'Why?' asked Kahu. 'Their usual targets are examples of our latest tech. Like that monorail.' She flicked her eyes to Nero.

'You're right,' Benjamin agreed, 'but the probability spikes converge on a particular date. February the twenty-fourth.'

'That's this week,' Harrison gasped. 'That's not much of a warning.'

Drake ploughed on. 'There's a gathering of security and technology companies converging on New York to meet with world leaders. The aim of the meeting is to promote technological advancement for the benefit of the human race.'

'The thing the Dheghomites hate the most,' drawled Chang.

'Precisely.' Benjamin ploughed on. 'It's just the sort of high-profile target that would get the world's attention and possibly make it think again.'

'It would certainly put us back a few years,' Chang observed. 'If half the world was to lose its leaders and the other half to lose its largest tech companies, progress would stall for sure.'

'And that's just what they want.' Benjamin waved his hand and the image disappeared. 'For starters, anyway. Then, they want progress reversed. Health interventions stopped. Technology halted. This could be the beginning of a major campaign that would set the world back hundreds of years.'

'So, what are they gonna do?' Kahu asked.

'Our stats are telling us it'll be a bomb, but not a conventional weapon.' Benjamin lowered his voice for dramatic effect. 'We believe they are planning to detonate an explosive device in the UN building.'

There was a rumble of muttered swear words around the room.

'How would they ever get past security?' asked Chang. 'It must be tight as a warthog's arse.'

'That's what we need to find out,' Benjamin smiled. He had clearly enjoyed Chang's analogy. Nero just knew he would be using it himself some time soon.

'What are our chances of success this time?' Nero asked.

'*This time?*' Benjamin looked at her quizzically. Nero looked away. 'Without our intervention, there's a ninety-five per cent probability that they'll succeed.'

'And *with* our intervention?' Harrison was hanging on his every word.

'We don't know this far out.'

Harrison slumped back in his seat and rolled his eyes.

'Our AI doesn't work like that. It's not predictive. It's deeper than that. As the probability spikes increase and the data converges, so we get a clearer picture.' Benjamin swallowed. 'We'll let you know as soon as we know.'

'Thank you, Benjamin.' Drake gestured that he take a seat. Benjamin swerved away from an empty chair right next to Nero and found another towards the back of the room.

Point taken, thought Nero.

'So, here's the plan.' Drake looked around the room at his assembled team. 'Alpha Squad will be placed among the UN Security staff. We have your passes in place and they are expecting you. It'll be your job to beef up the building's security, but also to keep an eye out for any irregularities, especially as we get nearer to the incident. Alpha Squad will comprise Kahu and Harrison.'

Harrison tried to make eye contact with Kahu. She looked away.

'Jones and Chang will be Beta Squad. It'll be your task to infiltrate the Dheghomite cell itself.'

Nero leaned forward, desperate not to miss a word.

'We've infiltrated their communications and pinpointed the exact location of the unit recruited to carry out the attack. It's a single Dheghomite operative but they're expecting support. That's where we come in. That support is due to arrive in twenty-four hours. Two female terrorists. Jones and Chang will find them, neutralise them, then take their place.'

Nero swallowed. The use of that word *neutralise* somehow made it all the more serious.

'This is where their aversion to modern tech comes in handy,' Drake continued. 'They're off grid which means they won't be being tracked by their leaders. They'll be relying on old school stuff, checking in at appointed hours, writing things on the backs of their hands, you know the kinds of things.'

Chang laughed. Nero tried hard to raise a smile.

'But seriously, it means you should be able to replace them almost unnoticed. If you're careful.' Chang exchanged a nod with Nero.

'Any questions?' asked Drake as he looked around the room.

'Just one.' Kahu raised her hand. 'When do we leave?'

Drake smiled. 'I'm glad you asked me that.'

13

The Lion's Den

Nero glanced round the cabin. She was part of what they used to call in the old movies her dad liked to watch, a *crack squad*. Kahu sat opposite her, staring straight ahead, betraying no emotion. Harrison was next to her, biting his nails.

'Wish we had a window,' he flustered. 'Why couldn't we have a window?'

'This is that big adventure you always wanted, Harrison,' Nero smirked. 'And you're complaining about the windows?'

Chang leaned back against the cabin walls, her lean frame seeming to fold itself around her seat.

A crack squad. Nero realised now how unlikely it would have been for the Bureau to send two raw recruits on a mission to the Clarke Elevator. It *couldn't* have been real. Could it? The further away Nero got, the more the whole event seemed like the product of a fever dream. Perhaps it was.

'Harrison,' she muttered, 'have you really not heard of the Bureau having any other facilities like the one beneath Fleet Street?'

'Nope. Why?'

Nero shook her head. 'It's nothing. Really.'

'Okay, listen up!' Chang had undone her seatbelt and risen to her feet. Holding onto a ceiling strap with one hand, she steadied herself against the turbulence.

'Here's what's gonna happen when we land.' She took a swig of water from a bottle. Nero noticed it was covered in the same mottled colours as the combat fatigues they were all wearing.

'The pilot is setting us down fifteen kilometres from the mark. There's a disused military compound in Grand Creek. That'll be our base for the night. We'll have twelve hours to gather our thoughts, then tomorrow we move out.'

She pointed at Harrison.

'You and Kahu are headed for the UN building where you'll be met by their head of security, Devlin Williams. His details are on your slates, so you can't miss him. He won't like you.'

Kahu squinted at the team leader. 'Why not?'

'He's jumped-up middle management. He'll think you're there to supervise his security procedures ahead of the meeting next month. Judging by his personality profile, it looks like he'll take it personally.'

'Great,' Kahu sighed.

'Jones and I are headed west.'

'Look who gets a holiday,' teased Harrison. Nero slapped his leg.

'We're looking for a party of two, heading to rendezvous with the Dheghomite cell. The Bureau has eyes on them already, so they should be easy to spot.'

'What sort of eyes?' Nero asked.

'Satellite, mainly. But also, surveillance cameras and Spyjacking.'

Nero gave her a blank look.

'The Bureau has the ability to hack any appliance or device on a network,' Kahu explained. 'Even old school. Radio, TV, wired or wireless.'

'I could tell you what they had for breakfast this morning if you really want to know,' Chang bragged. 'We'll take them out and assume their identities.' A broad smile spread across her face. 'That's the great thing about infiltrating a bunch of Luddites. They don't even know what these two goons look like. It'll be a cake walk.'

An electronic bleep chimed through the cabin.

'Okay,' said Chang as she strapped herself back into her seat. 'Looks like we're going down.'

The stealth carrier had stayed low across the Atlantic to avoid detection. The conditions on board the craft were cramped and uncomfortable, but it had sure been quicker than flying economy class to the Pacific. If Nero had ever *flown* to the Pacific. She frowned. She had a distinct memory of Meena telling her she'd trained at another Bureau facility at St Paul's. Yet Harrison had said there were no others. Perhaps he didn't know. Why should a rookie be party to Bureau infrastructure? Harrison was either mistaken, or Meena had lied. Or, and this was seeming increasingly likely, *it had never happened at all.*

Nero looked up to see Kahu studying her carefully.

'You look distracted, Jones.' Nero could hardly hear her above the hum of the engines. 'You need to get with the programme.'

Nero held on tight to her straps as she felt the craft banking. 'Thanks for the tip.'

A jolt in the cabin signalled that they had landed, and Chang sprang to her feet again.

'Okay, let's move out,' she barked. 'You'll find our overnight accommodation due north. Grab your bags, find your rooms and we'll meet in the old mess hall for some dinner.'

Dinner was hardly the word. Nero poked at the bland noodle soup before her.

'No one said it would be tasty,' grinned Chang, lifting a spoonful of thin broth to her lips.

'Whatever happened to an army marching on its stomach?' Harrison stared at his bowl in dismay.

'You're not in the army,' Chang snapped. 'This is much more dangerous.'

The military base had clearly seen better days. The grounds were overgrown and the runway cracked and uneven. The buildings were tumbledown, their smashed windows and missing doors leaving them open to the elements. All the furniture had been stripped, leaving the four agents to make do with whatever they could find.

Wooden pallets were put to use as tables, with great coils of cables and oil drums employed as chairs.

Nero leaned over the makeshift table to break the silence.

'What's with Kahu?' she whispered, nodding to where the last of their number sat alone in a corner, her backs to them.

Chang puffed out her cheeks. 'She's difficult, but she's good. Just don't think you're here to make friends.'

'How long has she been with the Bureau?' Harrison pushed his bowl away from him and reached for a protein bar.

'She was recruited at the same time as me. Drake found her in a frack house in Dresden.'

'Woah,' hissed Harrison. 'She was taking frack? And she *survived*?'

'Only because Drake put her through rehab.'

'What did he see in her?' Nero asked.

'The same he sees in all of us, I guess. Potential. That, and the fact that her mother would rather bankroll the Bureau's start-up costs than see her daughter exposed as an addict.'

Nero was aghast. 'Drake *blackmailed* her mother?' The more she learned of the man, the more she didn't like him.

'There was certainly some... coaxing involved.' Chang smiled. 'Drake can be quite persuasive. And her mother is *very rich*. She was the first Maori billionaire. Made her money in lithium at the start of the green energy boom.'

Nero sneaked a look at Kahu. 'She sounds like a liability. Why would Drake want her so badly?'

Chang swung back in her rickety chair. 'I didn't mention she killed her sister?'

Nero was appalled. 'How?'

Chang nodded, clearly delighted to be centre stage. 'She'd rigged up a chemical bomb in the woods behind her house. She wanted to clear some trees to build a camp. What she didn't know was that her sister was playing there, too. It was an accident, and luckily the courts saw it that way. She was a messed-up kid, but she had the skills. Now she's the Bureau's explosives expert.'

Nero looked over her shoulder again. With her back to the rest of them, it was impossible to know if she was eating or not. Just about everyone Nero had met at the Bureau was damaged goods. It seemed everyone had a story to tell. She wondered what Chang's was.

'So, the Bureau is Drake's baby?' Nero sat back in her chair.

'No government would listen to him,' Chang explained. 'He devised a system to predict huge events using Big Data and AI back in the days before anyone thought it would be useful for anything more than cheating in exams. He was a visionary, and visionaries are never believed. So, he used private money.'

Harrison whistled with admiration. 'Gotta respect the man.'

Nero wasn't so sure.

'Now,' Chang concluded, 'governments the world over pay him for the use of his services.'

'So, he's a mercenary.' Nero felt uncomfortable with the implications.

'You could think of him that way if you want.' Chang pushed her improvised chair back from the table and stood up. 'Or, you could just think of him as your boss.'

Fair point, thought Nero.

'I suggest you all get to bed soon,' Chang announced to the room. 'We move out in the morning.' She sauntered from the room towards the accommodation barracks, throwing her bowl in a rusting oil drum as she passed.

Nero and Harrison shared a look.

'You're lucky,' Harrison mumbled, 'I'm teamed with Little Miss Charisma over there.' He nodded towards Kahu.

'You've got to admire her,' Nero replied as she picked up her bowl. 'She's been through more than all of us put together and still come out the other side.' She rose from the table. 'Beside, she seems just the sort you'll need in your corner when the shit hits the fan.'

Nero slept about as badly as she had expected. Having hunted round the barracks for anything soft and vaguely comfortable, she ended up spending the night on a mattress of cardboard and polystyrene. Waking in the still hours of the night, she switched on her slate to remind herself of her cover story.

The basic facts were simple enough. Name, *Paola Merigan. Age, 23. Education, Degree – Biological Engineering (First), Oxford.*

Nero stopped reading. These were the details of the woman she was due to replace. By the evening, she would almost literally be walking in a dead woman's shoes. Paola Merigan was, no doubt, blissfully unaware of how her day was about to play out. That, by the end of the day, she would be *neutralised* and Nero would be in her place.

What had gone wrong? How had Paola ended up on the wrong side? Bad choices? Bad friends?

True beliefs?

Nero had heard how young people had been radicalised in the past. How they had been convinced to fight for a 'higher cause' through a process of grooming, desensitising and brainwashing. They were often troubled, looking for easy answers. Seeing only black and white in a world of grey. With a shiver, she realised her time at the Bureau had been little different. Nero could only hope she had chosen the right side. History would decide, no doubt. It always did.

A noise from the far side of the room told her Chang was getting up. Nero rolled from her makeshift mattress. 'What's for breakfast?' she yawned.

Chang nodded at an old rusty pipe that ran the length of the ceiling. 'Same every day,' she said. 'A hundred chin-ups. Wanna join me?'

As the morning sun glanced through the broken windows, Chang assembled her team and led them from the building. They had been given their orders. Once they had embedded themselves in their positions they were to report to Drake at the Bureau.

Kahu and Harrison, having changed out of their combat fatigues, peeled off to board a waiting car, its keys in the ignition, ready to drive.

As the car swept out of the airbase, Nero and Chang shouldered their bags.

'We're heading west,' Chang reminded her fellow recruit. 'Fifteen kilometres.'

Nero nodded. She was glad she had saved her protein bar.

The frost crunched underfoot. Fog swirled through the trees. It burned away as the sun rose and, gradually, the air warmed. Chang pointed out their destination on Nero's slate, then left her subordinate to map their way through the countryside. Nero chose to avoid roads and railways, the very places where surveillance might be at its heaviest. She led them, instead, through woods and barren scrubland. Three or four times, they crouched in the undergrowth to survey the way ahead.

A little under four hours later, Chang raised a hand to bring Nero to a halt. They both dropped to the ground, using a rotten tree trunk for cover. Chang gestured to Nero's map.

'There's the decommissioned substation,' she whispered. 'According to the Bureau computer, our two goons arrived there two days ago.'

Taking her Spi-Glasses from her bag, Nero peered through the foliage to the construction beyond. It was a single-storey building behind a tall fence. Clearly abandoned some time ago, it was surrounded by weeds and overgrown shrubs. Ivy was creeping up the metal links of the fence. The building's walls were cracked and crumbling. Nero could see half the roof was missing. They must have had an even colder night than she'd had.

'What are they waiting for?' she whispered.

'Collection,' Chang replied, coolly.

Nero flicked her eyes to navigate her way through her glasses' menu.

APPLICATIONS>VIEW>RADIOGRAPHY
>LOW
>MEDIUM

Soon, she was gazing through the brick walls at two figures. One was lying on some sort of bed or low table, the other was more animated, walking about the room in an agitated manner.

'I see them,' Nero reported. 'Two of them, just as you said,'

'Any signs of them moving?'

'Nope.' Nero could see bags stacked against the far wall. 'They're staying put for now.'

As she looked, she saw movement at the side of her glasses frame. A shape was barrelling towards the substation's fence, keeping low but moving fast. Dropping her glasses, she saw that Chang had disappeared from beside her. Looking again, she saw the squad leader squatting by an old-fashioned junction box. Unnervingly, Nero's Spi-Glasses showed Chang's bones glowing through her clothes. Chang reached into her backpack and withdrew a small tool. A laser torch. Within moments she was through the fence, moving stealthily so as not to make any sound. Nero watched as she flattened herself against the wall, just below an opening in the ramshackle roof. Chang reached into her bag again and pulled out a small ball that, through Nero's glasses, was glowing white hot. She saw Chang press a switch, then throw the ball up and over, through the hole in the roof and into the room below. Chang put her head low and squatted on her haunches. Nero could see the glowing ball had landed among the bags against the far wall. As far as she could see, the two people inside didn't suspect a thing.

There was a bright flash. So bright that Nero had to drop her glasses and shield her eyes. As she lowered her hands from her face, she felt Chang return to her side.

'A little gift from Kahu,' she panted. 'Pulse grenade.' Despite the tension, she seemed cool and detached. 'Now we need to help them forget. Come with me.'

She led Nero from their cover and through the fence to the building. They looked around them as they went, staking out the undergrowth for any unseen enemy agents.

'We're clear,' Chang announced. 'Let's go in.'

Nero had expected to see dust, smoke and debris from the explosion, but the air was clear. Everything was just as she had seen through her Spi-Glasses. The bags were still stacked in the corner. The furniture, sparse as it was, still stood. Even the two Dheghomite agents were just where Nero had seen them, except the one she had seen walking animatedly was now a crumpled heap on the floor. The other lay on the bed, just where Nero had observed her.

'The pulse grenade only affects organic matter,' Chang explained. 'There's no explosion, just a pulse of ultra-high sonic energy.'

'Then, they're not dead?' Nero was relieved. Peering closer, she could clearly see their chests rising and falling as they breathed.

'Just stunned,' Chang smiled as she knelt beside the woman on the floor. 'They'll be out for a few hours. Drake'll send someone to clear up after us. That'll be two fewer of them on the streets.'

Nero was searching through the bags stacked against the wall. 'There's not much here,' she reported over her shoulder. 'I don't think they've been here long.'

'Quick in and out, I guess,' replied Chang. 'They'd want to travel as light as they could.' She busied herself tying and gagging the two unconscious women.

Nero searched through the bags and found only clothes, toiletries, maps and books. *They really get off on their retro stuff*, she mused to herself. The only piece of tech that she could see in the room was a comms pad resting on the table.

'I don't understand,' Nero frowned. 'There's just the two of them. No weapons, no equipment. What are they bringing to the party?'

Chang shrugged. 'Expertise? Information?'

Nero thought back to her initial view of the women through her Spi-Glasses. 'Is this me?' she asked Chang.

'That's you. Paola Merigan.' Chang peered over. 'She's pretty. A perfect match.' Nero raised her eyebrows. Was she *flirting*?

'Search her clothes for any ID. You'll need to have it on you when we're collected.'

Nero rifled through Paola's pockets until she found an ID card.

'Pass it over,' Chang commanded, slipping her slate from her backpack. She tapped the ID card against a side port. The screen showed Paola Merigan's identification details, including a holographic representation of her face. As Chang swiped her hand across the screen, Nero watched the picture change to one of her own face. The accompanying statistics were updated to reflect her age and height.

'How long do you think we have?' Nero asked as she slipped the updated card into a pocket.

A beep from the comms pad brought Chang over to the table. Its screen showed a representation of their current location on a map, with a flashing dot moving ever closer. Chang turned to her young companion.

'I think our lift has arrived.'

14

Enemy Lines

'I'm Devlin Williams, head of security.'

'James Connor.' Harrison held out his hand. 'This is my colleague, Janice Tamati.'

The United Nations building soared high in the blue New York sky. Harrison was trying his best to not look overwhelmed at his surroundings. Even after all the catastrophes the city had suffered in the forties, it still managed to look imposing. Many of the more famous landmarks were gone, of course. Only the Statue of Liberty remained entirely intact. Almost every other building bore the scars of a desperate battle against dark forces. Even the UN building had been rebuilt and reconfigured following its almost total destruction.

The Plaza was spread before them, its fountains spraying water merrily at the few pedestrians brave enough to walk by. Here and there, Harrison saw armed guards dotted about the place and even along the skyline. It was a measure of just how nervous the world was in the face of its latest threat.

Williams looked at the surly woman in front of him. Like her partner, she was dressed in a dark suit and open-necked white shirt. From her evident discomfort, it was clear it was not the sort of thing she would usually wear.

'I can't pretend I'm pleased to see ya,' Williams drawled as he handed them their pass tokens. 'Just wish the company would leave me alone to do my job.'

'I'm sure they have complete confidence in you,' Harrison smiled.

'We're just here as an outside eye.' It was such a surprise to see Kahu smile that Harrison had to suppress a laugh. 'Pretend we're not here,' she concluded.

Williams sighed then turned to lead them across the Plaza to the security buildings. 'Well,' he began, 'I have eight teams of privately contracted security plus representatives of every government wanting to chew my ear about the security arrangements, so forgive me if I don't roll out the red carpet for y'all.'

'A look at your security strategy would do for now,' Harrison called ahead of him at Williams's back. 'The red carpet can wait.'

Williams showed them to a door at the side of the main building. 'You'll need to press your token in the slot there.'

The door hissed open for each of them in turn and Williams led them along a short corridor to his office. Harrison noticed the walls were lined with framed certificates declaring Devlin Williams as *Top Security Operative, 2053* and a recipient of the *Safe Hands Award* for 2051.

'They're industry awards,' Williams said proudly. 'Voted for by my clients.' He looked Harrison up and down. 'Which means they're *happy* clients.'

'We'll wanna see your level one through four security bands,' Kahu interrupted, clearly losing her patience.

Williams thought for a moment, then decided not to retaliate. Turning to his desk, he placed his pass token in another shallow slot. The screen blinked into life and a keyboard was projected into the air. He lifted his hands to input some key words and a series of schematics appeared before them.

'We got fourth generation bio-scanners at all entrances,' he sighed. 'And air sensors in each room.' He swiped his hand in the air as he talked, and the images scrolled from right to left. 'Every door and window is alarmed, we'll have armed military response on every vantage point and there'll be tactical support for every delegate.'

'Fourth generation scanners?' Harrison asked, thoughtfully. 'That's new tech.'

Williams nodded. 'The budget wouldn't stretch to having them at every door, so we got third generation only on the service entrance. Still, it's good enough.'

'Can we see the auditorium?' Kahu asked. 'And any other areas where the delegates might gather?'

Williams closed the screen with a wave of his hand. 'I guess lunch can wait,' he muttered to himself.

The main hall was huge. A central oval area contained an outer rim of tables and chairs, each holding a sign denoting the country of each delegate's origin. The floor in the middle displayed the flag of the United Nations, a garland of laurel leaves surrounding a representation of the nations under its jurisdiction. Beyond the ring of tables, seats were arranged around the great hall from where authorised spectators, journalists and the delegates' entourages could observe proceedings. To help them, great screens were hung around the hall, each of them displaying the flag until the conference got underway.

As Harrison and Kahu were led into the chamber, they noticed a team of staff busy making last minute preparations. Between them, a security squad was making a sweep of the hall, scanning the furniture and floor with a variety of handheld scanning devices.

'This whole room is a blast cage,' Williams was proclaiming. 'It's ringed with three hundred tonnes of reinforced titanium and a triple strength steel alloy mesh.' He turned proudly to his companions. 'It's the safest place in the United States of America, if not, the world.'

Kahu fought hard not to roll her eyes. 'Impressive,' she muttered, dutifully.

'Everyone you see around us,' Williams continued, 'has been security checked to within an inch of their lives. I'm talking biometric data, digital footprint, medical records, the works. Same goes with *everyone* who works in this building. No one gets in without my say so and they're all triple scanned on entry.'

'What could possibly go wrong?' Kahu muttered under her breath.'

This chamber is impregnable,' Williams concluded.

Harrison leaned to his fellow agent as they followed the American towards an exit.

'Didn't they say something similar about the Titanic?'

'And these are the holding pens.'

Williams laughed at his own joke as they entered another wing of the building. He shook his head at the lack of response and led his two new colleagues into a large, low-ceilinged room with comfortable furnishings and uncontroversial art hanging from the walls.

'I'm just kidding. In fact, they're our state-of-the-art guest facilities providing the very latest in comfort, information technology and communications. They are designed for a delegate and three-person entourage and have been especially designed with cultural sensitivities in mind.' He waved vaguely in the area of a small Hindu shrine that stood incongruously in a corner.

'That's an outside wall,' he continued, nodding towards the sweeping curve of the longest wall in the room. 'Two metres of steel reinforced concrete. Ain't nothing gonna get through that.' He folded his arms across his chest. 'But at the first sniff of trouble, all delegates will be corralled into the auditorium. It's – '

'The safest place in the world,' Kahu interrupted. 'What's the blast containment index for a wall that thick?'

For the first time, Williams looked flustered. 'I could look that up for you back at the office,' he spluttered.

'Mr Williams, sir?'

Williams looked around to see a member of staff approaching.

'What is it?'

'There's a fault in the feedback ring again,' the woman reported. 'Wondered if you wanted to take a look?'

'Okay Harley, I'll be right there.' Williams ushered the member of staff away and turned to his companions. 'That's my cue to leave you. Poke around all you want. You got any questions, you come to me.'

With that, Williams strode away, muttering something about company stooges under his breath.

15

Deep Cover

Nero couldn't see a thing.

Within minutes of storming the abandoned substation, she and Chang had had to stow the sleeping Dheghomite agents where they wouldn't be seen. Luckily their contact, a rather nervous looking man with a shaved head, had been too anxious to look around the inside of the building.

'Merigan?' he had snapped as he leaned from the Hoverjet's cockpit. 'Dumont?'

Chang had nodded. 'That's us.'

'Grab your stuff and put these on.' He had thrown a couple of cloth hoods to the ground. 'Then let's get out of here.'

Nero was conscious of the rise and fall of the craft through the air. She guessed they were keeping low to avoid detection. She also guessed, although she couldn't be sure, that Chang was sat beside her in the back of the small craft.

'Get out,' the pilot barked as Nero felt the Hoverjet settle on the ground. It was the first time he had spoken on the whole journey. 'Keep your hoods on and wait.'

Nero fumbled her way out of the tiny vehicle and stood as still as she could. Above the hum of the idling engine, she could hear Merigan and Dumont's bags being dumped beside her. At last, the Hoverjet's engines were engaged, and Nero listened as it rose into the air and faded into the distance. There was silence, broken only by the sounds of birdsong and leaves rustling in the wind.

'Walk towards my voice,' came a sudden command.

Nero did so.

'Stop,' came the voice again. 'You can take off your hoods.'

Nero was relieved to see Chang beside her as she threw her hood to the floor. They were standing in a clearing in dense woodland, a tall man with a straggly beard standing between them and a large tent. It was made of a dark green material that blended in perfectly with the undergrowth and was shielded from discovery by the tree canopy that swayed above it.

'You can call me Calian. It's Native American for *warrior of life*,' the man drawled. 'Seemed appropriate. Grab your stuff.'

The man walked away without waiting for a response, leaving Nero and Chang to follow him with their bags. As they walked through the opening of the tent, Calian stood before them, a wide smile on his face.

'Mind if I..?' He held an ID reader, expectantly. 'Can't be too careful.'

Nero almost held her breath as Calian swiped her ID card.

'Merigan,' he mused, comparing the picture with the young woman before him. 'What kinda name is that?'

'It's *my* name,' Nero snapped back.

'And Dumont?' He raised an eyebrow at Chang.

'French,' she replied, without missing a beat. 'On my father's side.'

'Take a seat, why don't you?' Calian gestured to an untidy bed. 'It's short on comfort, but I'm not gonna need it long. You two hungry?'

'Er, sure,' Nero piped up. She was having trouble reconciling her expectations with the man before her. He seemed... *normal*.

Calian ambled over to a small stove in the corner. It held a steaming pot and a dented, metal kettle.

'It ain't too tasty, but it's hot and wet,' he beamed as he ladled a thin soup into two cups 'Don't ever say I don't look after my guests.'

Nero sipped at the soup and wondered if she'd ever have a decent meal again.

Calian squatted on the floor in front of them and gestured out the door to the wilderness beyond. 'Not a bad way to spend your final hours, eh?'

'Final hours?' Nero asked.

Chang leaped in to cover for her. 'We've not been told the details,' she explained. 'Only that we're here in a support capacity.'

'Our Dear Leader keeping you both in the dark, huh?' Calian smirked as he stroked his beard. He reached under the bed and pulled out two notebooks. 'It's all in here, but I'll fill you in on the particulars.' He placed the notebooks on the ground in front of him and knelt with his eyes closed. For a moment, Nero thought he was going to pray. 'Year Zero,' he said finally, his eyes snapping open. 'It's a-coming!'

Nero shared a look with Chang.

'And I am the chosen one!' Calian had a broad grin on his face. He looked unhinged. 'If humankind is the virus, *I* am the vaccine.'

Calian handed over the notebooks to each of the two women.

'Welcome to the Great Reset. When you've finished with them, burn them,' he winked.

Harrison and Kahu had checked into their hotel for the night. Their fake identities had so far aroused no suspicion. It seemed that, as far as the whole world was concerned, they were representatives of Securol Inc, and in charge of monitoring proceedings at the UN building.

Kahu drew her slate from her bag and held the back of her hand up to the screen. With a soft *bleep*, the holographic display blinked into life. Kahu swiped the air to navigate to a private communications room and clicked *Enter*. Nathan Drake was already waiting. His head seemed to hang in the air as he spoke.

'Kahu, Harrison. I have updates for you.'

Another *bleep* signalled the arrival of Nero Jones. Her head hung in the air next to Drake, but Kahu could tell she was outdoors.

'Jones,' Drake nodded. 'You made it.'

Nero's voice was low. 'We're in the woods with our contact. He's calling himself Calian because it makes him sound like a warrior.'

'Has he told you their plan?' Drake asked.

'Only our part in it,' Nero replied. 'But he's holding something back.'

'What are you to do?'

'He's got enough explosives to make one hell of a bang.' Nero fought hard to steady her voice. 'Chang and I are to plant them at two separate locations tomorrow morning as the delegates arrive. I had to memorise the coordinates. He made us burn our instructions.' Nero's head bent as she turned her attention to her slate's keyboard. 'I'm sending them through... now.'

Three-dimensional representations of two buildings spun in the air.

'The Bureau computer is saying the tall building is a disused factory in downtown New York,' Drake reported, clearly looking at another screen. 'The other is by the quayside. It's an abandoned warehouse.'

Harrison reached forward to wave his hand across the display. The two buildings appeared to recede into the distance as they were placed on a map of the area. 'Each one is half a mile from the UN,' he said, confused. 'And if they're empty, that's no threat at all.'

'Do you know why you've been instructed to plant the devices there?' Drake asked.

Nero shook her head. 'Negative.'

'What explosives do you have?' Kahu asked.

'Bitrol. Ten kilos each.'

'Bitrol.' Kahu thought. 'It's a directional explosive. That's enough to blow the roof off, but leave the building standing.'

Harrison whistled through his teeth. 'That would get people's attention.'

'And what part does Calian play in all this?'

'I'm not sure. He says he's the vaccine. Called tomorrow Year Zero.'

Drake nodded thoughtfully. 'That's a common enough theme but it doesn't tell us anything specific.'

Another soft *bleep* alerted him to another participant waiting to join the call.

'Benjamin,' Drake said as another head joined the display, 'What do you have for us?'

'The data says there's a probability spike at nine thirty tomorrow morning. And it's centred in the auditorium of the UN building.'

'Just as the delegates arrive,' added Drake.

Harrison shook his head. 'There's no way anyone's getting in there. The security's watertight.'

'Pretty much,' agreed Kahu. 'Although the service entrance is a little vulnerable. The security scanner there isn't quite up to spec.'

'It's good enough,' Harrison snapped, a little too quickly. 'It'll still activate the blast doors if it detects anything. Then *nothing's* getting in.'

'We're due to move out at six in the morning,' Nero thought aloud.

Benjamin was punching at a keyboard. 'It's a two-hour journey so that would tally. Leaves you an hour to set the devices.'

'You're not actually going to let them plant those bombs?' Kahu was aghast.

'We need to let this play out,' Benjamin interrupted. 'We know those buildings are abandoned and we know the explosives will leave them standing. Those bombs don't go off, Calian will know he's been caught.'

'Why don't we bring him in now?'

'Because our evidence is circumstantial at best.'

Reluctantly, Kahu agreed. 'Bitrol is found in everything from fertilisers to water purifiers. He could be using it for anything.'

'And unfortunately,' added Drake, 'our computer's calculations aren't yet admissible in a court of law. It won't be enough to say we knew what he was going to do.'

'Pull him now,' Benjamin concluded, 'and Calian could walk free.'

'You have your orders,' Drake snapped, suddenly officious. 'Carry on as you are, report back when you can. Remember, we've got your back.' He nodded. 'Drake out.'

16

Year Zero

Calian spent the rest of the night outside. In between moments of fitful sleep, Nero could see him sitting cross-legged on the forest floor with his back to the tent. He seemed to be meditating. Preparing. Nero pulled a pen torch from her bag and swept the tent with its low beam. Beside the stove, she saw what she was looking for. A rectangular container about the size of a pencil case. Throughout the evening, whenever Calian had spoken about *Year Zero* or *being the vaccine*, she had noticed his eyes flick to it. She let the light rest on it for a while, then pulled her Spi-Glasses from her bag.

APPLICATIONS>VIEW>RADIOGRAPHY
>LOW

The forest looked even more eerie through the transparent tent walls. The trees were skeletons, looming ominously over the clearing. Looking down, she focussed on the mysterious box, eager for a glimpse inside. Instead, there was a black void. She adjusted the settings. Nothing. Whatever the box was made of, it was impervious to her glasses. Its contents were hidden from sight.

Nero sighed. For a group of people opposed to new technology, they sure knew how to use it when it counted. She slipped the glasses off and turned off the torch.

Chang was breathing softly beside her. Nero envied her composure in the face of the mission.

Perhaps she'd find it too, one day.

She was shaken awake by Calian.

'Today's the day!' he beamed. His eyes were wide and staring and his movements were jittery. Nero couldn't tell if it was the result of a sleepless night or something a little more... *pharmaceutical*. He had changed into smarter clothes. Black trousers and jacket and a white shirt. Nero guessed it was the sort of outfit that wouldn't draw so much attention at the UN.

'It's time to change the world,' Calian grinned.

Chang winced as he threw her a bag. It had been loaded with an explosive device the evening before.

'Relax, Dumont,' Calian laughed. 'It's stable until it's primed.' He looked at his watch. 'Which it will be in approximately three hours. Year Zero, baby!' He gave a whoop as he threw Nero her bag. 'Follow me,' he grinned. 'We're moving out!'

He brushed past Nero to retrieve the mysterious box beside the stove, then ran from the tent, leaving Chang and Nero to stare at each other in bewilderment.

As they followed, they saw him run into the woods and start lifting discarded and broken branches from a pile. Soon, a vehicle emerged from the debris.

'You're gonna get us into the heart of the city in *that*?'

Nero stared at the eyesore before her. It was an old internal combustion engine car. It had elongated wings that swept over the rear wheel arches and a wide windscreen. Its bonnet was pitted with rust and it sat low on four chrome wheels that had seen better days. Nero shook her head in dismay. It looked like something from the turn of the century.

'Er,' began Chang. 'Won't we, you know, *stick out a bit*?'

'No software!' boomed Calian with delight. 'So we can't be tracked.' He swung open the driver's door. 'Besides, this is only to get us to the suburbs. Once we hit the city roadblocks, we'll head underground.'

He threw himself into the seat and turned the key in the ignition.

'It's got a steering wheel!' Nero laughed as she slumped in the passenger seat. 'You're actually gonna *drive* this thing?'

Calian reached for the gear stick and smiled again. 'You just watch me.'

Nero felt herself thrown against the back of her seat as the car accelerated away. Looking behind her, she saw Chang hanging onto the headrest and quickly groping for the seatbelt.

They drove through the forest for an hour, then broke out into wide, expansive fields. Soon, the buildings by the roadside grew more substantial and more numerous until, just as the sun was rising, they found themselves in the outskirts of the city. Calian pulled over by the side of the road and turned to face his passengers.

'This is where we part company.' Nero and Chang looked around them.

'Where are we?' Chang asked.

'There's a storm drain five hundred metres north,' Calian pointed through the window. 'Follow it until it divides. Dumont, your target will be a kilometre to the right. Merigan? The other fork will take you down to the docks. You'll need these.'

Reaching into the glove compartment, he tossed them a couple of head torches. 'What are you going to do?' Nero asked as she unbuckled.

'I'm gonna catch the monorail to the city, then I'm gonna walk in the front door of the UN building… *and blow it up.*' Calian reached out to the back seat and picked up the small box.

'With that?'

Calian winked as he opened the door. 'Kinda.'

The three occupants of the car stepped onto the roadside, slamming the doors shut behind them. Without a backward glance, Calian set off down the street.

'How's he gonna walk in with a bomb?' Chang panted as they ran off the main road.

'They'll sniff it out a mile away.'

Nero fell into an easy jog. 'Maybe it's not a bomb.'

As the pair headed into a patch of scrubland, Nero couldn't help thinking she was missing something.

The storm drain was a large concrete construction two metres round. It meant the two women barely had to lower their heads as they ran. Slipping on their head torches to illuminate the way, they followed the course of the drain as it buried itself in the surrounding countryside. The first thing Nero noticed was the cold, damp air. The second thing she noticed was the smell.

'Drake,' Chang activated the comms buried in her ear. 'We're in a storm drain heading into the city from the east. Calian is heading into town on a monorail.'

'We've got you,' came Drake's voice. Nero heard it, too. 'There's a fork ahead. Do you have the explosives?'

'I'm trying not to think about it,' Nero muttered as she ran.

'We've got Calian on satellite now. He's about to board the monorail.'

'I still don't understand how he's going to get through security with a bomb.'

Drake hesitated. 'I don't see a bomb.'

'Small white box,' Chang explained as they reached the junction. 'He put it in a pocket as he left us.'

Nero peeled off to the left as her companion ran off down the other conduit. 'What's he playing at?' Nero was confused. 'How can he set off an explosion big enough to destroy the UN building, but not have a bomb?'

Benjamin Saal had been listening in. 'We don't know,' he said. 'But we know that he will, with a greater degree of certainty. We also know that he doesn't survive, so we're guessing the bomb must be on him somewhere.'

'Maybe he'll pick it up en route,' Chang suggested.

'Maybe,' Drake replied. 'Now we've got eyes on, we'll watch him like a hawk.'

'What are our odds, Benji?' Nero panted as she ran on.

'Fluctuating,' Benjamin replied, trying to hide his irritation at the misuse of his name. 'But generally favourable. Looks like at least one of you will make it out alive.'

'You have to tell us that now?'

'Sorry,' Benjamin whimpered. 'You *did* ask.'

A click indicated someone else had joined the conversation.

'Kahu here,' came a voice. 'The delegates are arriving. We found no holes in Williams's security. I honestly don't know how this guy is gonna get in.'

Harrison's voice joined in. 'You're sure the blast takes place in the auditorium?'

'There's a ninety-nine point nine percent chance that it does,' snapped Benjamin.

'Well, I don't mean to question your precious computer,' Kahu sneered, 'but that place is watertight. He'll be caught the moment he steps through the scanners at the entrance.'

'Then he's found another way,' Nero mused.

'There is no other way,' Harrison replied. 'Much as I hate to admit it, Williams has done a pretty good job here. Every entrance is covered. And besides, the auditorium is impregnable.'

Nero raised an eyebrow. 'How so?'

'Reinforced titanium, triple strength steel alloy,' Harrison explained. 'You could drop a nuke on that place and you'd barely hear the bang.'

'The only weak point is the service entrance scanner,' Kahu interjected, 'but it's still third gen. Should be secure enough.'

Drake attempted to sum up the situation. 'Okay. We'll keep running the probability stats through the computer and let you know if anything turns up. In the meantime, Nero, Chang, you've got bombs to plant. Nero, you're almost at the docks. When you exit the storm drain, your target is right in front of you. Chang, you'll be right underneath your warehouse in two hundred and fifty metres. Good luck. Drake out.'

One by one, everyone clicked off the call.

'F.A.B.' said Benjamin.

'What's that?'

'Stands for First Action Bureau.' He was losing confidence even as he spoke. 'I thought it could be a call sign or something.'

Nero rolled her eyes as she ran. 'I don't ever want to hear you say that again.' Benjamin tapped out.

Taking her slate from her bag, Nero held the back of her hand to the screen and scrolled through the display until she could see her location on a map. The exit to the wharf was displayed dead ahead. She crept forward until she found a grille in the side of the storm drain. It fell to the floor with a clatter following a swift kick, and Nero found herself in a large storeroom. She ran to the window to gaze out over the docks. The River Hudson was a busy waterway, bustling with leisure craft and commercial cargo ships. Nero could see security vessels weaving in between them. Further upstream, a cordon had been slung across the river, a series of buoys marking the limit beyond which no boats were allowed.

Swinging her bag from her shoulder, she turned her attention to the task at hand. 'Drake, I'm at my target site,' she reported as she removed the device, 'and setting the explosives.'

'Chang?' Drake asked.

'I'm in,' came the response.

'You have just over twenty minutes before they're due to blow. Prime the devices, then I want you down in the Plaza for whatever happens next.'

Nero set about priming her explosive device. It was a metal sphere twenty centimetres across. A small console on one side displayed some switches and a small screen. With the bomb in place by a supporting wall, Nero flicked the switches on. A series of numbers appeared on the screen, counting down from twenty minutes.

'I'm live,' she reported.

'Me too,' replied Chang. 'Let's go.'

Stepping gingerly away from the device, Nero turned to the nearest exit and broke into a run. She had just half an hour to reach the UN Plaza. What she would find when she got there, was anyone's guess.

'There!' Harrison tapped the screen to indicate the young man with a straggly beard walking coolly to the Plaza. 'I'm sure that's him.'

He and Kahu had commandeered the security building, much to Devlin Williams's annoyance. While they surveyed the security footage from a whole host of cameras, Williams had had to content himself with working on the shop floor. Kahu could see him on one of the projected screens now, taking out his frustration on some unfortunate underling.

Harrison pulled an image of the suspect getting into the monorail and displayed it side by side with the live feed. It was a perfect match.

'Bingo.'

Kahu nodded. 'Okay, but what's he doing? So far, the worst we can pin on him is loitering with intent.' She watched as the young man slowed to a stop by the fountains. 'Looks like he's waiting. But for what?'

She felt a sudden rumble in the floor. Then another.

'Two bombs,' she muttered. 'Right on cue.' Suddenly, she understood. 'A distraction.'

'The start of it,' Harrison said, rising behind her robotically.

'The start of what?'

She turned just in time to see Harrison had drawn a Tase Pistol. In the brief moment allowed to her, she could see it was set to maximum. A shot at this range would kill her.

'Year Zero,' Harrison grinned, a manic gleam in his eye.

And then, he pulled the trigger.

Two plumes of smoke curled into the sky from the horizon. Nero ran onto the Plaza to find it full of security personnel and members of the public come to see the delegates arrive. A large section had been cordoned off for the dignitaries' motorcades. Nero saw a whole line of driverless cars had already discharged their eminent passengers. She guessed all the delegates were inside now. Which made those two plumes of smoke all the more puzzling. Why set off explosives in deserted buildings half a kilometre away?

A line of demonstrators threatened to impede her progress. The explosions on the skyline had instilled a sense of panic in the crowd, but still some protestors took the opportunity to make their voices known. Some wearing masks chanted their all too familiar catchphrases.

'Kill the virus!'

'The Earth cries out!'

'We are the vaccine!'

The security services, who would normally have been only too happy to intervene, were distracted by the explosions in the distance. They ran from the Plaza or boarded driverless vehicles to take them to the scene of the explosions. Some passers-by ran in panic while others stood and stared. The general atmosphere was one of bewilderment.

'We've got him,' came Drake's voice in Nero's ear. 'Looks like he's picking up a communication.'

Nero frowned. 'Instructions, maybe?'

There was a pause.

'Yes,' said Drake at last. 'He's setting off. Round to the east of the building. Harrison, Kahu, can you intercept?'

There was no reply.

'Harrison? Kahu?' Drake tried again. 'Do you read me?'

The silence was profound.

'What the hell's going on?'

There was a click on the comms.

'I think I see him!' It was Chang. 'He's picking up his pace. But there's still no sign of any bomb.'

'The computer is spiking at a hundred per cent probability,' chimed in Benjamin Saal. 'He's definitely carrying something.'

Nero was thinking hard. 'Then how is he going to blow up that building?'

'We're seeing lots of movement inside.' Drake sounded more serious than ever. 'Judging from the internal security cameras, the delegates are being moved into the central auditorium. Probably as a result of the explosions.'

'But why?' Chang asked. 'Why would Calian want them in there? It's virtually nuke proof.'

Nero blinked as the penny dropped. 'The explosions,' she panted as she ran towards the Plaza. 'They were the cue.'

'Explain, Nero,' snapped Drake.

'They were Calian's cue to move.' Nero rounded the corner to see Chang ahead of her, in pursuit of the quarry. 'He knew the delegates would be moved to the auditorium for their own protection. The great and the good,' she breathed. 'The world's most important men and women. They'll be sitting ducks.'

'But why?' Chang asked in Nero's ear. 'He's never going to get in with a bomb.'

A sudden blow to her shoulder caught Nero unawares and she spun to the floor. Looking up, she saw a protestor ambling aimlessly, placard in the air.

'Watch where you're going!' he called. Nero read the placard.

WE ARE THE VACCINE!

A thousand thoughts collided in her head.

'Wait,' she gasped. 'He's not carrying a bomb. He is the bomb!'

'Nero?'

Nero was thinking through the implications. 'Calian said, *I am the vaccine.*'

'It's the Dheghomites' slogan,' Drake snapped back. 'So what?'

Nero scrambled to her feet. 'Not *we. I.* We're wondering how he was going to smuggle a bomb past the scanners. He's going to inject it. He is *literally* the vaccine.'

'A bio bomb.' Benjamin was following her train of thought. 'A serum that converts every cell of the human body into an explosive device, all delivered intravenously.'

Nero was aghast at where her own logic had taken her. 'Is there such a thing?'

'Theoretically it's possible,' Benjamin mused. 'But I was always convinced we were still a few years away from having the tech needed to produce it.'

'Well,' seethed Nero as she started running towards the building again, 'looks like the Dheghomites have it.' Even in her frenzied state, she was aware of the irony of the Dheghomites employing the very technology they opposed to bring about maximum destruction.

Nero heard Chang's voice in her ear. 'But how would it get through the security scanners?'

'There must be a hole in their ring of steel,' Drake answered grimly. 'A weakness somewhere.'

Nero rounded another corner to see Chang ahead. The Plaza and surrounding streets were in chaos. News of the two explosions had obviously reached everyone in the crowd and the sense of panic was growing. Nero saw security officers bundling delegates into the building towards the auditorium and supposed safety. Everyone else was turned away at gunpoint to take their chances elsewhere. A cacophony of alarms and recorded safety announcements filled the air.

'He's leading us round to the service entrance,' Chang panted. 'There's a security fence to climb and then the scanner to get past. If he's detected, the blast doors will close in front of him.'

'Harrison mentioned the staff entrance had an older type of scanner,' Benjamin interjected. 'Third generation, not fourth. Perhaps it's not sophisticated enough to detect a bio bomb.'

'But how would he know that?' Nero suddenly felt sick to her stomach. 'Unless…'

'Harrison!'

Nero flinched as Drake barked in her ear.

'Harrison, Kahu! Respond!'

Nothing.

'We have to assume,' Drake continued, trying to keep his voice under control, 'that Alpha Squad has been compromised.'

More pieces of the puzzle were falling into place.

'Overnight, I found the serum in Calian's tent, but I didn't know what it was. My Spi-Glasses couldn't see into the container.'

'It's obviously got some shield component,' explained Benjamin. 'Looks like he knew third generation scanners wouldn't pick it up.'

'I'm hit!'

There was feedback in Nero's ear as Chang screamed. 'One of the security team. It's my leg. I'm never going to make that fence.'

'I'm there,' Nero replied at once. 'And I can see him.'

Nero grabbed at the wire mesh and scaled the fence. As she reached the top, she felt a stabbing pain in her temple. She paused and shook her head, feeling suddenly dizzy. Dropping on the other side, she squatted for a moment on her haunches to catch her breath, then sprinted towards the staff entrance. The pain in her head was getting worse.

'He's through!' she called.

'You're going to have to be quick,' Benjamin warned her.

'I'm in,' Nero assured him, and she threw herself towards the entrance.

The moment she was through the arch, she saw people being ushered into another door to the auditorium. She just caught sight of Calian's sleeve as he slipped through.

'And so is he.'

Nero sprinted through the door to find hundreds of panicked delegates milling around the auditorium. She squinted to see through the pain in her head. Some were on their phones, others were crouching low on the ground or under tables. She noticed a rather officious looking security officer trying to calm the room.

'I can assure you,' he was booming above the din, 'This is the safest place in the country, if not the world!'

'Kill the virus!' came another shout. 'I am the vaccine!'

The crowd seemed to turn as one to see a striking looking man with a straggly beard standing in the middle of the floor. His feet were planted squarely on the flag of the United Nations displayed underfoot. He held a small syringe in his hand. Most strikingly of all, his skin was glowing. Every vein in his body seemed to be luminous, showing through the skin as if they were molten lava. Calian seemed to relish the pain.

'Welcome,' he called as he raised his hands into the air, 'to Year Zero!'

His eyes seemed to explode with an orange flame, then his whole body became a shaft of intense light. Feeling the scorching tendrils of the blast reaching out towards her, Nero turned away to find a familiar face right next to her.

'Duck!' screamed a voice.

As Nero blacked out, her aching brain somehow managed to reach through the confusion to form a word.

'*Meena..?*'

17

With Friends Like These

N ero tried to concentrate on physical sensations. She could feel the pressure of a mattress beneath her. She knew there were covers over her. Sheets? Blankets? Her mouth was dry and her eyes stung. Every limb ached. The pain in her head was subsiding, so she dared to open her eyes.

There was a bright light directly above her. She moved her head on her pillow to get her bearings. The room was small and brightly lit. Equipment lined the walls. Monitors displayed graphs and numbers. On one of them, an outline of a human form pulsed gently, the internal organs flashing various colours. Chairs stood by her bed. Looking down, she tried to focus on a logo embroidered on the sheets, a line of indistinct words arranged around a heart symbol. She saw a needle and line inserted into the skin of her left arm. The line was connected to a bag on a pole, its contents dripping into the tube via a hole at the bottom. Drugs. Good. Nero licked her lips. She was thirsty.

'Hey, Nero,' came a voice. 'Need some water?'

'Meena,' croaked Nero.

Meena turned from the water dispenser with a paper cup.

'That's me,' she purred. 'The one and only.' She cradled Nero's head in a hand and lifted the cup to her lips.

Nero gazed at her as she drank. The large, brown eyes, the hair swept back into a ponytail. She could barely believe her old friend was with her.

'Where am I?' she rasped.

'Somewhere safe. You're being well looked after.'

A sudden, recent memory crashed into Nero's mind.

'The explosion,' she spluttered.

Meena placed the cup on a table and drew up a chair. She reached out to hold Nero's hand, a look of concern on her face.

'That was four days ago,' she said, softly. 'You've been drifting in and out of consciousness since then. The doctors didn't want to revive you. They said it was the body's way of healing itself.'

'Four days?' Nero couldn't quite believe it. She lifted her head again. 'What happened?'

Meena patted her hand. 'You were right about Calian,' she began. 'He had injected himself with a DNA altering material, designed to turn every cell of his body into a bomb. That's how he avoided the scanner detecting him.' She leaned in and whispered, sadly. 'Nero, you didn't catch him.'

Nero's heart thumped in her chest. Her head swam. *'Didn't catch him?* Then – ' Tears sprang to her eyes. 'No,' she gasped. 'We failed? *I* failed.'

'Don't think of it like that,' Meena soothed. 'Everyone knew the odds were against you.'

Nero sobbed. So the Bureau computer had been right in its predictions. Had there really been any point in trying to beat it? She looked around the room.

'Then, how – ?'

'Drake sent me to watch you,' Meena explained. 'He thought you were too important to lose. He had me shadow you from the moment you arrived at the Plaza.'

Nero's head was hurting again. 'But, the explosion...'

Meena nodded. 'Killed just about everyone in the room. Every country in the world lost a prime minister or a president.'

'Then... how did I survive?' Nero was trying her hardest to contain her emotion.

'I got the blast door behind you open again. I just managed to pull you clear in time. Like Drake said, you're too important to lose.'

'But, Chang? Harrison? Kahu?'

Meena shook her head. 'You live to fight another day.'

Overcome, Nero struggled to swing her legs from the bed.

'Try and keep still, Nero,' Meena cautioned, standing to restrain her as softly as she could. 'You're no use to anyone until you're fixed.'

Nero slumped back into her pillow, the news almost too much to bear. Her mind raced over the events as she remembered them. The hideout in the woods, the planting of the explosives, running to the UN Plaza. Then, another memory asserted itself. One that she and Meena should share, if it had happened at all.

'The Clarke Elevator,' Nero gasped. Each word seemed more painful than the last. 'Tell me... *did it happen?*'

Meena looked at her for a moment. 'Of course it happened,' she said at last. 'And you acquitted yourself admirably.'

But something didn't add up. If the mission on the Clarke Elevator was real, then *how had she survived?* Her final memory had been of falling from the sky, the ground spinning up to meet her. Was Meena lying? Instinctively, Nero changed the subject.

'What about the Bureau?' she asked. 'Drake and Benjamin?'

Meena didn't reply at once. Instead, she let go of Nero's hand and rose silently from her bedside. She walked to the window and drew back the blind, gazing absently at whatever lay beyond. Nero struggled to catch a glimpse but could only see a steel grey sky.

'It's in the process of being disbanded,' Meena said at last, in measured tones. 'After two such high profile failures, the governments, intelligence communities and investors have lost confidence. First Action Bureau is no more.' She turned from the window. 'Although, a few of us are determined to keep the spirit alive.'

Nero's eyes widened. 'How?'

'The Dheghomites haven't gone away, you know,' Meena said as she walked back to the bed. 'The Bureau was the only credible threat to their existence. Our Pre-emptive Force agents are the only tools we have to defeat them.'

'But, with the Bureau disbanded, how can we carry on?'

Meena looked around as if to check no one was eavesdropping on their conversation. 'Nathan Drake and Benjamin Saal have been forced into hiding, but they left the Bureau's computer architecture alive and well in the quantum cloud.'

'Do you have access?' Nero's head was swimming. What was Meena suggesting?

'Almost,' Meena admitted. 'And that's where you come in.'

'Me?' Nero really didn't feel in any position to help.

Meena nodded. 'I know you've gained access before.'

Nero tried to shrug, but the pain in her shoulders prevented her. 'Only to get the intel I've been allowed.'

'No,' Meena smiled. 'I mean the other time.'

Nero swallowed. She meant the time she went digging for her father. Should she expose Benjamin?

'I know you gained access that night at Benjamin Saal's,' Meena continued, airily. 'If we are to use the Bureau computer to carry on fighting the Dheghomites, I'm going to need to know how you did it.'

'Benjamin Saal has higher clearance than me. I asked him to conduct a personal search – '

'For your father, yes,' Meena interrupted. 'But it was a secret search, wasn't it? You didn't want to be found out, so Benjamin got you in.' Meena leaned over the bed. 'How?'

Nero was looking at Meena's hand. She could tell she was hiding something in her palm, but she couldn't see what.

'He wouldn't let me watch.'

Meena laughed. 'Benjamin Saal has been trying to impress you since the moment you first met. He would be *dying* for you to watch. What did he do, Nero?'

Nero heard a threatening note in her voice

'How did he get into the computer without anyone knowing?'

'I don't know!' Nero shouted. Surely, if she was loud enough, someone would come running. But then again, in the time she'd been awake, she'd not been aware of any staff. No doctors or nurses. No noises beyond the door. Except for Meena, no one had been to see her since she had come to. Surely, her bedside should be a buzz of activity. *What was this place?*

'Tell me,' Meena hissed as she leaned forward.

Nero felt a stinging sensation on the back of her hand, and looked down to see a medical patch stuck to her skin.

'It's okay, Nero,' Meena was calm again now. 'You'll tell me soon enough.'

Nero's vision was starting to blur. The memory of that night at Benjamin's replayed in her mind. She could see him at the computer hub in his apartment. She watched as he flicked his hair from his eyes. *I mustn't tell her.* She saw Benjamin explaining to her how he was going to infiltrate the very computer he had built. He was proud of himself. He was trying to impress her. Nero fought hard not to speak her thoughts aloud. He kept repeating a phrase. The phrase Meena wanted to hear. Nero clamped her jaw tight.

'Tell me,' she heard Meena say. Somehow, her voice sounded far away and close at the same time.

Two words.
Just two words.
I mustn't say them.

She watched Benjamin as he repeated the phrase again. Watched as the words formed on his lips. Nero couldn't help herself. She could feel her own lips moving. She echoed him, heard her own voice copying his. She could fight no more.

'*Ghost Profile*,' she said, then slipped into unconsciousness.

The light is harsh.
The blade is sharp.
The pain, exquisite.
There's something inside.
Part of me
but not me.

The enemy
lies within
me.
Who
am
I?

'Nero! Nero Jones!'
    Another voice.
    'Nero, can you hear me?'
    Nero snapped her eyes open.
    'Ah,' Drake smiled. 'Glad you could join us.'

18

After the Storm

Nero found herself in the cabin of a small plane. Rain lashed at the window. There was the occasional flash of lightning. Chang lay along three seats across the aisle, her leg dressed in MediPlastic. Nero could see through the transparent outer layer to the viscous blue liquid inside. The wound would be healing already.

'Chang? You're *alive*?' Nero heard herself say.

Chang smiled. 'Last time I checked. You did good.'

'Where am I?'

Drake sat beside her, looking concerned. 'Heading home. We're going to get you checked out properly before we head back to the Bureau for a debrief.'

'The Bureau?'

'You okay, Nero?'

Nero tried to steady her breathing. *Has it happened again?*

'The UN building,' she stuttered.

'It's safe,' Drake answered. 'Thanks to your timely response.'

'Harrison? Kahu?'

It was as if Nero had flicked a switch. Drake looked furious. 'Harrison was a Dheghomite infiltrator. He alerted Calian to the weaker security scan at the service entrance. He knew it wouldn't detect the bio bomb.'

Nero couldn't believe what she was hearing. 'How did he become part of the Bureau? If he was an infiltrator, shouldn't you have spotted it?'

Drake shook his head. 'That's the trouble with Dheghomites. No digital footprint.'

'And Kahu?' Nero barely dared to ask.

'Casualty of war,' Chang replied. Nero got the impression she was being protected from the whole picture.

'She was a promising recruit,' Drake said, thoughtfully.

Nero chose her next words with care. 'Can you tell me what happened?'

Drake narrowed his eyes. 'The medics on the scene said we should expect this. The concussion you received has caused temporary memory loss. We were assured it wouldn't last.'

'You got him, Nero,' Chang said with a broad grin.

'How?'

Chang struggled to make herself comfortable. 'When I was shot by that doofus security guard, it was up to you to step up. And boy, did you step up.'

'What did I do?'

Chang chuckled. 'You threw yourself on his back. Crazy move, but turns out it was the only thing you could have done.'

Nero blinked. She had no memory of that at all. In fact, now she thought of it, her last memory was of being pulled from the auditorium as the bomb exploded, then lying in a hospital bed with Meena by her side.

'What happened then?'

'We came to clean up the mess,' Drake smiled. 'Including you.'

'So, you were in New York all the time?' Nero wasn't sure how she felt about that.

'It's like I said,' Drake said simply. 'The Bureau will always have your back.'

'And… when did all this happen?' Nero spoke with care.

'Just six hours ago, Nero,' Chang sighed. 'We were treated at the scene then put on this flight.'

'We're an hour and twenty minutes outside Heathrow,' Drake clarified. 'You *do* remember Heathrow?'

Nero managed a smirk and a nod, but she was troubled. Since joining the Bureau barely two weeks ago, she'd had two experiences that were… *strange*. Had they happened at all? If not, what the hell was wrong with her? If so, what the hell was wrong with everyone else?

'Why don't you try and get some rest?' Drake suggested as he rose to his feet. 'I'm going to head to the cockpit and open a channel to Benjamin. He'll need to know when we're due to land. I'm sure you have lots of questions for him.'

Nero managed a weak smile of thanks as he left, then shuffled over the aisle to Chang.

'Did Harrison kill Kahu?' she asked.

Chang shook her head. 'You don't need to deal with that right now,' she said. 'Why not make the most of that amnesia while you can?'

In stark contrast to when Nero had last sat in the briefing room, she found herself feeling very alone. It was difficult to believe the mission had cost them so dear. Nero needed answers about a great many things but, with Drake in the room with her and Benjamin, she would have to tread carefully. She had already exposed herself a little to Benjamin and, frankly, was ready to do so again in pursuit of the truth, but Drake was a different matter. For all that Nero felt she could now at least trust him, he was still something of an unknown quantity.

Benjamin was running satellite and surveillance camera footage of the incident at the UN building. Nero leaned in as she saw herself climbing the security fence in pursuit of Calian. That was when she had first felt the headache and paused at the top. Except, according to the footage, she didn't pause at all. She saw herself drop to the other side and break into a sprint. The camera switched to another angle as Nero rounded a corner, and she could plainly see Chang, writhing on the ground. She shouted something and slid a Tase Pistol along the floor. Without breaking her stride, Nero scooped it up and continued her pursuit.

Finally, with Calian in her sights, the Nero in the footage launched herself at his back, just as he passed beneath the scanner. The Tase Pistol in her pocket was enough to set off the alarm. An interior view showed the blast doors clanging shut. As Nero watched the ensuing struggle, she saw her past self reaching into Calian's pocket to pull out a small white box. She threw it away and it clattered to the ground, its lid springing open. A small syringe slid across the concrete, its contents leaking away as the glass shattered.

Within moments, a squad of security guards were on them. As Nero was pulled away, she caught a glance from Calian's fist and she fell to the floor, unconscious.

'That's when we picked you up,' Drake concluded. 'And Calian was apprehended for interrogation.'

Nero was uncharacteristically quiet.

Drake looked proudly at his young recruit. 'You got him,' he beamed. 'And that fact will be included and underlined in the official report. I just hope your memory returns soon. It's a terrible thing to save a hundred lives and not remember a thing about it.'

Nero didn't dare admit that her memory of events was very different indeed.

'There's one thing I don't understand,' she said.

'Fire away,' said Benjamin, regretting his use of the phrase almost at once. 'I mean,' he stammered, trying to recover himself. 'Let's hear it.'

'You said Harrison gave Calian instructions to head for the service entrance, knowing the security scanners wouldn't detect the bio bomb.'

Drake interjected. 'We saw the very moment Calian received his directions.'

'But Harrison was only on this assignment two days ago. How did he know he'd find a weakness in the building's security?'

Benjamin looked sheepish. 'Once our quantum data began to show there was an incident at the UN building on February the twenty-fourth, Harrison *knew* he would succeed even if he didn't know how. All he had to do was wait for the relevant information to fall into his lap, just as he knew it would. The data would be confirmed. He *became* the probability spike.'

Nero shook her head in wonder. 'A kind of self-fulfilling prophecy.'

Benjamin shrugged, apologetically. 'It's a design flaw I'm going to have to work on,' he admitted.

'Nero,' Drake said, perching on the edge of a desk. 'I want you to take some time out. Get a little *R&R*. With your mother's disappearance and the injury you sustained on this mission, I think you need some down time.' He walked to the door and held it open for her to signify the meeting was over. 'Go home and rest up. You've earned it.'

Nero found it hard to disagree.

'Home,' she called as the film came to an end, 'lights up, screen off.'

'Of course, Nero,' came the monotone voice. 'Did you enjoy the film?'

Nero nodded. 'One of my favourites.' A sudden memory came to mind. 'One of my dad's favourites.'

'Then might I suggest more films featuring Cary Grant?'

'Later,' Nero yawned. 'First, I need a coffee.'

'It would be a shame to negate the relaxing effects of watching a favourite film with a dose of caffeine.' Even in its expressionless delivery, it was almost possible to hear a note of disapproval in the computer's voice. 'Your blood pressure is at its lowest in several days. Your heart rate has settled at sixty-eight beats per minute. Caffeine will only – '

'Coffee!' Nero boomed. 'I just want a coffee.'

There was a momentary silence. Nero felt like she was being judged.

'Of course,' came the voice at last, and Nero heard the drinks dispenser in the kitchen begin to hiss.

'Okay, look,' she relented. 'How about I run every day and drink more water? Would that make you happy?'

'I am a computer. I cannot be *happy*.'

'Yeah,' muttered Nero under her breath. 'But you can sure be *judgy*.'

A ping from the kitchen told her that her coffee was ready, and Nero rose from her sofa. As she passed her computer hub, she noticed the photocube she had brought from home. With her coffee in one hand, she inserted the cube with the other and began to navigate through the albums of old photographs.

'Just what I need,' she sighed. 'A bit of nostalgia.'

She opened a folder that contained her favourite pictures of all. She smiled as the images scrolled before her. Her father fishing on a boat on a lake. The two of them making daisy chains in a park. Her father pushing her on a swing. They made her miss him all over again. She could almost smell his aftershave. She navigated back to the home page and opened another folder. This contained much older pictures, most of which Nero had barely looked at before. Her mother and father in front of their first house, with their first car. The two of them at a succession of parties and celebrations. A parade of friends.

Nero paused. She swiped back to a particular image of her mother standing with two young women. She couldn't have been older than twenty-five, in the early days of her marriage to Nero's father. But it wasn't her mother that had drawn her attention. It was the woman standing over her left shoulder. Nero scrolled on and found the woman again, this time raising a glass with her mother at a beachside bar. And there she was again, in a white lab coat, posing behind her mother near a table full of scientific equipment. Nero gasped.

The big, brown eyes and long, plaited hair were unmistakable.

19

Smoke and Mirrors

Benjamin Saal was a troubled man. He had spent years trying to perfect predictive quantum computing. The Dheghomite threat had seemed the perfect opportunity to put his theories into practice. Governments around the world had shown their confidence in his talents with their intel and their cash. Now, the whole programme was in jeopardy.

One thing had always attracted Benjamin to computing. There was only wrong or right. A program worked or it didn't. There were no shades of grey, only black or white. Until now.

Quantum computing meant that there was now black and white and every shade of grey in between. Harrison had used the system to his advantage. He had used it to insert himself into a probability and become the means by which it had become a certainty. Benjamin shook his head. How had he not seen the possibility? *Because it wasn't black or white.*

Sitting back in his chair, he sipped a glass of wine and stared at the projected screen hovering before him. Lines and lines of complex computer code swirled in the air. He was looking into the heart, *the guts*, of the Bureau computer. He hoped, if he stared long enough, an answer would present itself.

A soft chime interrupted his thoughts. With a wave of his hand, the rows of code were replaced by an image of a young woman at his apartment's door.

'Come on up,' he breathed. In the few seconds available to him, Benjamin prepared to make a good impression.

'Home,' he called, 'lighting level five.'

'Of course, darling,' came the soft, feminine voice.

'Play something by Rachmaninov.' A sudden thought occurred to him. 'And… maybe don't call me darling for the rest of the night.'

Soft piano music drifted through the air as Benjamin plumped the pillows on his armchairs. Finally, he undid the top button on his shirt and tested the quality of his breath in a cupped hand. Hearing Nero approach in the hall outside, he leaned casually on the back of a chair, glass of wine in hand.

'Home?' he said. 'Door.'

The door hummed open at his command and Nero barged in and slammed it shut behind her. Her hair was dishevelled and her eyes looked wild. Even through her obvious distress, she was able to look Benjamin up and down.

'You look ridiculous,' she said, tersely. 'You should do that top button up or people will mistake you for a perv.'

She marched into the room and slapped something down on Benjamin's computer hub. 'Home!' Nero barked. 'Turn the lights up and the music off.'

She looked at Benjamin. He was still fumbling with his top button.

'Do it, Home,' he said, deflated. He put his wine on the table.

'Of course, darling.'

Nero rolled her eyes and lowered her voice. 'Is it safe to talk while…' she pointed upwards to indicate the disembodied computer voice.

'Home?' Benjamin barked. 'Sleep mode, please.'

'Good night, darling,' came the response.

'She won't hear a thing until she wakes up.'

'And you have *no* idea how weird that sounds.' Nero threw herself into a chair and took a swig from Benjamin's wine. 'We need to talk.'

'Okay,' Benjamin replied carefully. 'About what?'

Nero looked him straight in the eye. 'Can I trust you?'

'You know you can.'

'This conversation stays between us?'

Benjamin pulled up a chair from the kitchen table and sat directly opposite her.

'Of course. What's the problem?'

Nero dropped her head into her hands. 'I think I'm going mad.'

'Why?'

There was a silence as Nero thought how to proceed. 'That night I came here, I didn't tell you everything.'

Benjamin nodded. 'But I'm guessing you *still* didn't succumb to my devastating charm.'

'Not even close.' Nero managed a weak smile. 'I asked you to look for evidence of where I had been following your tech briefing.'

'You said I should humour you, and I did. But you never did tell me why.'

Nero took a breath. *How the hell do you tell someone something like this?*

'I have... memories,' she began slowly, 'of things that may not have happened.' Benjamin frowned. 'What, like dreams?'

'More real than dreams. Actual *physical* experiences. Whole days. People.' She met his gaze again. 'Assignments.'

'When?'

'Since I joined the Bureau. The first happened shortly after your briefing when Drake took me into his office. It was to instruct me on my first assignment. There was going to be an attack on the Clarke Elevator and I had to stop it.'

'The Clarke Elevator?' Benjamin's eyes were wide. 'That's what the briefing was about?'

Nero nodded. 'I remember the mission. The whole thing. As if it happened. The flight to the Pacific, the journey in the elevator, disposing of the bomb.' She didn't mention Meena for now. 'Falling.'

'*Falling*?'

'From seven and a half thousand kilometres.'

Benjamin was aghast. 'But then, you'd never have survived. Doesn't that tell you that it never happened?'

'Maybe,' Nero agreed. 'But then why do I *feel* like it did?'

Benjamin noticed she was shaking with fear.

'I can remember the lurch in my stomach as the elevator lifted off. The smell of the air in the maintenance corridor, the cold of the atmosphere outside as I fell.' She shivered. 'I remember it all.'

'Anything else?' Benjamin was staring at her intently, his face a mask of concern.

Nero looked at her hands. 'It happened again, just after the UN mission.'

'Your amnesia? We've been assured that's entirely consistent with your injuries.'

'It's not that I don't remember what happened,' Nero insisted. 'It's that I remember *something else.*'

Benjamin swallowed. 'What do you remember?'

'Waking up in a hospital bed. Talking to a friend who turned out not to be a friend.' She looked up. 'She was asking about the Bureau computer.'

Benjamin frowned. 'BRAINS?'

Nero sighed. 'Whatever. But she *knew* you got in undetected the other night to search for my father.'

Benjamin shrugged. 'But it wasn't real, so it doesn't matter.'

'It *felt* real.'

'Nero, you were treated at the scene. Then you and Chang were recovered by Drake and brought home. There was no hospital bed. There's no time for your memory to have happened.' He gnawed his lip as he thought. 'I can prove it,' he said at last and turned to the computer hub. 'I've been poking around in BRAINS in the light of our recent, uh, discrepancy. While I'm there, I can access the security logs.'

'Why?' Nero turned to face him. 'Won't Drake find out?'

Benjamin shook his head. 'I'm conducting an internal investigation. Drake has sanctioned it. It'll all look above board.'

He waved his hand above the desktop and frowned at the display before him. Using his fingers, he navigated his way to a virtual room labelled SURVEILLANCE and isolated a camera feed.

'Here we go.' An image of a room appeared, as if filmed from above. 'Drake's office. Just need to find the right time stamp.'

He placed his fingers in a virtual dial that hung in the air and spun it to the left and right. The image moved in response. The footage played out, but sped up. Nero watched as Drake sat at his desk, made calls and moved about the room in agitation. At last he exited and Benjamin withdrew his hand. The playback stopped.

'This is the moment before your meeting, Nero,' he explained. 'Ready?'

Nero rose to stand by his side and nodded. The first thing she noticed was an absence. *Meena was missing from the room*. Nero swallowed.

Benjamin waved his hand and the playback began again. This time, there was sound. Nero heard the hum of the door as Drake showed her into the room.

'This'll just take a moment, Nero,' she heard Drake say. 'I don't want to interrupt your training. Take a seat.'

Nero saw herself pull up a chair as Drake seated himself behind his desk.

'The military police are continuing to look for your mother,' Drake began, 'but I think it's important that you don't give up. Why don't you take the rest of the day off?' Drake was saying from the screen. 'We'll see you tomorrow.'

Nero saw herself nod silently then rise and leave the room. Benjamin stopped the playback with a wave of his hand, 'Well,' he sighed, 'There's one man who would know for sure.'

'I'm not going to Drake,' Nero insisted. 'He'd think I was crazy. I'd be thrown out of the Bureau, for sure.' She slumped back down in her chair.

'Then,' Benjamin said, softly, 'there are three possibilities. Either you're right and this never happened or you're wrong and it did.'

'What's the third?'

Benjamin thought back to the shades of grey. 'You're both wrong *and* right.'

'Huh?'

'It both happened and *didn't* happen.'

'Okay, Schrödinger,' Nero scoffed, 'what do you mean by that?'

Benjamin was thinking on his feet. 'Perhaps these experiences feel real, because they are real. At least to you. As far as you're concerned you experienced everything you've talked about. So, how would that be possible?'

Nero followed his train of thought. 'Lucid dreaming? Hypnosis? Mind control?'

'Maybe. Or memory implantation.'

'Is that even possible?'

Benjamin stared at her for a while, as if measuring her up.

'What?' Nero asked. 'What is it?'

Benjamin sat in a chair directly in front of her and leaned in. 'What I'm about to tell you is beyond classified.'

'Okay,' Nero replied cautiously.

'I mean, it's top, *top* secret.'

'I get it!'

'And I'm only telling you because it sounds like you ought to know.'

'Know what?'

Benjamin thought for a moment, then seemed to come to a decision. He moved back to the computer hub and waved his hand over the desktop. 'Before I moved to First Action Bureau, I worked for Psi-Ops.'

Nero could scarcely believe it. 'And you seem like such a nice guy.'

Benjamin nodded. 'I was in their tech division, of course,' he continued. 'Working on the code for an experimental prototype. The project was abandoned as a costly dead end but, when I moved to the Bureau, I ported over all the work I'd done to the computer's database.' He smiled at Nero. 'I thought it might come in useful one day.'

Nero attempted a smile back. 'Well, that day has come.'

A myriad of cascading code was illuminated in the air.

'You understand all that?' Nero asked.

'More than any other language I know.' Benjamin's fingers were waggling in the air as he searched through the directories to find his work.

'Here we are.' He flicked through folder after folder. 'We had been in receipt of new tech. New to us, that is. It was developed years ago in the US but then abandoned as unethical.'

'But it was good enough for you?'

Benjamin shrugged. 'Needs must.'

'How did it come to you?'

'Black market, probably.' He seemed remarkably unconcerned. 'It became the basic architecture for the whole of the Bureau's systems. Including BRAINS.'

Nero sighed. *He wasn't giving up, was he?*

'We identified the tech as being the work of three people. There are three distinct styles of coding in there. I call them the Architects.' A folder flashed green. 'Ah, okay.' With a double-tap in the air, Benjamin opened the folder to read its contents. 'This was their work on self-monitoring. It seems that memory implants, if that's what it is, can be unstable. After all, you're dealing with the subconscious.' He smiled at Nero. 'And some people's thoughts are more dangerous than others.'

Nero groaned inwardly. She hated it when he tried to be cute.

'Anyway,' Benjamin continued, 'to keep the program from veering into the realms of unreality, a monitor sub-routine is inserted to keep it on track. It's visible by the subject within the implanted memories, usually as an object or even a person. So, you're probably looking for a recurring character or item. Ring any bells?'

Nero's mouth dried as she tried to speak. 'I think so, yes.' She pointed to the photocube she had placed on the computer hub. 'She's in there.'

'Her name is Meena Aziz.'

They were staring at a picture of a young woman with brown eyes and long plaited hair. She stood proudly behind a laboratory table.

'I know her from my time in the Dump. That photo is from a collection of pictures belonging to my mum. They're over twenty-five years old, from before she met my father. And she looks exactly the same in my memories.'

'Then she's the control,' Benjamin whispered. 'Whoever implanted those memories picked her as the monitor sub-routine, perhaps thinking you wouldn't recognise her.'

Nero's legs felt suddenly weak. She lurched towards the chair before she fell. 'Then,' she began, 'has she *ever* been real? She was there in the Dump. Does that mean *none of that happened?*'

'Not necessarily,' Benjamin tried to reassure her. 'But it is a possibility.'

'Then where have I been for the last nine months?' Nero's head was swimming.

'Well,' said Benjamin, 'we know Drake recruited you from the correctional facility – under my recommendation – so I can assure you that it *was* real.' He coughed, awkwardly. 'At least some of it.'

'It all started at the Dump,' Nero thought out loud. 'The headaches, the flashbacks.'

'Flashbacks?'

Nero swore under her breath. She'd let it slip.

'If that's what they are. Maybe they're false memories too.'

Benjamin's interest was piqued. 'Memories of what?'

Nero shook her head. 'They're hazy. Some sort of room. Like a hospital. And there's someone there... *doing something.*'

Benjamin frowned. 'To who?'

'I'm not sure,' Nero admitted. 'To me? Perhaps?'

'And they started while you were at the Dump?'

Nero nodded.

'Then I think that's where we start.'

As Nero thought through the implications of his remark, Benjamin turned back to his computer hub and requested a search for the plans of government youth correctional facilities.

20

Break In

Nero never thought she'd be breaking back *in*.

Benjamin had dropped her in the woods about a quarter of a mile south of the perimeter fence. Her small backpack held everything she'd need for the expedition, including one or two special items that Benjamin had managed to take from the Bureau stores.

'I'll log them out as stationery,' he'd said. 'Drake'll never know.'

Nero slipped on her Spi-Glasses.

APPLICATIONS>VIEW>NIGHT VISION
>ON

The trees around her seemed to pulsate with an eerie glow. A full Moon dominated the sky beyond the canopy, almost bright enough to hurt her eyes. Keeping low, Nero skulked through the undergrowth, being careful to place her feet where they'd make no noise. Soon enough, she could see the watchtowers looming through the trees.

Nero crouched in a leaf strewn gully and reached into her bag. The overall was light and flexible. It was made, so Benjamin had told her, from a material called Deep Black, a lightweight polymer capable of absorbing light rather than reflecting it. As such, it was practically invisible to any night vision viewers or scanners. It would even, Benjamin had assured her, fool the heat sensitive goggles that had been her downfall previously.

With the zip pulled up to her chin and the hood pulled tight over her head, Nero made her way to the ditch that surrounded the perimeter fence.

It was a good three metres deep. Teetering on the edge, she pulled a spike from her bag and jammed it into the compacted earth. As it made contact, three prongs sprung out from its hilt and drove themselves into the ground around it, holding it fast. Nero attached a rope to a loop at the spike's base and lowered herself to the ground beyond the sheer drop. Once there, she flicked the rope. As if it was a signal, the prongs retracted, pulling the spike from the ground. Nero caught it with one hand and threw it, almost at once, to the top of the trench behind her. Again, the spike embedded itself, and Nero gave the rope a sharp tug to test it. Satisfied that it would take her weight, she pulled herself, hand over hand, to the top and swung her legs over the lip of the ditch. With a flick of the rope, the spike was released and placed carefully back into Nero's bag.

She lay on the ground for a while, waiting for her breathing to settle, then inched her way slowly towards the fence. She had chosen a point equidistant to the two watchtowers on the south side, judging that it would be on the very edge of vision should the guards choose to look at that particular moment.

Beyond the fence, the compound was flooded with bright light. Nero remembered how the light had been kept on all night while she was kept within the building's walls, almost turning night in her little cell into day. It had taken her a couple of weeks to get used to it.

Nero took some small tools from her bag. Connecting some lengths of wire to the mesh in front of her, she isolated an area of the fence that she could cut through without setting off the alarm. She pulled out a tiny circular saw, a miniature blade held suspended on the end of a shaft no bigger than a pencil. Benjamin had thought it would be harder to detect than Nero's choice of a laser torch. He was probably right. The small blade cut through the wire with barely a sound until there was a space big enough for her to crawl through.

She reached into her hood to pull a gauze mask over her face. Made from the same material as the overall, it allowed every inch of her body to be covered whilst still letting her see her way. With a start, she realised she had entered the site at almost the same place she had tried to leave it just a few weeks ago. Ironically, she was having much more luck breaking into the place than breaking out.

So far.

Crouching beyond the glare of the lights, Nero took a small box from her bag. A console on the top held a switch and a touch panel. Flicking it on, Nero swiped her finger slowly across the panel, looking for its effects on the harsh light in the compound. At last, the bulb shattered and the area of ground directly in front of her was plunged into darkness. Benjamin had described it as having the same effect as an opera singer smashing a glass with their voice. Nero switched the unit off with a smile. She knew it wouldn't be long before the bulb was replaced and the light was fixed.

Keeping low, she ran towards a cluster of power generators, reasoning that their background hum would mask any noise she might make. Almost as soon as she'd ducked behind them, the light in the compound snapped back on. Nero let out a sigh of relief, but she knew the hardest part was yet to come.

With her back to the generators, Nero readied herself for the next stage of her assault on the building. It was unnerving to have no communication or promise of backup from Drake and the Bureau. Even Benjamin was unreachable. The danger of any communication being discovered had been considered too great. This time, she was alone.

Just as she was about to move towards the building, Nero heard a noise. She pressed herself between two power generators, taking advantage of the shadow between them.

'Just a blown bulb,' came a crackly voice as a guard passed a few metres away.

'They order the cheapest of everything,' the guard retorted. 'You ask me, you get what you pay for.'

The voice at the end of the comms laughed. 'Does that include the guards?'

'Yup,' replied the guard as he moved away. 'You pay peanuts, you get monkeys.

Nero waited as his footsteps receded into the distance. Sensing her opportunity, she broke cover and made a dash for the down pipe that connected to the guttering on the roof. The same guttering she had tied her improvised rope to during her escape.

The grips on the palms of her gloves and the soles of her shoes helped her gain purchase on the pipe. Inch by inch, she hauled herself up to the roof then rolled over the parapet. Resting for a moment on the gravel, she took the opportunity to get her bearings. There, just a few metres away, was the entrance to the ventilation duct. They hadn't even bothered to secure it against another escape. *I guess they thought no one would be that stupid*, Nero smirked.

She crawled on all fours to the duct. With a final look around, she clambered into the funnel shaped vent and slid inside.

Another rest.

Nero knew she was directly above the shower block, the only area of the facility not covered by security cameras. The minute she left that room, she would be being watched.

Nero stretched her legs out in front of her and felt for the bend in the vent. Lowering herself down carefully, she found the very same footholds she had used on the way up. She looked between her feet to see the fan in its housing. This time, thankfully, it was still. With the showers standing empty, there was no need to ventilate the room. Which made Nero's job so much easier. With a kick, she dislodged the unit from its moorings, and the fan swung down to hang on its hinges.

Nero braced herself for the drop, then let herself fall through the gap to the floor beneath, rolling to break the impact of her descent. Scrambling back to her feet, she pressed herself against the tiled wall. The room was dark, just as she had expected. After a minute or so, it became clear that no one had heard her breaking in. Reaching into her backpack, she snapped the elastic of a head torch round her head and flicked it on. Looking around, her light fell upon a cupboard door in the corner. She skulked across the room, her ears alert for the sound of approaching footsteps.

Once at the door, she pulled a Bureau standard issue explosive tab from her pocket. Moulding it around the lock, she tapped it lightly with a finger to activate it. With the quietest of puffs, the lock was dislodged. Nice one Benji, she smiled. Perhaps he was good for *something* after all. Pulling the door open, she stepped inside the cupboard and switched on the light.

Cleaning products lined the shelves and mops and brooms stood propped up against the wall. Cleaners' overalls hung from a peg. From her time in the Dump, Nero knew most of the cleaning was done at night. From the number of overalls left, she guessed the night shift had already started work, locking the door to their supplies cupboard as they left. Nero shrugged into a pair of overalls, cursing at the tight shoulders. Pulling up the zipper and jamming a cap on her head, she grabbed at a mop and bucket and made to leave the room.

The corridor outside was quiet as the grave. It was strange to be walking these familiar routes again. Past the canteen and through the exercise block, nodding at the other cleaners busying themselves about their tasks. Once or twice, she found herself passing groups of guards. Keeping her head low to avoid eye contact, she strode purposefully towards the lift. Experience had taught Nero that the key to convincing anyone that you had a right to be in a place, was to act as if you had.

The lift took her down to the basement. She conjured an image of the building's footprint in her mind's eye. If Benjamin was right, there was a whole suite of rooms that weren't marked on any official plans. The lift door opened with a soft chime, and Nero stepped into another deserted corridor. Here, the brick walls were bare. Harsh strip lighting hung from the ceiling. The floor was plain, unfinished concrete. Following the directions in her head, Nero scurried past store rooms bursting with bedding, equipment and old uniforms. Just as she'd hoped, the area was unguarded. Finding herself at a dead end, Nero cut a left into a storage bay. Moving between shelves of stored equipment, she finally reached a plain brick wall. She reached up to tap the frames on her Spi-Glasses and, with a flick of her eyes, navigated her way through the menu.

APPLICATIONS>VIEW>RADIOGRAPHY
>LOW

Even the lowest setting was powerful enough to see through the brick. Nero gasped at the view beyond. Her blood ran cold in her veins. It was a room both strange and familiar.

White walls.
Sterile.
Clinical.
A metal chair.
Straps.
A figure, bending. Leaning forwards.
An instrument. A tool. No, a blade.
Pain.
A harsh light.
Pain.
A scream. Mine?
I scream.
So much pain.
It's done.
My brain is a fog.
A question forms.
From the fog, a question.
Who
am
I?

Nero felt her legs buckling beneath her. She leaned against the wall for support, her head spinning. She could hear the pulse of her heart, thumping in her ears. Louder and louder. She fought for breath. The air seemed thick. But with what? Memories? *Had she been in that room before?*

Nero felt herself dropping. She seemed to fall for hours. If anything, the soft crack of her cheek against the tiled floor and the oblivion of unconsciousness that accompanied it came as a relief.

21

Questions and Answers

S he became aware of a rocking motion.
 Daring to open her eyes, Nero peered into the darkness.
There were shapes stacked all around her. Boxes. She
recognised some as the same from the storeroom in the
Dump. They had clearly been loaded on board along with
her.

There was a squeak of brakes and the truck came to a
halt. Nero heard the opening and slamming shut of the cab
door, then footsteps behind her. She rolled to her feet then
crouched low in the furthest corner as the shutter was lifted
to the compartment.

'Okay, Nero,' came a voice. 'You're safe. Come out.'

Nero breathed a sigh of relief. She never thought she
would be so happy to hear Benjamin Saal. She scuttled to
the open shutter and dropped to the ground beyond. It was
only then that she realised her head hurt.

'Here.'

She felt something cool against her cheek. An analgesic
pack. The relief was immediate.

'Hold it there for a few minutes,' said Benjamin, a note
of concern in his voice.

'You got me out?' Nero mumbled.

'As planned,' Benjamin replied. 'Just about. Luckily they
were expecting a supply swap, and it was easy enough to
commandeer this truck once I'd traced it.'

Nero nodded. She didn't want to know what he'd done
with the driver.

'Although,' Benjamin continued, 'you made life difficult when you – '

'Fainted, yeah. Sorry about that.'

'Luckily, they gave me access to the stores without question. I don't think they even know what's down there.'

'I do,' Nero rasped. 'I know exactly what's down there.'

Benjamin led Nero from the road and sat her on a fallen tree. She gasped as she looked into the shallow valley beneath them.

'I know that place.'

'The Pelham Reactor,' Benjamin nodded as he sat beside her.

'But,' Nero spluttered. 'Are we safe?'

'At this distance, sure.' Benjamin gazed down upon the wrecked buildings. 'For maybe an hour or so.'

'*Maybe?*'

Benjamin shrugged. 'At least we won't be interrupted. No one else dares come here since the explosion, so it's a handy place to grab some *we* time.'

Nero blinked. Did he really just say that? She looked down at the scene beneath them. As the first rays of the morning sun touched the complex beneath them, she could see the damage quite clearly. A gaping gash ran the entire length of the reactor building, the result of a strike by the Dheghomites. Just as the Holy Grail of clean, abundant energy had been within humanity's grasp, they had destroyed it. In their subsequent claims of responsibility, the Dheghomites delivered a long treatise detailing how they disagreed with the project's aims. Nuclear fusion, they had said, was simply a way of extending humankind's dominion over the Earth. A way of aiding its proliferation. If the Earth was to heal, the human race must be curtailed. Projects such as the Pelham Reactor were legitimate targets. To drive home the point, the explosion was just one of a series that were detonated simultaneously at similar sites around the world. Each had involved the use of a dirty bomb, an explosive device coupled to a small quantity of radioactive material. It had been enough to render the surrounding countryside out of bounds. Lives had been lost and the search for abundant energy had been set back years.

'This was the incident that led directly to the First Action Bureau. Governments around the world started looking for a way to predict terrorist acts. Without those bombs, we wouldn't be sitting here now.'

Nero sneered at the irony.

'We'd spent years on the back foot,' Benjamin continued. 'Those bombs forced us to confront the threat they posed.'

'And without them,' Nero noted sardonically, 'we would never have met.'

'Every cloud,' Benjamin grinned. 'Give me your glasses.'

Nero was surprised to find she was still wearing them. Reaching up, she snatched them from her face and handed them over. Benjamin took out a computer pad and inserted one of the Spi-Glass arms into a port.

'Let's see what you found,' he said.

The screen flickered into life and Benjamin found himself sharing Nero's view through her Spi-Glasses. He felt Nero tense beside him as she looked over his shoulder, then looked away. On the screen, a wall dissolved to show the interior of a clinical white room. A reclined medical treatment chair stood in the middle of the floor, a lamp suspended from the ceiling above it. Nearby, a shining metal table stood empty. A bank of instruments lined the furthest wall. Benjamin recognised a centrifuge and sterilising equipment. A tall cabinet stood in a corner, its shiny metal doors reflecting the dismal scene.

'It's the room from my flashbacks,' Nero whispered. 'It's the same room.'

Benjamin flicked the screen off to spare her any further discomfort.

'So,' Nero began, slowly, 'how do I know what's real and what's fake?'

Benjamin looked uncomfortable. 'It seems that whenever Meena is around,' he said, 'it's fake.'

Nero was thinking. 'Meena was by my side when my mother told me my dad had died. She came with me to his funeral. Was that an implanted memory?'

Benjamin raised his eyebrows. 'Maybe.'

'Then he's alive?' Nero felt her heart racing.

Benjamin was non-committal. 'Possibly.'

'Who's implanting these memories?' Nero's mind was whirling. 'And how? What do they want?'

'There would be a physical implant,' Benjamin explained. 'Straight into the hippocampus. The part of the brain where memories are created and indexed. Like slipping extra pages into a book.'

Nero was aghast.

'If your false memories and flashbacks began at the Dump,' Benjamin continued, 'I think it's a pretty safe bet that the device in your brain was implanted in that room.'

'But I was scanned by the Bureau when I joined, and by just about every form of transport I've taken in the last three weeks. Nothing's been picked up.'

'We know the Dheghomites have shield tech,' Benjamin replied. 'Just like they used on their bio bomb.'

'The Dheghomites?' Nero was appalled. 'You think they've been poking about in my brain?'

Benjamin looked at her with something approaching sympathy. Nero didn't like it.

'I think,' he said, 'you should accept the possibility. You would make an excellent target. Young, impressionable and, as of three weeks ago, at the heart of the only organisation capable of stopping them.'

'Then how did they get hold of this technology? I thought the Bureau computer was meant to be impregnable?'

'That's a very good question,' Benjamin replied.

Nero was determined to stay calm. 'Okay,' she breathed. 'That's the how and the who. What about the why?'

'Information and control,' Benjamin said. 'During these experiences, have you given them any intel they could use against the Bureau?'

Nero bit her tongue. Of course she had. *Ghost Profile*.

'No,' she lied.

'Good.' Benjamin looked relieved. 'If it happens again, try not to give anything away.'

Nero was feeling lost. The only thing that would help, she reasoned, was action. What could she do?

'We need to get this thing out of me,' she said, tapping her temple with a finger.

'Too dangerous,' Benjamin sighed. 'But there might be something else.'

'What's that?'

'Memory transplants are essentially chaotic. They're at the will of the subconscious, so the control program – in this case, Meena – would try to impose order wherever it can. Are there any connections or patterns you remember from your experiences? It might give us a clue as to where they're coming from.'

Nero thought hard. Patterns. Connections

'It could even be a concept. Or a place.'

'A place?'

A sudden memory flashed before Nero's eyes, though whether it was real or not, she couldn't tell.

The boat captain at Clarke Island, leaning over the tiller.

'Is it always so humid?' Nero had asked.

'Gotta love this sea air!' the captain had replied with a laugh. 'I'm a Utah boy. It's so dry there, you can feel your skin crack like baked mud.'

Another memory crashed in with such force, it almost took Nero's breath away.

A hospital bed. Clean sheets. Nero lying, broken, as Meena looked on. A pattern on the sheet caught Nero's eye. She struggled to focus on a label. A logo. UNIFIED TRAUMA and ACOLOGY HOSPITAL.

A final memory.

Meena sitting at Nero's side, holding her hand for support. Helene sitting the other side of a table, her face stern. 'It was a plane crash,' she was saying. 'In Utah. He wouldn't have known anything about it.'

Nero took a breath and fixed Benjamin in her gaze.

'I know exactly where I need to go,' she said.

22

Absent Without Leave

Nero didn't sleep at all well. All night, she felt like she was free-falling through a world that was only partly real. Twice, to affirm her identity, she asked her Home computer to tell her who she was. It rattled off her Bureau profile detailing her childhood, education and her time at the Dump. With a jolt, she realised even the Bureau's records could not be trusted. At the hospital with Meena, Nero had handed over the means to infiltrate the computer by using a Ghost Profile. Perhaps they had done so, already. She scratched her head, aware that, somewhere deep in her brain sat a device that controlled her very perception of reality. After seven hours of turning fitfully in her bed, Nero got up, showered, and made her way to Bureau headquarters beneath St Bride's in Fleet Street.

'You want to go to Utah?'

Nathan Drake sat behind his desk. Nero was wary. The last time she had stood in this office, her memory of the event had been flatly contradicted by the security camera.

'On Bureau business?'

Nero shuffled, uncomfortably. Just what should she tell him? That the Dheghomites had access to Bureau tech? They'd she'd given them the means? That she wasn't sure what was real any more?

'I'm following a hunch,' she said finally.

Drake raised his eyebrows. 'Not good enough,' he growled. 'What hunch?'

'I've reason to believe there's a Dheghomite cell operating out of Utah,' Nero said, carefully.

'*Reason to believe?* What reason?'

Nero knew she had to tread gingerly. 'While we were undercover with Calian, he made a joke about the *dear leader*. He said he took his orders straight from Utah.' It was a straightforward, bare-faced lie. But what was the alternative? Tell Drake about her implanted memories? About Meena? Her father?

'Utah's a big place,' Drake grumbled. 'It'd be like looking for a needle in a haystack.'

'Benjamin Saal is triangulating some communications,' Nero lied again. 'Should put me within sixteen kilometres of their base.'

There was a pause.

'What's going on with you and Saal?'

The question took Nero by surprise. She blinked, unsure how to answer.

Drake raised his eyebrows, expectantly. 'You must know that the Bureau computer continually monitors our agents, so we know where they are at all times?'

Nero swallowed. 'Yes.'

'Then perhaps you can tell me why you've been to see Benjamin so frequently over the last week?' Drake held her gaze as he spoke. 'The Bureau's records place you in his apartment twice in four days.'

It wasn't a question Nero had been prepared for.

Drake cleared his throat and walked awkwardly to a set of shelves behind his desk. He pretended to be enthralled by a photograph of a mountain scene.

'I don't encourage workplace romances here,' he spluttered. 'But I am aware that such things happen.'

Nero couldn't believe her ears.

'It can lead to both parties being compromised and leave them vulnerable. That is not a good position for any agent in the field.' Drake turned to face his young recruit and looked her squarely in the eye. 'So, tell me truthfully, are you and Benjamin romantically involved?'

The awkward use of the phrase almost made Nero laugh.

'I'm not angry,' Drake assured her. 'I'm just trying to protect you. From yourself.'

Nero bit her lip while she considered her response. It would save her a lot of bother if she admitted it. But, *Benjamin*?

'Yes,' she said, as seriously as possible. 'We are… romantically involved.' She tried hard not to laugh.

Drake nodded. 'I would advise you to tread carefully.' He looked knowingly at Nero. 'And, next time you speak to Benjamin, ask him about Claudia Chambers. Then you'll understand.'

Nero frowned. *Claudia Chambers*? What the hell was he on about? Did Benjamin have a dark past? She doubted it.

'But,' Drake continued, 'for now, I'm afraid I can't sanction a trip to Utah.'

Trip?

Nero understood. 'You don't trust me.'

'I trust you implicitly,' Drake countered. 'But it's not many hours since you were lying unconscious on the ground in New York.'

Here it comes, Nero thought.

'And frankly, your memory loss is… concerning.'

'I'm fine,' Nero snapped. 'It's all coming back to me.'

Drake studied her intently. 'Is there something you're not telling me, Nero?'

Nero felt herself flush. *What did he know*? She shook her head.

Drake nodded. 'I want to give you a full medical before I put you on another mission. Including a psych test.'

That sounded like a bad idea.

'But, the Dheghomite base?' Nero knew she had already lost the argument.

'Get better,' Drake said softly, 'and bring me evidence. More than a hunch.'

'I'm… sorry to interrupt.'

Nero turned to the source of the noise and saw Benjamin Saal standing in the door to the office. Drake sighed and shot a meaningful glance at Nero. She shrugged.

'What is it, Benjamin?'

Benjamin walked gingerly into the room, pulling at his fingers in agitation. 'Nero,' he stuttered. 'I think we should tell him everything.'

Was he crazy? Nero thought hard. 'It's okay, Benjamin,' she blurted. 'I've already told him.'

Benjamin was taken aback. 'Really?'

'Er, sure,' Nero spluttered. 'You know. *Our relationship.*' She raised her eyebrows meaningfully.

Benjamin frowned. 'Relationship?'

'That's right, Benjamin,' Drake interjected with a note of impatience. 'I know all about it.'

Benjamin shuffled nervously from foot to foot.

'And I'll tell you what I told Nero.' Drake leaned in, conspiratorially. 'Tread carefully.'

Benjamin swallowed. 'Yes,' he whispered. 'Of course.'

Drake turned back to Nero. 'Now, get yourself home and get yourself better. And I'll book you in for that psych test. Benjamin? Could you see that she leaves the building?'

Nero took a breath. 'Actually, I think I want to leave the Bureau.'

There was a silence in the room. Drake looked astonished. 'Leave?' he gasped at last. His eyes flicked to Benjamin who shook his head to show his ignorance.

'Well,' said Nero boldly. 'If the only way to pursue our *relationship* in the open is to leave the Bureau, then so be it.'

To Benjamin's surprise, Nero suddenly sprang to his side and dropped her hand in his.

'I don't want us to have to hide our love,' Nero continued. 'Having to pretend there's nothing going on between us – '

'Er,' Benjamin began.

Nero put a finger on his lips. 'No, darling,' she breathed. 'We're worth more than that.'

Benjamin was clearly at a loss for words.

'What's the protocol for leaving the Bureau?' Nero asked, boldly.

Drake thought. The blood had drained from his face. 'There *is* no protocol,' he said. 'Because *no one's ever left before*.'

'Well,' Nero smiled sweetly, 'get back to me when you can.'

'I don't think you understand,' Drake hissed, suddenly furious. 'The knowledge you have makes you dangerous.'

'To who?'

Drake gestured around the room. 'To us! To the Bureau! If you leave us, you'll effectively be public enemy number one. We will have to watch you everywhere. All the time.'

Nero held his gaze. 'I thought you said you trusted me. *Implicitly*.' She could see Drake struggling.

'I do,' he said, at last.

Nero nodded. 'Then let me go.'

Drake gave a sharp bob of his head.

'Thank you,' Nero whispered. 'And you can start by turning off all your monitoring programs. The minute I walk through that door, I'm a free citizen.'

Drake was cowed. 'I'll see to it.'

Much to Benjamin's surprise, Nero looped her arm through his and planted a kiss on his cheek. 'Right,' she said breezily. 'You may now escort me from the building, darling.'

Drake slowly nodded his assent.

Benjamin turned to leave with Nero clinging onto his arm. They marched through the door together and turned down the corridor without saying a word. Just once Nero looked back to see Nathan Drake alone in his office, his face frozen in a look of sheer astonishment.

'What the hell was that all about?'

Nero sat opposite Benjamin outside a small café in Covent Garden. A cold breeze was whipping through the street.

'I'm guessing you didn't mean a word of it?'

Nero shook her head, sadly. 'Sorry, Benji.'

Benjamin grit his teeth. 'So, it was a ploy.' He looked disappointed. 'It's always a ploy.'

Nero sighed. 'I had to get Drake off my back. He wasn't happy with me going to Utah without a decent lead and I really don't need a psych test right now. God knows what it would find.'

Benjamin turned his collar up against the cold. 'You can't blame him.'

'Maybe not. But no way was I going to tell him that the only lead I've got is from a dream and a photocube.'

'You really trust him to stop monitoring you?'

Nero remembered the look Drake had given her in his office. 'I think so, yes.'

She noticed Benjamin looking at her intently.

Something's coming, she thought.

'That was cruel, Nero,' he said. 'What you said in there about us.'

If I were to dig deep enough, Nero thought, *I might almost feel a tiny pang of guilt.*

'Benji,' she said, kindly. *'Benjamin*. We are never going to be a *thing*.'

Benjamin looked like a broken man. 'I can feel the whole *it's not you it's me* thing coming.'

'Oh, no,' replied Nero emphatically, 'it's *definitely* you. And, if it's any comfort, there's nothing you can do to change that.' She nodded down to his lap. 'Except maybe surgery.'

A light seemed to dawn in Benjamin's eyes. 'Ah,' he smiled. 'I see. So it's not *just* me then. It's everyone *like* me.'

Nero rolled her eyes. 'Sure. If that makes you feel better.'

A young waiter came with a tray of coffees. Nero knocked back an espresso.

'Another one of those, please,' she beamed. 'Make it a double.' She winked at Benjamin. 'Gotta keep my wits about me if I'm public enemy number one.'

Benjamin took a sip of his own drink and looked at his watch. 'A pressing engagement?'

Benjamin shrugged. 'You could say that.'

Nero rolled her empty cup between her hands. 'Benji, why are they doing it to me?' Benjamin had no answer.

'Why put this thing in my head? And why implant those false memories? What's the point?'

'I don't know, Nero.'

Nero gnawed at her lip. 'There *has* to be a reason, and that's worrying me.'

'I mean,' Benjamin mused aloud, 'If I got my hands on some tech, especially untested tech, I'd want to try it out.'

'So I'm a Guinea Pig?'

'Perhaps.' He fell silent as the waiter delivered Nero's next cup of coffee.

'You think those first experiences were tests?' she said as the waiter moved back out of earshot.

Benjamin felt his way as he spoke. 'Maybe, at first.'

'And now?' Nero wasn't sure she wanted to hear his reply.

'They're obviously using it to get intelligence from you. You mentioned Meena was asking you questions about the Bureau computer while you were in hospital?'

Nero nodded.

'Did you tell them anything?'

'Nope.' She still daren't tell him about the Ghost Profile intel she'd given them.

'Good. Maybe whatever is in your brain isn't just a receiver, but a transmitter too. So, whatever you say while under their influence, they would hear.'

Nero wondered what damage she had done.

'So,' she whispered, suddenly afraid. 'Last night, you mentioned two things they could use the implant for. Information and *control*.'

Benjamin clearly didn't know what to say.

'Come on, Benji,' Nero rasped. 'You put a device in someone's brain. First, you test if you can implant fake memories, then you test if you can interact directly with your subject.' Her eyes were welling with tears. 'Then you take control.'

The word seemed to hang in the air.

'I was thinking out loud,' Benjamin said at last. 'I mean, control you to do what?'

'*That's* what worries me.' Nero wiped her eyes with a napkin. 'Maybe it's just as well that I left the Bureau. Drake could be right. I could be public enemy number one. I just don't know it yet.'

Benjamin was following her train of thought. 'Then, maybe we need to get to Utah.' He checked his watch again, then looked over Nero's shoulder to the street beyond.

'Drake was right,' Nero sighed. 'It's a big place.'

'True,' Benjamin agreed. 'But I think I've found someone who could help.'

Turning to follow his gaze, Nero saw an elegant, older lady walking towards them. She looked in her fifties, but was wearing her years well. Her big brown eyes were still bright and her long hair, though now iron grey, looked lustrous in the sunshine.

'Nero Jones,' Benjamin began as he rose to his feet. 'Allow me to introduce you to Meena Aziz.'

23

Meena

The woman radiated calm. Even the wind seemed to leave her entirely unruffled.

Nero blinked, then stared.

'Nero,' Benjamin nudged her. 'You're being rude.'

Nero shook her head and held out her hand. 'Nice to meet you,' she spluttered. 'Again.'

'Again?' Meena smiled, confused. 'I'm not sure – '

'Have a seat,' Benjamin interrupted. 'Can I get you anything?'

Meena shook her head as she pulled up a chair. 'No thank you, but you can tell me what this is all about.'

Nero couldn't take her eyes off the woman. It was Meena but not Meena. She was older, of course, but she seemed... different. Nero couldn't believe that this woman could ever have been her Meena. But then her Meena had probably never existed at all.

'I'm not entirely comfortable meeting a pair of complete strangers.' Meena sat awkwardly, her body tense. 'You said it was about Helene Jones?'

Benjamin nodded and held out a hand. 'This is Nero Jones, Helene's daughter.'

Meena's eyes widened. 'Goodness me,' she beamed. 'You look just like her.'

It was all Nero could do to stare back in awe. Meena's features, lined though they were, looked so familiar.

Benjamin tried to break the awkward silence. 'I called you because you might be able to help us.' He leaned forward across the table. 'I have some news about Helene.'

Meena looked surprised. 'I haven't heard from her in over twenty years,' she said, confused. 'And I haven't thought about her much, either. Why should I be interested in her news?'

'My mother has gone missing.' Nero had found her voice at last.

'Missing?' Meena repeated. 'When?'

'Over a week ago,' Nero continued. 'There's been no trace of her since.'

Meena shook her head. 'I'm sorry, Nero,' she said, carefully, 'but I really don't know how I can help.'

She had a quizzical expression on her face. 'Sorry... you keep looking at me like that. Like you know me.' Meena frowned. 'Have we met before?'

Nero smiled. 'In a manner of speaking.'

Meena was about to respond but Nero ploughed on.

'I visited my mother's house the day she disappeared. I found an old photocube with some pictures on. Mostly of the family. But there were some older pictures that I'd never really looked at before. They were of you and my mother.'

Meena nodded. 'We were very close,' she admitted. 'Both professionally and personally. You have to remember we weren't much older than you are now. It was all a long time ago.'

'What were you and Helene working on?' Benjamin asked.

Meena hesitated. 'It was top secret. I'm not sure how much I can tell you, even now.'

'Tell us what you can,' Nero insisted. 'Please.'

Meena thought for a while. 'I think I will have a drink, after all,' she said at last. Raising her hand, she beckoned the waiter over. 'Camomile tea,' she purred. 'With a spoonful of honey.'

The waiter nodded and walked away, clearly intrigued by the unlikely party.

Meena turned to face Nero directly. 'Was your mother happy?'

The question took Nero by surprise. It was something she had never considered before. 'I think... she could've been happier.'

If it wasn't for me, Nero thought to herself.

'Did she marry? Have more children?'

'There's only me.' Nero felt a lump in her throat. 'Her husband, my father, died in a plane crash. They had been divorced for some time.' For the first time, Nero wasn't quite sure she was speaking the truth. But what would Meena think if she admitted she wasn't entirely sure what the truth was?

'I'm sorry to hear that.' Meena looked genuinely sad. 'She was a wonderful young woman. She deserved more.'

Nero swallowed. That was undoubtedly true.

'And you really have no idea where she is?'

'Not a clue,' Benjamin interjected, seeing Nero was struggling. 'We were hoping you might be able to shed some light. Even inadvertently.'

Meena leaned back as the waiter brought her tea, then stirred in the honey as she thought.

'We were working on various areas at once,' she said at last. 'Your mother's field was behavioural implants. Mine was augmented interfaces.'

'What was that?' Nero asked.

'To allow humans to integrate with computers on a synaptic level.'

'Wiring people up to computers?'

Meena blew on her tea to cool it as Nero and Benjamin exchanged looks.

'There was one other. Levchenko, her name was. She worked on theoretical predictive computing. Forecasting the future.'

Nero flicked her eyes to Benjamin. *The Architects.*

'Our work was deemed unethical,' Meena continued, 'and our experiments were shut down.'

Nero fixed her gaze on the woman opposite. 'How far did my mother get?'

Meena took a sip of her tea. 'Rodents mostly, although I understand she went a little off-piste.'

'How so?'

'I heard she had experimented on some higher primates. A pair of macaques.'

'With success?' Nero was appalled to think she might just be the latest in a line of experiments.

'That I don't know,' Meena admitted. 'These were just rumours, you understand.'

Benjamin leaned forward again so as not to miss a word. 'Tell me how. What was the procedure?'

'It was revolutionary,' Meena answered, proudly. 'She used the rodents' own tissue and bone to create a control receptor. With no external technology required.'

Benjamin looked at Nero, who nodded in understanding. So that would explain why her own implant was never detected.

'She was able to influence their behaviour on a very basic level,' Meena continued, looking around her as she spoke to check no one was listening in. 'To increase their cortisone or serotonin levels and thus control elements of their personality in real time. All it took was a flick of a switch.' She held her cup suspended in the air as she remembered. 'Remarkable,' she muttered to herself.

Nero had the impression Meena had never been asked these things before. She was clearly enjoying reliving the memories.

'To what end?' Benjamin asked. 'What was the ultimate application?'

'Military, of course,' Meena scoffed. 'Isn't it always?'

Benjamin frowned.

'Imagine a battalion of soldiers whose behaviour you could control remotely. You could make them stronger, more adaptable, quicker thinkers. Couple that with a knowledge of your enemy's future tactics.' Meena shrugged. 'Your army would be unbeatable, able to outsmart your adversary at every turn.'

'That's sick,' Nero sneered.

She noticed a flash of something in Meena's eyes. Anger?

'The battle would be over quicker,' Meena snapped in reply. 'There would be fewer casualties, fewer deaths.' She sipped from her tea. 'Our funding was withdrawn when Helene's unauthorised experiments were discovered.'

'What exactly were the rumours?' Nero felt they were closing in on something vital. Something that would explain her own predicament.

Meena took a breath and paused, clearly weighing up her options. Was it long enough ago that she could speak frankly without consequences? She considered the company she found herself in. A determined but anxious looking young man. A frightened and confused young woman. What harm could they do?

'False memory implantation.'

Nero's mouth ran dry. *Helene worked on the very programme that had resulted in her own implant? And the Bureau itself?*

'Helene saw it as the next logical step,' Meena continued. 'Our financiers disagreed.'

'What did she do?' Nero almost didn't want to know the answer.

'She started on apes, implanting false experiences to help them learn faster.'

Benjamin was enthralled. 'How?'

'Using the tech we had developed so far, Helene gained access to the memory centres of the apes' brains. She implanted false memories of solving puzzles. Simple things at first. Using sign language to communicate, completing jigsaws. So when they were presented with the real problems, they were convinced they had encountered them before and knew just what to do. Soon, they were using complex mathematics to solve puzzles and even using tools and heavy machinery. All without having to be trained.' Meena smiled in admiration. 'Because they had a false memory of having done it before.'

Nero's blood ran cold. Which of her memories could be considered as training? And training for what? Just what lay ahead?

'What happened to you both when the project was abandoned?' Benjamin asked.

Meena looked sad. 'I dropped out of research completely and became a teacher. As for Helene,' she shrugged. 'I heard she stayed in America for a while, then came to the UK to work as a chemist.' She nodded at Nero. 'And start a family. That's when we lost touch.' Meena reached across the table and clasped Nero's hands in hers. 'I hope you find your mother. She was a remarkable woman.'

Nero swallowed. 'Then, this work you did... it was in America?'

Meena nodded. 'A secret government facility.'

Nero's blood ran cold. She didn't even have to ask where.

Benjamin leaned in closer, keen to hear the details. 'Could you tell us the location? It's important that you're as precise as possible.'

Nero noticed the bead too late. A tiny point of red light trained on Meena's forehead for just a moment. As Meena opened her mouth to answer, the dull thud of a bullet rang out and she slumped back in her chair.

'Down!' Benjamin shouted as he lurched towards Nero, throwing her to the floor. She looked up from beneath the table and saw Meena's head hanging limp. Blood trickled from the entry point in her forehead.

'No!' screamed Nero. 'Meena!'

'It's too late, Nero,' Benjamin panted. 'We've got to get out of here.' He had already noticed the terrified waiter reaching for his phone. The security forces would be here within minutes.

'But, Meena!' Although they had only just met, Nero felt she had lost an old friend.

'Go!'

Benjamin scrambled to his feet and pulled Nero up behind him. Pushing her out into the street, he pulled her hood over her head and guided her to the shadows.

'Keep low and head to my apartment. Take the long way round and I'll be there before you to let you in.'

24

Rendezvous

Benjamin let Nero sleep on his sofa for the night. For some reason, she hadn't felt like going home. It wasn't that she needed his company, or that he could offer her anything in the way of protection. It was simply that she didn't want to be alone. Even the sound of his snoring drifting in from the bedroom was preferable to silence.

It was the first time she had ever seen someone die. Right in front of her and so quickly. It had shocked her. She dreamt, as she knew she would, of Meena. But, strangely, not the Meena she had met in the café, *her* Meena. She felt a pang of guilt at not mourning for the woman with the iron-grey hair, but then, she had never known the *real* Meena. Her Meena, Nero knew, was a phantom. But still, she felt real enough to grieve for.

Nero refused Benjamin's offer of an elaborate breakfast in favour of a strong coffee, then he booked her a Skycab to the airport. The journey took longer than expected. Twice, the driver had to take a detour due to protests on the outskirts of the city.

Nero gazed through the window as the military police arrived to cart the protestors away. Not for the first time, she wondered why such ordinary people would ally themselves with the Dheghomites' deadly cause. Perhaps she shouldn't have been surprised. Increasingly, it had seemed that the technology that had been supposed to set people free had enslaved them.

The Utopian dream of the machines doing the labour while the populace enjoyed the benefits had been reversed.

Artificial intelligence had taken all the most rewarding jobs, the creative jobs, the technical jobs, and left the dregs for humanity. Many people felt powerless, mere drudges in the service of AI. The Dheghomites offered a return to simpler, preindustrial times. It was an enticing prospect.

Heathrow, as Nero expected, was heavily guarded. Having passed safely through security with the false ID Benjamin had provided, she slipped her passport back into her pocket with a smile. This time, she had insisted on choosing her own name.

'Ms Hudson?' came a voice as she passed through a facial recognition point. Nero looked round to see a smartly dressed young man with an implausible smile.

'Would you care to avail yourself of our Premium Lounge?'

Nero raised an eyebrow. Good old Benji.

'Thank you,' she smiled back. She ducked her head as she passed. She had confidence in Benjamin's ID cloning skills, but still couldn't bring herself to make eye contact with anyone.

The lounge was positively luxurious. Tinkling piano music played over hidden speakers to calm the nerves of passengers. Large leafed plants rose from colourful pots. Tasteful furniture was placed in discrete areas to create cosy nooks. Tables groaning with food lined the walls. Nero took a plate, helped herself to a hearty breakfast and took a seat next to the low window that ran the length of the furthest wall. She looked out onto the tarmac as she ate. Almost directly below her, she could see her flight waiting at the end of a connecting conduit.

The Empress Delta Wing was a distinctive looking craft, its shape reminding Nero of an arrow head. A narrow fuselage swept back from the pilots' cockpit, embedded down the centre of the airplane's two wings. Each had an engine mounted at its rear. The cargo and fuel were carried in the wings themselves, giving the vehicle increased efficiency and, above all, increased speed. Travelling at a height of sixteen kilometres at a speed seven times faster than sound, the Empress would make the trans-Atlantic trip in a little over an hour.

Nero finished off a Danish pastry and heard the click of her comms.

'Just a little parting gift.' Benjamin's voice sounded in her ear. 'Besides, I didn't want you travelling on an empty stomach.'

Nero smiled. 'Your concern is touching,' she muttered.

'And,' Benjamin continued, 'I didn't want you travelling alone.'

'Huh?'

'Look to your right. About three o'clock.'

Of course, he had access to the Premium Lounge's security cameras. Nero knew Benjamin was risking Drake's wrath for misappropriation of Bureau tech.

She spun round in her chair to see a familiar face beaming at her from across the room. Nero could barely believe her eyes. She rose from her chair and walked towards the huddle of comfortable sofas in the corner.

'Chang!' she almost called, but stopped herself in time.

Chang held out a hand. 'Ms Hudson?' she said. 'I'm Beverley Noh. I think we're both speakers at the TechCon conference?'

Nero slid onto the sofa beside her. 'I see your injury has healed,' she said, gesturing to Chang's leg.

'The wonders of modern science,' Chang nodded. 'That'll teach me not to try and out-ski my instructor.'

Nero looked around her. The lounge was filling with expectant passengers.

'So,' she began, carefully, 'you're coming to Utah, too?'

'Wouldn't miss it for the world,' Chang replied, reaching for a cup of coffee from a small glass table.

Nero nodded. She wondered how to phrase her next question. 'Travelling light?' she asked, at last.

Chang understood at once. 'I've had everything I need sent ahead of me.' She sipped from her coffee. 'My personal assistant has seen to it.'

'Your personal assistant?' Nero glanced around.

'He's very good,' Chang chuckled, tapping her ear so Benjamin would hear. 'If a little needy.'

Nero stifled a laugh. She was glad Benjamin was thinking ahead.

'Do you know the exact location of the conference?' Chang asked, innocently.

Nero started to relax. 'I'll share the details with you on the flight. I imagine the company has given us seats together.'

Chang leaned towards her. 'What are you hoping to find?'

Nero frowned as she thought. 'Answers,' she said, simply.

The soft chime of the PA system interrupted their conversation. 'The gate is now open to Premium passengers for flight number AV281 to Denver.' The voice was clear, soothing and almost certainly computer generated. 'Would passengers in the Premium Lounge please make their way to the gate for boarding?'

'That's us,' Chang said as she rose. 'I guess we'd better take our seats.'

25

Flight Into Danger

The take-off was almost silent from inside the low passenger cabin. Nero watched as the runway dropped away beneath her, then felt her stomach churn as the plane accelerated away, banking alarmingly to the left as it rose.

She and Chang had indeed been placed in adjacent seats. A low table was situated between them, holding more food and two glasses of sparkling liquid. The table top screen displayed a representation of the Earth's surface, with their progress across the Atlantic indicated by a tiny red V moving inexorably across the map.

'So, where we headed?' Chang asked quietly.

'A secret US Government facility in Utah.' Nero looked apologetic. 'Unfortunately, it's so secret no one knows where it is. Not even the Bureau.' Following an extensive search for the facility, even Benjamin had thrown up his hands in despair.

'Then how have you heard of it?'

Nero thought back to the previous night's conversation with Meena. 'Let's just say an old friend told me,' she said, obtusely.

Nero turned to look out the window. Far below her, through the dotted clouds, she could make out the swirling blue-grey of the sea. They were over the Atlantic already. Looking up, she was faced with the blackness of space. She shivered, involuntarily, and for a moment she was caught in a memory of falling through the cold void.

'That can't be all,' she heard Chang say.

Turning, Nero saw her companion staring at her inquisitively.

'No,' she admitted, 'That's not all.' She took a breath to steady herself. 'Chang,' she began, 'I'm not all I seem – '

She was interrupted by a sudden lurch in the cabin. Nero reached down to clutch instinctively at her armrests. The great globe of the Earth filled her window. She felt the whole craft pitching to the left. The passengers panicked, grabbing at the seats in front of them for stability. Nero heard someone scream. Somewhere, a child started crying.

'What's happening?' Chang hissed, pushing herself back into her seat.

'We're turning,' Nero replied through gritted teeth. 'Sharply.'

The light from the sun glanced through her window and onto the overhead lockers opposite her. By watching its course through the cabin, Nero was able to take a guess at their new trajectory.

'We're heading south.'

'What?' Chang sounded worried. 'Why?'

As the craft settled back into a less erratic flight path, a voice came over the speakers. But it wasn't the cool professional voice of the attendant announcing the availability of hot and cold drinks. And it wasn't the voice of the pilot informing them of their height, air speed and expected arrival time in Denver. It was a voice belonging to someone altogether more desperate.

'Ladies and gentlemen,' it began. Nero could tell the voice's owner was out of breath. 'Stay calm and no one will get hurt.'

Almost at once, Nero felt the atmosphere in the cabin shift. Where before she had heard the gentle hubbub of conversation, now she could feel a rising panic among the passengers. It reminded her of the mercury rising on her dad's old thermometer.

'We have radioed our demands to the United Nations,' the voice continued. 'We demand the cessation of all technological advancement. We demand the enforced destruction of artificial intelligence, the halting of genetic manipulation and the dismantling of all industrial developments. Humankind is a virus...'

Like just about everyone on the plane, Nero knew exactly how that sentence would end. The speaker crackled as the owner of the voice held the intercom just a bit too tight.

'We are the vaccine!'

The moment the voice had finished, the cabin was alive with sudden activity.

Nero heard people shouting. Some of the passengers screamed.

'Sit forward and put your hands behind your heads!' a male voice commanded. A voice Nero felt sure she knew. She cast a glance at Chang who sat, alert. Nero could tell she had noticed it, too.

A blow to the back of her neck forced Chang forwards on her seat until her head was against the headrest in front.

'I said, *sit forward and put your hands behind your head*!' A man in a balaclava hurried past, his hand in the air.

Nero leaned forward to press her forehead against the seat in front, taking advantage of his instructions. If she recognised him, she thought, he might very well recognise her.

She shared a look with Chang who nodded. The man was the right height and build. There was no doubt about it. It was Harrison.

The man had ripped open his jacket to reveal a series of gel packs strapped to his chest. Nero frowned. *How the hell had he got through security with a jacket full of explosives?*

'Inside job?' muttered Chang, having clearly had the same thought.

Nero nodded. That was the only answer. The security team at Heathrow had been compromised.

'If I press this trigger,' Harrison shouted down the cabin, 'this flight is over.' He nodded down the aisle. 'There are two more packs of explosives planted in the hold.' He tapped the gel packs on his chest. 'One in each wing. They are paired wirelessly to this trigger. If you do as we say, no one will be harmed. If you don't...' A sick smile spread across the only part of his face that was visible. 'Boom!'

'Benjamin,' Nero whispered to activate her comms. She was struggling to hear herself speak above the whimpering of the other passengers.

'Go ahead,' came the response in her ear.

'We're in the middle of an incident here. A hijack.'

'I'm tracking you.' There was a sudden note of tension in Benjamin's voice. 'Got you.' Nero could hear him breathing. 'You're way off course, Nero. How many are there?'

Nero thought. 'Unknown. One in the cabin. It's Harrison.'

'Harrison?' Benjamin spluttered. 'Are you sure?'

'He's standing right in front of us,' Chang interjected. 'There's no mistaking him.'

'So, it's a Dheghomite action.'

'Gotta be,' Nero agreed. 'But where are we heading?'

'I think I can answer that.'

Nero imagined Benjamin's fingers dancing over his computer hub controls. 'I'm sending your current trajectory to your slate.'

Nero looked down to where her computer pad was resting on her knees. A red dot flashed on a map of the Atlantic, Africa to the right, the Americas to the left.

'If you carry on at this speed and direction, you will be *here* in thirteen minutes.'

A line was traced from the red dot to another point in the middle of the sea. The image zoomed in to show a huge steel and concrete construction looming over the ocean surface.

'The Cambria Three Tidal Dynamo.'

A picture emerged of a circular structure arranged around a central concrete pylon. This housed the engineers and managers who were tasked with manning the station. They were responsible for its smooth running as well as the transfer of the hundreds of gigawatts that it generated into the network of cables that ran along the ocean floor to the North American continent. It had been the biggest logistical and engineering feat of the 2030s, a symbol of the world's desire to move away from polluting fossil fuels towards greener, more sustainable energy. As such, it was the perfect target for the Dheghomites.

The central tower rose from the sea bed some three thousand metres below the seething surface. Around it, a large, circular platform stretched out into the sea. As the ocean rose and fell, so the platform moved with it, the resulting energy being transferred via huge dynamos connected to the tower.

'I guess we have to work on the assumption that we're going to crash right into it,' Chang whispered.

'There are thirty men and women on that station,' Benjamin said. 'Not to mention the two hundred on board your plane.'

Nero stole a glance around the cabin. Most of the passengers were sitting just as they had been commanded, their hands behind their heads. Some were crying, a few were praying. Nero noticed fidgeting children with tears in their eyes. A baby was wailing from the rear of the plane.

'This is huge, Benjamin,' Nero gasped. 'The hijacking of an aircraft, the murder of over two hundred people and the destruction of an entire energy network. How come your fancy computer didn't predict this?'

Benjamin was hesitant. 'Because my fancy computer has been compromised.'

Nero was aghast. 'By who?'

'By person or persons unknown. But we have to assume it's the Dheghomites. Who else would stand to gain so much?'

'So, I guess you can't give us our chances of success? Isn't that how it normally works?'

'Afraid not,' Benjamin admitted.

'How did they get in?' Chang hissed.

'I'm looking into it, but it seems they were given some sort of key to the system.'

Nero swallowed. *Ghost Profile.*

'Does Drake know?'

'Not yet.' Benjamin lowered his voice. 'It means we're flying blind. We have no idea what they're planning, their chances of success or how we should deploy to defeat them. They've got us exactly where they want us. In the dark.'

'So, we're on our own,' Chang said, quietly.

'Not quite,' cautioned Benjamin. 'Looks like you've got company.'

Chang looked across Nero to the window and the sky beyond. A fighter was taking a position beside them.

'The military are on us,' Chang whispered. 'They'll shoot us out the sky without hesitation.'

'There's another on the other side,' Benjamin reported. 'I've got them both on comms. I'll hold them off as long as I can.'

Nero was seized with a sudden urgency. 'Then Chang and I have got eight minutes to stop this plane going down. We need to get into that cockpit.' She shared a look at Chang, who nodded in return. Over two hundred souls were depending on them. 'Nero, out.'

Just as the comms clicked off, Nero felt a stabbing pain at her temples. She pressed herself back against her seat, suddenly feeling light headed.

Chang looked worried. 'You okay, Nero?'

Nero's mouth felt dry. This was a sensation she recognised, and it usually meant one thing.

Ducking over Chang's lap, she looked up and down the aisle.

Harrison was standing at the front of the cabin, his trigger hand raised high in the air.

'Who are you looking for?' Chang hissed.

Nero sat forward again and turned to face her companion. Her eyes looked wild.

As the plane gave another lurch, there came a commotion by the door to the cockpit. Two burly men had decided to confront their hijacker. As one threw himself at Harrison, the other swung wildly in an effort to snatch the trigger device from his hand.

'We're not going to die with you!' the first man cried as he barrelled into Harrison's stomach. The hijacker took a step back and brought his free hand down on the back of the man's neck. There was a groan as he sunk to the floor.

Harrison kicked at the man's head as he pulled a Tase Pistol from a harness fastened under his arm. Some of the nearest passengers screamed and called out in fear, some covered their eyes, others stared in disbelief. Turning to confront the second man, Harrison pressed the gun into his chest and fired. At such close quarters, Harrison knew there was no threat to the plane. He also knew the shot would be fatal. The screams halted. There was an eerie silence as the man slumped to the floor, landing spreadeagled across his companion. A young woman called out and leaped from her seat. Harrison pushed her back with the palm of his hand.

'That's a warning not to be a hero!' he called down the cabin. The woman sat, sobbing and shaking with fear amid the cries from other passengers.

Nero was looking wildly around her. 'Is this real?' she asked suddenly.

'What?'

'Is this really happening?'

It was clear that Chang didn't quite know how to respond.

'Tell me if this is really happening,' Nero demanded, looking between the seats at the passengers in front.

'It's happening,' Chang replied, nervously. 'Who are you looking for?'

'Meena.' Nero whispered.

'Who's Meena?'

A sudden change came over Nero. Her breathing settled. She looked at Chang, eerily calm. 'I have so much to tell you,' she said. 'But first, we need to take control of this plane.'

'Agreed,' Chang nodded sombrely, 'but we need to be careful, the guy's armed.'

As she spoke, she noticed Nero reach down to unclip her seatbelt.

'Okay, but we need a plan,' Chang warned her. 'Nero! A plan!'

But it was too late. As Harrison took up his position by the cockpit door, Nero slipped below the seat in front of her and wriggled her way between the other passengers' feet and legs. One or two looked down in alarm, only to be confronted by the sight of a young woman peering back at them, her finger on her lips.

Meanwhile, Chang fumbled with her own seat belt to release the catch, eager to offer assistance the moment Nero attacked.

That moment came quickly.

Chang saw Nero crouched among a row of seats to Harrison's right. Her eyes were on him, waiting for a sign of weakness. One moment when he might drop his guard. As she watched and waited, a groan came from the cabin floor and one of Harrison's attackers stirred. The hijacker instinctively dropped his gaze.

That was all Nero needed.

In a blur of speed, she rolled into the aisle and, landing crouched on one leg, swung the other in an arc through Harrison's feet. With a yelp of surprise, he stumbled back against the cockpit door. Taking advantage of his momentum, Nero sprung to her feet and slammed her whole body against his chest. Winded, he let go of the trigger device. It spun through the air before landing several feet away down the aisle. The surprised passengers looked on as Nero jabbed Harrison in the windpipe with a clenched fist. As he gasped for breath, Nero reached into his shoulder harness and drew out his Taser Pistol. Harrison slumped to his knees and fell forward, his hands grasping maniacally for the trigger device. With one deft move, Nero somersaulted over him and slid her foot along the ground, sending the device into Chang's waiting hand. Spinning round, Nero fell to her knees, pulled up Harrison's balaclava and jammed the gun against his temple. The whole sequence had lasted no more than eight seconds.

'No one else dies today,' Nero hissed as she jabbed the pistol against Harrison's head.

'Nero Jones,' Harrison groaned. 'You're fighting on the wrong side again.'

'I'm fighting on the winning side,' Nero snapped.

She nodded at the nearest passengers and they sprang forward to subdue the hijacker. Almost comically, two elderly women squatted on Harrison's back while a businessman secured his hands with a necktie.

Chang joined Nero by the cockpit door. 'Way to go,' she beamed. 'I would've joined in, but you seemed to be in a hurry. Where did you learn those moves?'

Nero seemed surprised. 'Bureau training,' she replied. 'Didn't they teach you that, too?'

Chang shook her head. 'Uh, uh.'

Nero looked suddenly worried, her eyes darting around the cabin. For a brief moment, she was sure she saw one of the female passengers duck behind a seat, her long, plaited hair swinging behind her.

'Who is this Meena you keep looking for?' Chang asked, trying to follow her gaze.

Nero could feel the plane dropping through the air. 'No time,' she barked and she thrust the nozzle of her pistol against the cockpit door control. She pulled the trigger and a fizz of electricity rippled across the console. The door slid open with a hum.

'I thought we agreed no access – '

That was as far as the woman behind the controls got. As she turned to face the door, Nero launched herself into the cockpit. Almost at once, she had the woman's head by her hair. With lightning speed, she slammed it into the controls, rendering the unfortunate pilot unconscious.

Looking round, Nero saw Chang was wrestling with a stocky, powerful-looking man who was armed with another Tase Pistol. Chang had her arm outstretched, her flat hand directing the weapon away and to the floor. The man had his hand at her throat. He grimaced with effort as Chang's eyes bulged through lack of air.

Sensing her companion's distress, Nero reached past the pilot hijacker to grasp at the plane's controls. Throwing her weight against the central lever, she sent the craft into a nosedive. Caught off balance by the sudden movement, the stocky man was thrown back towards the flight deck, his arms flailing about him as he tried to regain his balance. Seizing the initiative, Chang planted a fist in his stomach. As the man doubled over in pain, he released his grip on the pistol and it clattered to the cockpit floor. Finally, Chang put all her weight behind a mighty uppercut that shattered his teeth and sent him sprawling across the flight deck, unconscious.

Breathing heavily, Nero walked across to a tall cabinet by the cockpit door. Snapping it open, she let out a yelp as the body of the pilot tumbled out, his neck clearly broken.

'Bastards,' she hissed.

'Er, Nero,' came Chang's voice from behind her.

Spinning round, she saw Chang gazing at the windscreen in terror.

An alarm started to sound, along with an automated voice. '*Warning!*' it rasped. '*Collision imminent. Automatic controls disabled.*'

As the message was repeated, Nero lifted her gaze to the view outside the plane.

The Cambria Three Tidal Dynamo loomed large in the middle of a boiling sea. Nero could make out the observation windows dotted along its central tower and even, she thought, people moving about inside.

'*Collision in twenty seconds,*' chimed the automated warning voice. '*Nineteen... eighteen...*'

'Now what?' cried Chang above the scream of the engines.

Nero knew there was no time to think. Instead, she sprang to the pilot's seat and pulled the unconscious hijacker to the floor where she settled into an ungainly heap. Nero threw herself into the vacant seat and scanned the flight deck controls before her.

'Automatic controls are disabled,' she muttered to herself as she mentally ticked off the controls she recognised. 'Altimeter... axis stabilisation... pitch axis trim...'

Chang stared at her, open-mouthed. 'You know how to fly this thing?' Nero flicked her a look.

'Piece of cake.'

As she reached forward to flick a row of buttons, the automated voice continued its inexorable countdown. '*Fourteen... thirteen... twelve...*'

The airplane bucked and jolted as it was buffeted by the wind. They were now so low that Nero saw sea spray splashing against the windscreen.

'We spent an intensive week on hyper sonic flight during training, remember?'

Chang gave her a blank look.

Shrugging, Nero pulled back on the flight controls. She noticed the two military jets that still flanked the plane were pulling back, no doubt taking up positions to fire.

'Don't you dare...' Nero rasped.

'*Eight... seven... six...*'

Nero felt herself pushed back into her seat as the thruster engines engaged. Chang was pressed suddenly against the cockpit wall, struggling for breath as the G forces kicked in. She could swear she heard the passengers screaming beyond the cockpit door.

'You're going straight to hypersonic?' she yelled above the noise. 'You'll break the plane apart with the stress.'

But Nero wasn't listening. As the engines ran up to speed, she was struggling to angle the craft's nose up above the horizon.

'*Three.. two... one...*'

Under Nero's control, the plane veered suddenly to the left. The tidal dynamo's central tower passed within feet of the cockpit windscreen. Nero was sure she could see the whites of the eyes of the few people who had stopped at the observation windows to watch in horror as the plane passed. A sudden jolt told her that the port side wing had grazed the brickwork. Not too much, she hoped. She was relying on those engines.

Luckily, they kicked in with a roar. Nero's fingers danced along the flight deck, flicking switches and nudging slide controls into place. The engines were at full power within moments. A scream filled the cockpit as the plane leaped into the clouds. Within seconds the ocean, the tidal dynamo and, it seemed, even the Earth itself, were far behind them. The blue sky faded to black as they punched through the atmosphere and the plane levelled out. The shrieking sound in the cockpit receded.

'*Automatic controls engaged,*' came the computer voice. Outside the cockpit window, the two military jets peeled away.

Nero sat back in her seat and ran her fingers through her hair. She looked suddenly scared. 'How the hell did I do that?'

Chang moved towards her. 'That was extraordinary,' she panted. 'You seemed to know exactly what to do. Every step of the way.'

Nero was at a loss. 'I can't explain it.'

'I'm afraid I can,' came Benjamin's voice in her ear.

'Benjamin!' Chang called having heard him in her own comms. 'What's going on?'

Benjamin sounded sheepish. 'I'm afraid I've hacked into Nero's hippocampus.'

'You've what?' Nero was aghast.

'I found a route into your implant,' Benjamin explained carefully, 'and planted some false memories.'

'What have you been doing inside my head, Benjamin?'

'Giving you exactly what you needed to resolve your situation,' Benjamin replied. It was clear from his tone of voice that he was trying to calm her down. 'Memories of classes at the Bureau that would be useful. Combat training. How to fly an Empress Class Hypersonic plane.'

'Like *that'll* ever come in useful again,' Chang scoffed.

'Classes that *never happened*. But I was able to trick your memory into believing that they had.'

Nero sat in stunned silence for a while.

'Nero?' Benjamin knew he was in trouble.

'I am fed up with feeling violated,' Nero whispered at last, almost to herself. 'Poked, prodded, abused, used.' Her voice was getting louder. 'Invaded.' She slammed her fist on the flight deck controls. 'You stay the hell out of my mind! You had no right.'

'You were going to die,' Benjamin pleaded. 'Along with everyone else on that plane.'

'I don't give a shit!' Nero screamed. 'Stay out of my head!'

There was silence again, broken only by the sound of the engines propelling the plane through the upper atmosphere. Outside, the velvet blue sky was studded with evening stars, the horizon streaked with flashes of sunset orange.

'Wait,' said Nero at last. 'How did you get in?'

'You want the long version or the short version?' Benjamin asked, clearly relieved she had decided to change the subject.

Nero rolled her eyes in exasperation. 'The short version.'

'I'm a genius,' Benjamin replied. 'Your implant is based on the original template built by your mother. It utilises the Hewlett-Savage Zero One algorithm, the same architecture as all Bureau tech.'

'But, if it's Bureau tech, how did the Dheghomites get hold of it?'

Benjamin chose his words carefully. 'Either they stole it – '

Nero completed the thought. 'Or someone gave it to them.' She rubbed her eyes with the heel of her hands. 'Then someone in the Bureau is a traitor. But who?'

'Someone who agrees with the Dheghomite agenda,' Benjamin said quietly. 'Or someone who would have the most to gain.'

The silence between them was thick with meaning.

'I'm glad I asked,' Nero mumbled to herself at last. She turned to Chang, only to find her standing open mouthed in disbelief at the conversation.

'Could someone tell me what the hell just happened?'

26

En Route

Nero sat rocking in the pilot's seat, her eyes staring wildly like a hunted animal. Chang had bound the two hijackers and dragged them into the passenger cabin. She had been greeted by whoops and a prolonged round of applause as she explained the situation. The gratitude among the passengers was palpable. A queue formed almost the entire length of the plane to thank her, clap her on the shoulder and even offer tearful hugs. Under her instruction, a group of the most capable men and women were recruited to guard the hijackers at the back of the plane. The two men and single woman, bound and gagged, were regarded with contempt by the other passengers, and it was all Chang could do to keep the more determined of them from delivering a swift kick as they passed.

With the atmosphere settling into something approaching grateful relief, Chang made her way back to the cockpit and shut the door behind her. Seeing Nero's distress, she put a hand on her shoulder.

'You wanna start at the beginning?'

Nero shrugged. 'I don't know where the beginning is,' she simpered.

'Benjamin mentioned an implant?'

Nero nodded and tapped her forehead. 'It's here, inside me. And it means the Dheghomites can manipulate my memories. Now, I don't know what's true anymore.'

Chang sat in the co-pilot's seat and shook her head. 'Did they put it there?'

A white room.
A blade.
Pain.

'I don't know. I think so.'
'When?'

Pain.
The blade again.
A scream.
Her scream?

'I don't know.'

A hand.
A figure.
A voice.

Nero pressed her temples to make the pain go away. The cockpit was swimming before her eyes. She forced herself to focus on the horizon and the red clouds gathered along the curve of the Earth.

'Do you still trust me?' she asked quietly.

'Way I see it,' Chang began, 'you could've nosedived this plane right into the sea any time within the last fifteen minutes.' She smiled. 'So, yeah. I trust you.'

Nero just managed a smile back, but her eyes looked sadder than ever.

'Is that why we're going to Utah?' Chang asked.

Of course. Benjamin hadn't told her. How could he? Nero nodded. 'My subconscious has been leaving clues in my false memories.' She swallowed, uncomfortable at having to admit it to somebody else. 'I think the Dheghomite base is in Utah. But Drake wouldn't let me go.'

Chang leaned back in her chair. 'What's the plan when we get to Utah? All Benjamin would tell me is that there's a hotel room with a stash of equipment waiting for us on arrival. He'd managed to log into a secret Bureau account away from prying eyes. He put it down as office supplies.'

Nero grunted in reluctant admiration. She had to hand it to Benjamin Saal. He was a good man to have on your side in a crisis. Perhaps she'd been too hard on him. 'I think I need to go deeper.'

'Deeper?' Chang threw her a look. 'Deeper where?'

Nero tapped her forehead. 'I get the feeling that everything I need is inside me. I just need to find it.'

'Will it be dangerous?'

'Danger is my friend,' Nero winked, playfully. 'Or at least, my acquaintance. I've got to know him quite well in the last few weeks.' She thought back to her days at the correctional facility. The Princess, Tank, Meena. With a start, she realised she couldn't be sure how many of those memories were real. They felt as real as the non-existent flight classes that Benjamin had embedded in her brain. So, not real at all.

Chang seemed to sense her disquiet. 'This is real,' she whispered, kindly. 'All this?' She gestured around the cockpit. 'This is happening.'

Nero looked deep into her eyes. All she could do was trust. It was all she had left. 'Thank you,' she said, her eyes filling with tears. As much as she wanted it to be true, she knew she couldn't be sure. For all she knew, perhaps she was still in that sterile, clinical room with the white walls. Perhaps everything since that moment, whenever that moment was, had been a lie. Perhaps she no longer existed at all.

'It's a new day,' Chang suddenly announced, nodding through the windscreen.

Nero turned to see the sun rising over the globe, spilling over the horizon to the east like liquid gold. 'A new day,' she breathed.

And she wondered what it would bring.

27

Utah

The Empress was brought in by guided control. The control tower paired with the plane's automatic flight systems and, between them, they brought the craft down with a barely noticeable bump. The passengers on board erupted into applause once more and then waited while US Special Forces entered to detain the Dheghomite hijackers.

The passengers were then corralled into a conference room at the airport to begin their debriefing. It wasn't long before stories of a thrilling confrontation emerged. Of how a young woman, barely out of her teens it seemed, had subdued the lead hijacker – indeed, had appeared to actually know him – before storming and taking control of the cockpit. There was another young woman with her, the passengers related, but she seemed just as astonished by the turn of events as they had been. When they were pressed by the interrogating team to identify the two women, the passengers seemed to turn as one to look around the room. There was no sign of either of them.

Nero and Chang had evaded the special forces at the airport, then simply climbed the perimeter fence in a security camera blind spot. Clearly, American civilian airports were not as secure as they could have been. The car had been waiting as Benjamin had promised.

After their exertions, Nero had fallen into a sullen silence for the entire journey. The vast, open road wound up into the mountains, the morning sun painting the rocky landscape a vivid orange. They drove for almost three hours to Benjamin's designated location and, in all that time, they barely saw another living soul.

Benjamin Saal knew that America had yet to fully embrace driverless technology, so he had deliberately chosen a car Chang could actually drive so as not to be conspicuous. Truth be told, she had enjoyed the feel of the wheels turning beneath the steering wheel and the hum of the road through the foot pedals.

Chang brought the car to a stop outside the seediest motel she had ever seen. Slamming the door shut with a satisfying clunk, she headed for the reception desk. Nero, she noticed, didn't follow her. She remained in the car, staring straight ahead, until Chang returned with the keys.

'Benjamin was right,' she said. 'No questions asked.'

She nodded over towards a row of single floor rooms, each with the same colour curtains at the window and the same front door.

'Number twenty-four,' she said, gesturing to the last door in the row. 'Should have everything we need right inside.'

Finally, Nero looked at her, her face a mask of defiance. 'Let's get this over with,' she said.

The room was tiny. It was dominated by a double bed and a single wardrobe. The bathroom was functional at best. The wallpaper was a lurid yellow, the bedding was stained and the exposed pipes were rusting and dripped water onto the floor. Nero was sure she heard the scurrying of rats as they opened the door.

'Christ, Benjamin,' she breathed. 'This the best you can do?'

'You're welcome,' came the response in her ear. 'It's as off-grid as I could find.'

'You're telling me. We're in the middle of nowhere.'

'That's why it's perfect.'

Chang had walked over to a stack of black boxes. They were made from a dull, matt material and showed no signs of a lid or hinges.

'What have we got?' she demanded.

'Everything you need,' came Benjamin's reply. 'I think.'

Chang placed the cases side by side on the bed. The springs creaked and groaned in complaint at the increased load. She waved the back of her hand over the tiny sensors she knew were embedded in their sides and, one by one, they each displayed a small, white light along one edge. The light grew into a line that ran along three sides of each box, creating a lid. At last, they sprang open to reveal the boxes' contents. Deep Black overalls were folded carefully alongside laser cutters, Spi-Glasses and grappling hooks.

'All standard issue,' Benjamin continued, 'but there are a few surprises, too. The small box.'

Chang held up a box containing a dozen or so squares of material resembling sticking plasters. They each contained a blob of a blue-green gel.

'Explosives,' Benjamin announced over comms. 'Enough to blast open a door. You'll also find some sedation darts and a Tase Pistol each.'

'It all sounds refreshingly lo-tech,' Chang sneered.

'It has to be,' Benjamin retorted. 'The Dheghomites would sniff out anything more advanced at a hundred paces. Wherever they are.'

Chang turned meaningfully to Nero who had stretched herself out along what little room there was left on the mattress. 'I guess that's where you come in.'

Nero nodded and took a deep breath. 'I'm ready,' she exhaled. 'But this is the last time.'

'Understood,' replied Benjamin guiltily.

'And this time, I'll be there with you. So don't think you're going to go snooping around.'

'Wouldn't dream of it.'

'Okay,' said Nero, resigned. 'What do I do?'

'Just lie back and think nice thoughts.'

First time for everything, Nero thought to herself as she settled back, closed her eyes and drifted into oblivion.

They were standing in a nowhere space.
Nero was a child again, no more than six or seven. She was holding on to someone's hand. The void around them coalesced into

flickering flames. The roar of a fire filled her ears. Sirens wailed. She felt the pavement beneath her feet. She recognised where they were.

'What's this?' came a voice, but not the one she was expecting.

Nero looked up to see she was holding Benjamin's hand. He wore a long coat. The same coat her father had been wearing the night they had watched her school burn.

She tried to snatch her hand away but it was locked, immovable, as if that was the way things had always been and always would be.

She felt odd. Light yet heavy. The tiniest movement required the most enormous effort. Her eyelids felt like lead, her arms and legs like concrete.

'This is the first fire,' she heard herself say.

'The first?'

In an instant, the scene changed. Nero was sitting on a chair in a drab room. She noticed the concessions to childhood in the corner. A stuffed teddy bear, some building blocks. Just as she remembered them. She looked down to see drawings of burning buildings scattered around the floor. Childish drawings, full of anger and movement.

'Can you tell me why you like fire, Nero?'

She looked up to see Benjamin sitting where her therapist should be, a ream of notes on his lap. He looked serious.

Nero shrugged.

'How do you feel when you see it?'

'I don't know.'

'You must know.'

Nero thought.

'Powerful.'

'Why are we here?' Nero asked.

'These are your most formative memories. The ones that shaped you.'

Nero looked away. 'I don't want you to see this.'

'Your implant is trying to distract you,' Benjamin explained, squeezing the young girl's hand. 'To keep you from looking where we need to look.'

The room dissolved before her. Where the walls had been, faces loomed. Teachers, therapists – endless therapists – friends, family, the old lady who had lived down the street and the young man who had cared for her. They were huge and distorted, as if they were outside, trying to peer in. They seemed to merge from one to the next, but all distinct.

Nero smelled cut grass after rain, strawberries, farmland, vomit. The smells of childhood. Her head was invaded by sounds. Traffic.

There was blood on her lip. She heard the whistle of movement, and another scratch grazed her cheek. She reached out and grabbed the girl by the hair. It seemed quite natural that she had Benjamin's face. Nero took great delight in landing blow after blow.
'Jones!'
She turned to see another Benjamin striding towards her, wearing the clothes her headmaster used to wear.

She was in another room. She had been in so many like this. Grey, functional. She was older now.
'I'm sorry Mrs Jones, but Nero cannot stay in her current place of education.' Benjamin sat behind a desk, addressing the woman who stood beside her. 'It is my profound belief that she would be better off in a correctional facility. There, she would learn what it is to be a useful member of society. I shall be saying as much in my report, together with a recommendation that she receive therapy from a state sponsored professional.'
Nero felt the woman beside her tense.
'Happy now?' her mother hissed. Her cruel lips were pressed together. Her eyes blazed in fury.

'She always hated me.'

Nero was alone in a hallway. A door stood before her, white, smooth and metallic. Her mouth dried. She knew what awaited her.

'Don't make me go in.'

'Nero!'

She felt someone take her hand – and she was flying through an infinite reflection of memories. Moments from her life replayed and refracted through a lens.

'Don't let them distract you.'
Benjamin stood beside her on a mountain top. Nero had camped here with her school when she was, what, ten? She had been sent home early for swimming naked in the lake.
'We need to find an inserted memory,' Benjamin said, though he seemed not to move his mouth at all. Nero nodded.
'Then we need to find Meena.'

The mention of her name summoned her.
Nero found herself in another room, sitting at a table, just months ago. She couldn't help staring at the young woman by her side. Meena's long hair was fastened into its usual plait. Her dark eyes looked more mysterious than ever. Her regulation clothing looked clean and freshly pressed. Nero knew she wasn't real. She was a figment of her imagined memories. The control programme. She was the signal that this particular event had never happened. Just like the Clarke Elevator and the explosion at the UN Building in New York. Nero felt betrayed all over again.
On the opposite side of the table, sat her mother.
This was the day Nero learned her father had died.
'I don't want to feel this again.'
Behind her, she noticed Benjamin standing, impassive in a guard's uniform. He answered, but she heard his voice inside her head.
'You don't have to feel it,' he explained, 'just watch. Imagine you're a spectator.'
'That's pretty much how I've felt my entire life,' Nero scoffed. She knew at once that wasn't true. In fact, since joining the Bureau, she had never felt so… alive.
'How are they treating you?' her mother asked. Nero had forgotten she could sound so snide. She realised with a jolt that she felt no sadness at her disappearance. In fact, she didn't miss her at all. But then, thought Nero, if the tables were turned, her mother wouldn't miss her either. What was the phrase? No love lost?

'They feed me three times a day,' Nero heard herself answer. 'Sometimes it's edible.' She turned to the guard. 'What am I looking for?'

'I'm trying to force the OC into the open,' Benjamin replied.

'OC?'

Nero knew that, while she could see him in the room, he was in fact sitting at his own computer hub in his apartment.

'Origin Code. If they're using Zero One, it should have a geographical tag, the location where the code was written.'

'Will I see it?'

'You should. Just keep watching.'

'I have some sad news, darling,' her mother was saying. Nero had to admit, she didn't look that sad.

'It's your father.'

Nero felt Meena squeeze her hand in support. She would have been touched if she had known she was real.

'I'm afraid he's dead,'

That was it. That was exactly the way she had said it. Cold. Emotionless. Factual.

'I'm so sorry,' soothed Meena. Nero ignored her.

'I've almost got it,' came Benjamin's voice. 'Keep watching.'

'It was a plane crash,' Helene continued. 'In Utah. He wouldn't have known anything about it.'

'When?' Nero asked.

'Two days ago. They came down near a town called Eureka.'

'Wait.'

Nero blinked. Meena, her mother and the guard disappeared in an instant. She was back in front of the metal door.

'What is it?' came Benjamin's disembodied voice.

'She was never that specific before.'

'You're sure?'

Nero thought hard. Her head was hurting. 'She mentioned Utah, but not the site of the crash. Eureka.'

'That must be it. Now get out of there!'

But Nero stood, transfixed. The door in front of her was slowly swinging open, the crack of light around its edges widening into a harsh glare.

'How?' cried Nero, shielding her eyes from the light with her hands. She knew what was inside.

A chair.
A blade.
Pain.

Nero cradled her head in her hands, the throbbing in her temples increasing as the door opened wider.

A presence.
A voice.
Pain.

'Get out, Nero!' screamed Benjamin, his voice shaking.

'I... must... go... in...'

'Nero! No!'

Benjamin's voice merged with her screams of pain as the light increased. A blast of icy air roared from the room beyond the door, chilling her to the bone. She pressed her hands against her ears to muffle the maelstrom.

'Wake up, Nero!'

There was someone beyond the door. She could feel them. She could hear them.

'I need to know who's in there!'

'Wake up!'

The wind dropped. The sound ceased. There was a silence so profound it was equally deafening. And then, two words. Spoken by a voice she knew.

'Hello, darling.'

Nero woke in a tangle of sheets. Her face was wet with sweat.

'Nero, it's all right.' Chang was leaning over her, concerned. 'You're fine, everything's fine.'

Nero sat up and swung her legs off the bed.

'Did you get it?' she cried. 'Benjamin, did you get it?'

Her comms clicked on.

'I got it.'

28

The Valley of Death

Nero was studying a map on her slate. With a wave of her hand, she swiped it over to Chang's tablet.

'Eureka,' Chang muttered as she peered at the map. 'About a half hour drive from Delta Municipal Airport.' She tapped the screen to reveal a slideshow of images. They all showed the same building from different angles. It was of a dull, nondescript construction, utilitarian and bleak. High concrete walls contained small, rectangular windows that reflected the sky. It was the sort of building that, in ordinary times, no one would want to go near. For miles around, a blasted landscape stood, barren and forlorn.

'It's about thirteen kilometres out of town,' she continued reading. 'Hidden in a valley near Packard Peak. The building itself looks impressive enough, but it sits on a network of tunnels from the old mining days.'

Nero nodded. 'Perfect for setting up a secret base.'

'What's inside?' Chang asked, carefully. 'Do you know?'

Nero sighed. 'It was the site of some… *questionable* experiments twenty-five years ago.' She looked at Chang, meaningfully. 'Led by my mother.'

Chang's eyes widened. 'Your mother?'

Nero nodded. 'Long story. And I'm sorry to get you involved.'

Chang smiled. 'I was involved the minute I joined the Bureau and the minute I met you. Now, what's in this building?' She gestured to the images on her slate.

'I can't be sure,' Nero replied honestly. 'But my implanted memories all originate from there. That's where they were transmitted.'

'So it's a Dheghomite base?'

Nero nodded, silently.

'And your mother worked there?'

'A long time ago.'

Chang's next question hung in the air, unsaid. Nero had been asking it herself.

Is your mother a Dheghomite?

'So what's the mission?' Chang asked, finally. 'Infiltrate? Disable? Destroy?'

Nero shrugged. 'All the above.'

'Actually,' came Benjamin's voice in her ear, 'it might be more serious than that.'

'Listening in on a private conversation between two young women isn't a great look, Benji,' Nero sighed.

Benjamin ignored the barb. 'You've got company. Don't say I didn't warn you.'

There was a knock at the door.

Nero and Chang exchanged a look. At an unspoken signal, they both dropped to the floor, out of sight of the only window in the room.

'Who is it, Benji?' Nero whispered.

'Can you think of anyone else who could track you to the most remote motel in the whole of the US, then commandeer a private jet to follow you across the Atlantic?'

'Drake,' Nero grumbled.

'I've got him on a live satellite feed,' Benjamin continued. 'He'll know I'm watching.' He sounded resigned. 'Believe me, I'll be in as much trouble as you are.'

The knock came again.

'Is he alone?' Chang asked, keen to know what to expect.

'Yes, I'm alone!' came Drake's voice from behind the door. 'And getting more pissed off by the minute!'

Nero heard the click of Benjamin closing his comms. So, he'd left her high and dry. Taking a breath, she rose to her feet and walked to the door, twisting the latch before walking back to sit on the bed, expectantly. The door swung open slowly to reveal Nathan Drake, seething in the hot Utah sun. The dust was settling round a Hoverjet behind him.

'You realise you disobeyed a direct order by getting on that flight?' he fumed from the doorway. 'And everything you've done since.'

'I'm on leave,' Nero snapped back from the bed. 'Medical grounds.'

Drake wasn't amused. 'And Chang?'

'I'm her carer,' Chang replied with a mischievous smile.

'So, you tracked me after all,' Nero sneered. 'You lied.'

Drake stomped into the room. 'I told you, Jones,' he seethed, 'the knowledge you have is dangerous. No one has left the Bureau before, and I won't allow it now. Not like this.'

'So, what,' Nero retorted, rising to her feet, 'you've come to wipe my memory and send me on my way?'

Drake looked flustered. 'What are you talking about?'

Nero narrowed her eyes. She trusted him even less than before.

'Wait,' she said. 'You didn't come all this way just to give me a bollocking.'

Drake marched to the window to stare out at the desert beyond. 'You mean Benjamin hasn't filled you in on the details?' The inference was clear.

Nero sighed. 'We're not as close as I led you to believe,' she admitted.

'So I understand,' Drake replied. 'It was all a ruse to get to Utah.' He turned from the window. 'To follow a hunch!'

'A hunch that your presence here would suggest has paid off,' Nero teased.

Now it was Drake's turn to sit on the bed. 'I want you to know that this is in no way an endorsement of your behaviour,' he began, 'but perhaps there is something here after all, in Eureka.'

Nero looked at him, carefully. 'What do you know?'

Drake looked deep into her eyes. 'Enough,' he said, simply.

Nero wondered just what Benjamin had told him. Or rather, what he *hadn't* told him. She was certain he would have kept the details of the implant being Bureau tech to himself. To admit to *that* knowledge might prove dangerous.

'That you've been experiencing hallucinations due to some implant. That you think the origins of the signals that control it may be here.'

'Some guys just can't keep a secret,' Nero sighed, dramatically.

'Benjamin Saal's allegiance is to the Bureau, Nero,' Drake snapped. 'Something you could learn, too.'

'So,' interjected Chang, impatiently, 'what's in Eureka?'

Drake looked back at her. 'Nero and Saal are right,' he began. 'It's a Dheghomite base. We've had eyes on it for months.'

'*Months?*' Nero echoed. 'And you've just left it alone?'

'We've been waiting.'

'For what?'

'For the Dheghomites to reveal its purpose.' Drake looked at a loss. 'We've really no idea what it's for. And now we've lost control of the Bureau's predictive AI systems, we might never know.'

'So, what's the plan?' Chang asked.

'Our conventional tech has pinpointed a spike in power usage in the area. Too much for a small town like Eureka. So, they're planning something. Imminently. We just don't know what.'

Nero gulped. A surge in power at the very place that controlled her implant didn't sound great.

Drake was looking over the boxes arranged on the bed behind him. 'It looks like Benjamin has given you all the equipment you need.'

Nero nodded, guiltily.

'That would account for the increase in the stationery budget,' Drake mused to himself. He rose to his feet and turned to the two young women before him. 'So, get in that base and find out what's going on. I'll be monitoring you from my Hoverjet. It's armed, so just give the word if you need back up.'

Nero nodded.

'Whatever's going on in there,' Drake concluded, 'it's something they want to keep secret. Which means it's gonna be bad news for us.'

'I never thought I'd miss Benjamin and his predictive powers,' Nero smirked. 'I'd love to know our chances of success right now.'

'That's something I can't tell you,' Drake replied without humour. 'But I can tell you that you'll both face disciplinary measures the moment you get back.'

'*If* we get back,' Nero corrected him, grimly.

29

A Single Random Event

The temperature dropped like a stone with the setting of the sun. As Drake ferried the two agents to their destination, he kept the Hoverjet low to avoid detection. He flew so close to the ground, Nero felt she could almost reach out and scoop up a handful of soil, or at least pluck a leaf from a tree as they passed overhead. The mountains on the horizon looked like they had been cut from black paper and stuck against the purple sky. The first stars pricked the velvet void above. Nero shivered. Whatever happened in the next twelve hours, she hoped she would at last get the answers to so many questions. And not die in the process.

She glanced across to where Chang sat, tensed for action. Like Nero, she had donned her Deep Black suit in anticipation of the assault. Like Nero, she had her backpack slung over her shoulders. Unlike Nero, she stood to gain nothing from the adventure except the respect of her peers and the knowledge she had done her duty for the Bureau, the country and the world. Nero couldn't help but hold her new friend in awe.

At last, Nero saw the lights of a small town twinkling in the distance. Eureka. Drake guided the Hoverjet to a gully between two tall peaks and set her down by a dry riverbed.

'The complex is a kilometre that way,' he said, pointing through the windscreen. 'I'll be here, ready, if you need me. You listening Benjamin?'

Nero heard the comms click on in her ear.

'Um, yes, I'm listening.' Benjamin answered timidly.

'You have some explaining to do,' Drake snarled. 'But first, I want you to use whatever we have left to assist Nero and Chang. Hack into every local surveillance system, security camera and wireless network you can. Call up traffic details, rail, air and bus schedules and local transport manifests.'

'Will do,' Benjamin replied. 'I'll get back to you just as soon as I can.' His voice softened. 'And Nero? Good luck. I hope you find what you're looking for.'

The comms clicked off and Drake nodded his head for the two young women to move out.

The ground was hard underfoot. Nero's head torch lit the way as she and Chang scrambled for purchase in the darkness. Their feet slid away from beneath them more than once as they picked their way over the loose rock. The cold was biting, even through their all-enveloping Deep Black suits, and Nero felt her lungs sting as she inhaled the freezing air. Occasionally, her slate would ping from her backpack, indicating which direction to take. Without it, she had no doubt they would soon have been lost in the forbidding darkness. Except the twinkling lights to her left, there were no landmarks to speak of. Every turn looked much like the last. Tufts of hardy grass sprang from rocky outcrops, their roots tapping the stones for whatever moisture they could absorb. Above them, the last vestiges of the day had receded into inky night. A crescent Moon hung low on the horizon as if tethered there, like a boat. As Nero sprinted on, she felt her muscles beginning to warm. She looked back to see if Chang was keeping pace. Her companion was breathing hard but powering through.

'I'm with you,' Chang panted. 'But I wouldn't stand a chance against you in a race.'

Nero thought back to the time she had sprinted a kilometre and a half in under six minutes on board the Clarke Elevator, then remembered she had done no such thing. Misremembered memories were so tiresome.

Picking up the pace, Nero suddenly felt the ground drop away from beneath her. She was suspended in the air for a moment then, her arms flailing, she dropped to the rocky ground, twisting her ankle painfully as she landed. She stifled a scream as she clutched at her leg.

'You okay?' Chang skidded to a halt beside her and knelt to feel for any damage.

Nero winced with the pain. 'I'm okay,' she rasped.

Chang peered ahead into the darkness. 'We're over half way. Less than a quarter of a mile to go.'

'I'm fine,' Nero responded, louder. 'Just give me a moment.'

'Shall I call Drake?'

Nero shook her head vehemently. She was damned if she'd turn back now. Now she was so close. Swinging her backpack from her shoulder, she propped herself against a rock and drew out her Spi-Glasses.

APPLICATIONS>VIEW>RADIOGRAPHY
>LOW

'Nothing's broken,' she said as she studied her ankle through the glasses. 'It's just swollen.' She thought for a moment. 'Pass me one of those explosive gel packs.'

Chang was confused. 'What? Why?'

'Just do it!' Nero snapped. She regretted it at once. 'Look,' she began, quieter this time, 'the darkest part of the night only lasts four hours here. It'll be getting light soon and we'll lose the cover of darkness. We've got to move quickly. The gel packs work by heat exchange. They take the heat out of the surrounding air to ignite the explosives. But they also work the other way round.'

Chang nodded as she reached inside her own backpack. 'So, you're going to use it to cool the site of the injury.'

'And try not to blow my leg off in the process,' Nero smirked.

Chang passed her a small pack of blue green gel. It was, Benjamin Saal had assured them, enough to blow a door off its hinges.

Nero carefully twisted the trigger valve with her fingernails, then stuck the pack to her ankle. She felt the affected area begin to cool immediately.

'That's feeling better already,' Nero smiled. 'But there's something else that'll make it heal quicker.'

She reached towards Chang and pulled her nearer. So near, that Chang – just for a moment – was sure she was going to kiss her. Instead, Nero reached beneath the sleeve of Chang's Deep Black jumpsuit and pulled.

'Sorry,' Nero grinned mischievously as the material from Chang's shirt came away from beneath her suit. 'But you're way skinnier than me, and this needs to be tight.'

Stretching the sleeve over her shoe, Nero snapped it back over her ankle, partly to provide support and partly to hold the gel pack in place. Taking a breath, she reached out to support her weight on a nearby rock and rose gingerly to her feet.

'That's good,' she sighed with relief, pressing her foot against the ground.

'Good enough?' asked Chang.

Nero nodded. 'You bet.'

With that she turned. Uncertainly at first, but with her confidence increasing with every step, Nero struck out into the arid landscape, being more careful where she placed her feet. Soon, the building loomed on the horizon, dark and forbidding against the low Moon. When they were barely a hundred metres from the wall, the two agents ducked into a dip in the dirt.

'You ready?' Chang panted.

Nero nodded towards the building. 'Born ready.'

She swung her bag from her back and slipped on her Spi-Glasses.

APPLICATIONS>VIEW>
>NIGHT VISION

'Come on,' she muttered to herself as she scanned the walls. 'All those windows and not one left open?'

'It's weird,' whispered Chang beside her. 'There are no lights on at all. The place looks deserted.'

Nero let her gaze wander to the roof. 'Bingo.'

Chang was peering through her own Spi-Glasses. 'What is it?'

Nero reached out and grabbed the image in her fist, throwing it to her companion as if it was a ball. Reacting to the gesture, Chang's glasses displayed what Nero saw.

'Flue-stacks,' explained Nero as a collection of squat chimneys glowed red through her lenses. 'Relics of when this place produced chemicals. I doubt the Dheghomites have much use for them now.'

'Then, that's our way in,' said Chang, reaching into her backpack.

As Nero pulled down her Deep Black face covering, Chang drew a grappler pistol from her bag. Aiming it high, she fired the projectile at the roof. The line unspooled as the spiked hook flew towards the flue-stacks, embedding itself in the brickwork with a puff of dust. Driving the pointed handle of the pistol into the dirt at her feet, Chang flicked a switch to extend four metal prongs into the rock. The gun was held fast. Nero reached out to test that the line was taut.

'Nice work,' she said, approvingly.

'I learned from the best,' Chang grinned back. 'Now get in there and find out what the hell's going on.'

Nero nodded curtly. Chang held out her hand to pass Nero a set of roller grips. Nero took a few steps forward until the line was directly above her. Reaching up, she snapped the roller grips over the wire, then folded her fingers around it. Pressing a button with her thumb, she felt herself slowly lifting from the ground and being propelled forwards towards the building, the taut line taking her full weight with ease.

Nero felt her stomach turn as she reached the top of the building. She must have been twelve metres in the air with just a thin line between life and a rather unpleasant death. Lifting her legs clear of the brick parapet, she swung herself onto the roof and relaxed her hold on the roller grips.

Rolling across the roof, Nero let her own momentum carry her as far as the flue-stacks. Pressing herself against the brickwork, she paused to catch her breath. For all that she knew the Dheghomites were resistant to technology, she was grateful for her Deep Black suit in case any security cameras had been trained upon her during her ascent. She knew that, if they had been, all their monitors would have shown would be a small ripple in the picture that could easily be blamed on a local atmospheric disturbance.

'Chang,' Nero whispered to activate her comms. 'I made it.'

'Okay,' came Chang's voice in her ear. 'I'll release the line so you can lower yourself down. Stand back.'

Nero scurried round the corner of the stack and lowered her head in anticipation. Soon, she heard the whistle of the wire as it cut through the air and the mini-motor in the grappling hook whirring as it pulled the line in and wound it round an internal spool.

A red light flashed on the hook's central prong and there was a soft *bleep* to indicate the line was safely housed within. Nero crept forward to pull at the wire's end.

'Got it,' she reported to Chang. 'I'm going in.'

'I'll scout the perimeter,' Chang responded. 'If there's any sign of movement, I'll let you know.'

The comms clicked off as Nero attached the end of the line to her belt. Giving a swift tug to ensure the grappler was secure, she scrambled to the top of the flue-stack and peered into the darkness below.

If I can break out of the Dump, then break back in, I can break in here.

Nero paused on the lip of the stack.

Had she really broken out of the Dump? Had she broken back in? She knew now that Benjamin had infiltrated her brain and implanted false memories. Had he done it before? *Was he doing it now?* Is that how she knew how to break into this building, just as she had known how to fly a hypersonic airplane?

Nero's head began to swim. There was a pain at her temples. Her vision began to blur. She lifted a hand to her

head to pinch the bridge of her nose as the scene before her
began to dissolve.

Pain.
A harsh light.
Pain.
A scream. Mine?
I scream.
So much pain.

'Hello, darling.'

Nero fought to regain control. With an effort, she pulled
her thoughts back to her current situation. *This is real*, she
told herself. *This is happening.* She stared down into the flue,
into the darkness. Into the void. Then...

She jumped.

30

The Descent

The wire stayed taut all the way down, depositing Nero safely on the concrete floor beneath.

'Chang, I'm in.'

Before her fellow agent could respond, Benjamin clicked on comms.

'Nero, I've noticed a huge energy surge in your vicinity.'

'What sort of energy surge?' Nero flicked on her head torch to look around her.

'A power build up of some sort, at your exact location.'

'Well, that's weird.' Nero frowned. 'There isn't so much as a light on anywhere.' She directed her head torch down the corridor. 'The place seems completely empty.' She walked carefully to a nearby stairwell. 'I'll try the other floors.'

'I'm just looking through the energy stats for the local grid,' Benjamin muttered as she descended to the next level. 'Looks like this isn't the first time this has happened. There's records of multiple surges over the previous four nights. At about the same time.'

'Why?' mused Nero as she peered through an open door to the next floor. 'There's literally nothing here.'

Her torch picked out scattered pieces of paper littering the floor and dirt and grime smeared on the windowpanes. There were signs in the dust of furniture having been moved out, but for now, the large open-plan room was completely empty.

'I tell a lie,' Nero corrected herself. 'Water cooler.' She tapped the plastic cylinder that stood beside her, the only sign that there was ever any life in the building. 'I'm heading down.'

She snapped on her Spi-Glasses and navigated through the menu with a few blinks of her eyes.

APPLICATIONS>VIEW>
>REMOTE SHARING

'Got it on my screen,' Drake confirmed. 'Be careful down there. I'll keep your comms open.'

As Nero turned back to the stairwell, she heard Chang's voice in her ear.

'All quiet out here, Nero,' she reported. 'Though the surge seems to be affecting the town. The lights all went out five minutes ago.'

'Any signs of movement?' Nero asked.

'None.'

'And there hasn't been for weeks,' Benjamin interjected. 'I followed Drake's instructions and took a look at the local traffic hubs. Nothing's been near the place in months.'

'Not looking much like a terrorist base, is it?' Nero sneered back. She had reached another level and, just like the first two, had found it abandoned. 'No signs of life,' she muttered to herself.

'Perhaps we could have just walked in after all,' Chang interjected.

A sudden thought occurred to Nero. 'Chang, you mentioned tunnels beneath the building?'

'That's right,' Chang replied, the penny dropping. 'That must be where you'll find whatever is drawing all that power.'

'But you can bet there won't be a handy door. Can you help, Benjamin?' She had chosen deliberately to use his full name.

'Let me see,' came the response. Nero could almost hear his hands waving above his computer hub, his fingers dancing at speed across the virtual keyboard.

'There's a public domain map from 1879,' he said at last. 'Seems pretty detailed.'

'Can you jack it straight into my implant? So I can find the way?'

Benjamin was understandably hesitant. 'I thought you wanted me staying out of your head?'

'Think of it as sharing an apartment with a best friend. I might invite you into my room occasionally, but I wouldn't want you barging in unannounced.'

'Understood.'

Nero could hear the amusement in his voice. 'Not that I would want to share an apartment with you,' she added.

Benjamin sighed. 'Of course.'

'A quick in and out, you understand?'

'Got it.'

There was a brief pause then, suddenly, Nero knew exactly where she was going. Every corner and corridor looked familiar. Every stairwell led exactly where she expected. It was as if she had been there before.

'This is weird,' Nero muttered to herself, forgetting her comms were still active.

'Welcome to the Bureau,' Benjamin shot back. 'Weird is what we do.'

'Then I can see why you got the job,' Nero sneered. 'Now, let's see how to get into those tunnels.'

She quickened her pace as she descended through the building. Every floor was deserted, just as she expected. Her footsteps echoed back to her from the tiled walls and concrete floors. Every now and then, a spinning logo was displayed on a VidScreen. Nero guessed it might provide a clue as to the building's use and why it now stood empty. There was no time now for such mysteries, she mused as she reached the lowest levels. She noticed with a start that she had seen no exterior windows for several minutes. She instinctively knew she was underground. Her head torch picked out stains on the walls left by water leaching from rusty pipes. Light fittings hung loose from the ceiling.

'Looks like this part of the building has been empty the longest,' she panted into her comms. 'I doubt many people came down here even when it was occupied.'

'The power surge is continuing,' Benjamin reported back. 'Any sign of an entrance to the – '

Nero gasped as a searing pain pierced her skull. She clutched the sides of her head.

'Nero, are you okay?'

Nero blinked as the room began to sway around her. Her legs beginning to buckle beneath her, she leaned against the wall for support.

'Nero!'

Chang's voice felt close and far away at the same time. The beam of light from Nero's torch made her eyes ache. She reached to switch it off, but even the impenetrable darkness seemed somehow too bright. She pressed the heels of her hands against her eyes as an image began to form.

A white room.
A chair.
A blade.

The visions were getting worse.

'Benji,' she gasped. 'You still in my head?'

'I got outta there as soon as I implanted the map. Just as you told me.'

'Nero?' came Drake's voice, suddenly urgent. 'What's happening down there? Do you need back up?'

Nero shook her head as the pain subsided. 'No,' she said at last. 'I'm fine. I'm proceeding as planned.' She tried to sound calm but, in reality, felt anything but. She noticed her clothes were wringing with sweat. Her heart was pounding and her mouth was dry.

'Take it easy, Nero,' said Chang, soothingly. 'You're doing fine.'

Nero took a breath and switched her torch on again. Almost at once, the light fell upon a pile of debris in a far corner.

'I think I've found something,' she whispered as she crept slowly forwards. Reaching out, she pulled a metal bar free of the pile, then a length of plastic sheeting.

'Careful Nero,' warned Drake over her comms, plainly keeping an eye on proceedings via her Spi-Glasses. 'You don't know what's under there.'

'I'm guessing,' Nero rasped as she pulled a pipe from the pile, 'that it's a way in.'

Even as she cleared the debris, Nero couldn't help wondering just why this was all so easy. Where were the surveillance cameras? Even armed guards? If this was really a secret Dheghomite base, wouldn't it be better protected?

She paused. 'Guys. Do you think this is a trap?'

'No one knows you're coming Nero,' Benjamin reassured her. 'Our comms are secure and your fake ID is infallible. There's been nothing to mark you out as suspicious since you left London.'

Nero nodded. She wondered just how far she could trust Benjamin Saal. She never had asked him about Claudia Chambers. Who was she? And what had Drake meant by mentioning her? Nero smiled to herself. She had never felt so in the dark, both figuratively and literally.

With a final plastic tube pulled clear, Nero found herself looking down at an improvised hatch that had been set into the concrete floor. Knowing how easy her progress had been thus far, she wasn't at all surprised to find that she could lift it easily.

'I get the feeling someone's expecting me,' she muttered, almost to herself.

'I'm standing by, Nero,' Drake assured her. 'Give me the word and I'll be with you in three minutes.'

'And I'm at the main entrance,' Chang added. 'Making my way in.'

Nero slung the metal grating to one side and directed her head torch into the abyss beneath.

'Looks like quite a drop,' she reported, 'but there's definitely something down there. I'm guessing it's strong enough to take my weight.'

Before any of her companions could object, Nero pitched herself forward and down through the hole in the floor. She landed with a *clang* on a grated metal panel. Having bent her knees to soften the impact, she straightened up to her full height to look around her.

'I'm in an old miner's elevator,' she said. She leaned over the side to see the lift's cable dropping beneath her. 'And it looks like it's gonna take me a long way down.'

Looking up, Nero noticed a series of buttons arranged on a handle. She grasped it firmly in both hands and pressed the button marked with a *down* arrow. With a jolt, the lift began to move. The grinding of gears and rattling metal accompanied her descent into the gloom. The air was getting noticeably cooler and, within minutes, Nero was sure she could see her breath in her torch beam.

'Nero,' came Benjamin's voice over comms, 'I'm losing you... There... to be... ference... I... th...'

'Benji?' Nero instinctively tapped the side of her head. 'Benji?'

Nothing.

'Drake? Chang?'

Her appeals were met with silence. Nero tapped her Spi-Glasses.

>>*CONNECTION LOST...*

She frowned.

'Guess I'm on my own for now.'

The lift came to a halt with a judder that threatened to knock Nero off her feet. Steadying herself against the low cage fence, she fumbled for a latch in the door. It swung open with an almost comical squeak. Nero stepped from the lift to find herself, quite unexpectedly, on a smooth, metal floor. Just as she swung her torch down to inspect it, the lights flicked on. Nero squinted into the glare, raising her hand to her eyes until they were accustomed to the light.

She was standing in a tunnel, its walls, floor and ceiling all lined in a smooth, reflective metal. The result was an infinite number of Neros all staring back at her. They looked as bewildered as she felt. The effect was quite disconcerting, and it was all Nero could do to keep her balance as she walked. She could feel her head was starting to ache again. Squeezing her eyes tight shut, she tried in vain to *will* the pain away. It didn't work. For now, it seemed to settle behind her eyes as a dull throb. Nero focussed on a single door at the end of the tunnel. She could see it was slightly ajar. Every now and then, flashes of light appeared from the room within. Nero was sure she could hear the buzz of machinery. Afraid of what she might see, and feeling hopelessly alone, Nero reached out her hand to the cold, metal door and pushed it open.

At first, she couldn't quite take in what she saw. She was in a circular room lined with equipment and cables. Holographic images were projected above workstations. Numbers and letters scrolled through the air in a blur. Here and there, Nero saw images of a human figure, its organs highlighted in a variety of colours. Above one desk, she saw a revolving representation of a brain. Certain sections of it pulsed a lurid green, others a bright red. A text box beneath it flashed neon-coloured digits that rose and fell in value. The hum of electrical activity was constant. The sensory onslaught disoriented Nero for a moment, and she struggled to make sense of the scene. *What was all this equipment for?*

Turning to the centre of the room, she was confronted with a sight that made her gorge rise. The cables from the workstations led to a central structure, a tall column that seemed part mechanical, part organic. It wasn't the twisted arrangement of pipes and sinews that made her head spin, nor the throb of electrical energy that seemed to pop and fizz along the entire construction. It was the sight of a human female hanging suspended at its core like a piece of meat on a butcher's rail.

Nero recognised her at once. 'Mother!' she screamed.

As Helene looked down, Nero saw that her eyes blazed with a fierce energy.

'I saw you,' Helene said, with an eerie calm. 'I see it all!'

Nero ran to the base of the tower and pulled at the cables to release them. They were stuck fast. In frustration, she kicked at the structure and reached up to her mother's feet.

'I see it all!' Helene repeated. '*I AM THE VACCINE!*'

Nero stood, breathing hard, uncomprehending. Her thoughts were a whirl. And then she heard another voice, clear and calm above the all-pervasive hum.

'*Hello, darling.*'

It cut Nero to the quick. Tears pricked at her eyes. A lump came to her throat. It was a voice she had thought she would never hear again. She dared hardly turn round but, slowly, she forced herself to face the familiar figure before her.

'It's so lovely to see you again.'

There stood her father, looking just as she remembered him. His arms were spread wide and he was smiling.

'This is quite the family reunion,' he beamed.

And Nero fainted clean away.

31

Vincit Qui Se Vincit

The headache was worse than ever. Nero's temples felt like they would burst. A sharp, stabbing pain stretched from the nape of her neck across her skull to just behind the eyes. The discomfort made her wince. She tried to raise her hands to her face, but found they wouldn't budge. Finally opening her eyes, Nero saw she had been bound to a chair near a workstation. She heard fragments of a muted conversation between her father and mother.

'Connected,' her mother hissed. She seemed to be in pain.

'Then that's the last one,' her father replied. 'I think we're ready.'

Looking across the room, Nero saw Doctor Jonathan Jones busying himself at a computer console. Nero doubted what she saw. This *had* to be an implanted memory. Perhaps she was still in Benjamin's apartment, sleeping on the couch, waiting for her flight to Utah.

Her father was dead.

Wasn't he?

'Nero is awake,' her mother suddenly announced, her eyes blazing.

Jonathan whirled round. 'Sorry about that,' he said kindly, gesturing to the cable ties that bound Nero's hands behind her back. 'But I can't let you interfere.' Incredibly, he laughed. 'In fact, I know you won't. Just as I knew you'd come here tonight. Just as I know how it'll end.'

'How what will end?' spat Nero from her chair.

Jonathan walked towards her and placed both his hands on the chair's armrests. He leaned in so close that Nero could smell his aftershave. It smelled familiar. *Comfortable.*

'Everything,' he smiled. Giving her a ghastly wink, he sauntered back to his console. 'I'm very proud of you, you know. You've done so well at the First Action Bureau. They could learn a thing or two from you.'

Nero couldn't help herself. 'I thought you were dead!' she blurted, straining against her restraints. '*She* told me you had died!'

Her father turned from his work, a look of pity on his face. 'Did she, though? Are you sure about that?'

Nero's whole head throbbed. She could feel the pain moving down to her shoulders as she struggled to order her thoughts. Of course. Meena. She had been with her when Helene had told her of the plane crash.

It had never happened.

A word formed in Nero's mind. A small word, but she knew it held a universe of potential.

'Why?'

Jonathan folded his arms across his chest as he surveyed his daughter. 'You, Nero,' he said at last. 'I did it all for you.'

The idea revolted her.

'What have you done to my mother?'

Jonathan looked up at the central column where his wife hung, entwined in cables.

'It's quite impressive isn't it?' he began, breezily. 'Of course, she's not really your mother any more. She's more computer than human.'

Nero saw Helene twist and writhe in pain.

'Accessing,' rasped her mother in a voice that only just seemed human.

'Good!' Jonathan replied, rubbing his hands. 'You're just in time, Nero. But then, we always knew you would be.'

'Accessing what?' Nero spat. 'What is she doing?'

'Helene practically built the original computer architecture,' Jonathan boomed as he sprang back to the console. 'The same architecture that the Bureau used for their quantum predictive computer. And you gave us the way in.'

Nero swallowed. It was all her fault.

'Oh, don't blame yourself,' Jonathan purred, as if he had read her mind. 'There was really nothing you could do.'

Nero's eyes flicked to her mother.

Helene's face was contorted with pain. 'Probability... shift...' she groaned. Nero's eyes narrowed. What did she mean?

'She sees everything now,' Jonathan continued, oblivious. 'In many ways, she is the computer.' He spread his arms wide in an expansive gesture. 'She's everything, everywhere, all at once!'

'Probability... shift...' Helene moaned again.

Nero started to struggle with the cable ties that bound her hands behind her back. A probability shift? If Helene was hooked up to the Bureau computer's predictive systems, she would be constantly monitoring the outcome of an infinite number of variables. It would be more than the human mind could bear.

'Did you put this thing inside my head?' Nero hissed.

Jonathan smiled. 'With a little help, yes.'

Help? thought Nero. *If it had been fitted at the room in the Dump, who had helped him?*

'What do you want with me?'

Her father reached his hands out towards her. 'Come on Nero, isn't this touching? The three of us against the world, just like it would've been had your mother not left me.'

Nero narrowed her eyes. 'She was always an excellent judge of character.'

Jonathan shrugged. 'You know, I think she secretly hoped the Bureau would keep you safe. In fact, it put you right where I needed you. The irony.'

'*Ghost Profile*,' Nero groaned.

'Exactly. And with that one innocuous phrase, you granted me access to the greatest computer ever built. I just needed someone who could control it.'

'My mother?'

Jonathan clasped his hands to his heart. It made Nero feel sick. 'My darling Helene. She was never a natural mother, we both know that.'

Nero was enraged. 'She was a better mother than you ever were a father!'

Jonathan seemed completely unmoved by the outburst. 'But now she has the opportunity to put things right for you.' He gestured around him. 'In the very same room where she began those covert experiments all those years ago. With Levchenko and Aziz. The very core of what would eventually become the First Action Bureau. It's beautiful, isn't it?'

'It's sick!'

'All we have to do is wait for the next energy surge, and we'll bring the modern world crashing down.'

There was a triumphant note in Jonathan's voice. Nero grimaced as she loosened the ties around her wrist. Looking back at her father, she was sure she could see tears in his eyes.

'I'm saving the planet for you, Nero. For you and your generation.'

Nero was aghast. 'By joining with the Dheghomites?'

Jonathan threw back his head and laughed. 'It doesn't work like that. I haven't joined the Dheghomites. I've just found a cause that aligns with my values.'

'Is she hanging there because of your values?' Nero gestured to where Helene writhed in agony. 'You'd see people die for your values? The bombs in London? Around the world?'

'All spearheaded by individual cells. There's no one at the centre of things.' Jonathan leaned towards her on his chair. 'That's what makes us so dangerous.'

'So how many are there that share your *values*?' Nero was trying desperately to free her hands.

'You've seen the protesters,' Jonathan explained patiently. 'Even the most peaceful participant can be tipped over the edge given the right cause.'

'Probability... shift...' Helene repeated, her eyes rolling back in her head.

RICHARD JAMES

Nero's mind was a whirl. If Helene was part of the Bureau computer's predictive systems, she would know exactly how events were to play out. That's what her father had meant when he had said he knew Nero would come here tonight. But, what was a *probability shift*? Had something changed? Nero groaned, inwardly. *Where was Benjamin Saal when you needed him?*

'Humankind is the virus,' Jonathan intoned. 'We've been allowed to grow unchecked. The Earth cries out!'

'*POWER SURGE IMMINENT*,' came an automated voice from the console. A row of rolling digits hung in the air, representing a countdown.

'*THIRTY SECONDS.*'

'Thirty seconds to what?' Nero rasped, her mouth dry.

Her father stared straight at her as he spoke. 'Until the end of the modern world. At the peak of the next power surge, Helene will have all she needs to enter every online portal in the world from personal slate computer pads to banking, corporate and military mainframes.'

Nero's eyes were wide. She heard Helene moaning in a delirious agony. 'What are you making her do?'

'Switch them off,' Jonathan replied, simply.

Nero reeled at the implications. 'There'll be chaos!'

'Yes! Jonathan screamed, maniacally. 'Beautiful chaos!'

'*FIFTEEN SECONDS.*'

The hum of building power was almost unbearable now. The lights blazed.

'We gouge the ground for the metals to drive our machines,' Jonathan was shouting above the din. 'We build higher and stronger in the search for abundant energy. And, all the time, we multiply. New mouths to feed, new lives to support. We proliferate.' He patted the computer console. 'Well, no more! In just five seconds, the twenty-first century will be erased. Humankind can start again!'

'*Probability shift*!' Helene screamed as the air fizzed and popped with energy. 'Now, Nero!'

With a mighty roar, Nero pulled her hands free from the ties that had bound her to the chair. Keeping her head low, she barrelled towards her father. He had swivelled round at the sound of her scream, his features set in an expression of surprise. Reaching down, Nero snapped the explosive gel pack from her ankle.

'*They take the heat out of the surrounding air to ignite the explosives,*' she had explained to Chang in the desert. It was her only hope.

Nero slammed into her father, her momentum carrying them both on his chair towards the central column that dominated the room.

'No!' her father roared as Nero wrapped her arms around him and clasped the explosive with both hands behind his back.

'*THREE, TWO, ONE...*'

Nero looked up to see her mother smiling down at her. Through all the chaos, Nero was sure she heard her speak.

'*I love you.*'

And then, Nero twisted the trigger.

32

The White Room

'Chang says Nero had a fall in the desert,' Benjamin explained. 'It seems that it created a single random event resulting in a probability shift. Enough to put a spanner in the works and change the future. Even the quantum computer can't foresee such small, seemingly innocuous events.'

Drake raised his eyebrows. 'A bug?'

'An anomaly,' Benjamin mumbled. 'I'll see that it's fixed.' He nodded down at Nero, eager to change the subject. 'Looks like you got to her just in time. She lost a lot of blood but the medics say she'll be okay.'

Drake nodded.

'And the fractures?'

He stared gloomily at Nero's unconscious form. She lay, inert, on a metal chair in the centre of the room. Holographic displays danced in the air around her, indicating her state of health. Drake could see the blue-green liquid through the MediPlastic casts that encased her right arm and her left leg.

'She'll be up and about in a matter of days.' Benjamin couldn't help noticing Drake's total lack of emotion at the prognosis. If anything, he looked worried.

'She can't be allowed to remember any of this,' Drake said at last.

Benjamin blinked. 'Sir?'

'She's a compromised agent. Don't think that's the last we'll see of the Dheghomites, Benjamin.' Drake looked back down at Nero. 'As long as Nero has that implant in her brain, she's susceptible.'

'What are you suggesting?' Benjamin was worried. 'It's too dangerous to remove it.'

'So I understand. But it could be restored and all the information in it erased.'

Benjamin's eyes were wide in disbelief. 'That would mean a hard restore of all her cognitive functions. It would be like – '

'I know,' Drake nodded grimly. 'Switching her off and switching her back on again.'

Benjamin felt movement behind him. The young woman who had been watching them from the shadows stepped into the glare of the light.

'Could it be done?' Drake asked.

'I think so,' the woman responded.

Benjamin couldn't believe what he was hearing. 'You *think* so? You could leave her with permanent brain damage!'

'I promise I'll be careful.'

'There has to be another way!'

'We don't want another Claudia Chambers on our hands,' Drake snapped. Benjamin was stunned into silence by the remark. 'Nero Jones knows too much. Her knowledge is dangerous, both to herself and the Bureau.'

'Is the Bureau *that* important?' Benjamin muttered.

'In the fight for the future,' Drake hissed, 'it's the most important thing of all.'

Benjamin fell silent.

'You must never speak of this again,' Drake continued, his voice low. 'Or any of the events that have occurred since you met Nero Jones. If you do, your association with Agent Chambers will be made public and you will be ruined. And behind bars.'

Benjamin swallowed.

'Is everything ready, Agent Aziz?'

The young woman beside him nodded, her long, plaited hair swinging behind her.

'Thank you for your assistance, Meena,' Drake smiled. 'Your conduct has been exemplary.'

'Thank you, sir,' Meena replied, her dark eyes shining.

Drake nodded curtly. 'Begin the procedure. Authorisation, Zero One.'

White walls.
Sterile.
Clinical.
A metal chair.
Straps.
A figure, bending. Leaning forwards.
An instrument. A tool.
No, a blade.
Pain.
A harsh light.
Pain.
A scream. Mine?
I scream.
So much pain.
It's done.
My brain is a fog.
A question forms.
From the fog, a question.
Who
am
I?

33

Nothing Is True

Just as she had done for the last two hundred and seventy-eight days, Nero Jones woke to the sound of the morning alarm blaring from the speaker by her cell door. She pulled the pillow over her head as she waited for the alarm to end, then threw it to the floor with a scream. Angling her head, she squinted through the bars of her window to the sky beyond. It was still dark. The strip light above her flickered on and off for a few seconds before settling on an unrelenting glare. Nero squeezed her eyes tight shut. Despite the government's insistence that the Dump *wasn't* a prison, it sure felt like a prison to her. Taking a breath to steel herself, she swung her legs to the floor and sat for a moment, her head hanging almost to her knees. Then, she remembered.

Today was the day she would escape.

OTHER GREAT TITLES
BY ANDERSON ENTERTAINMENT

Five Star Five: John Lovell and the Zargon Threat

THE TIME: THE FUTURE
THE PLACE: THE UNIVERSE

The peaceful planet of Kestra is under threat. The evil Zargon forces are preparing to launch a devastating attack from an asteroid fortress. With the whole Kestran system in the Zargons' sights, Colonel Zana looks to one man to save them. Except one man isn't enough.

Gathering a crack team around him including a talking chimpanzee, a marauding robot and a mystic monk, John Lovell must infiltrate the enemy base and save Kestra from the Zargons!

Five Star Five: The Doomsday Device

THE TIME: THE FUTURE
THE PLACE: THE UNIVERSE

The Zargon home world is dying. With their nemesis in prison on trumped up charges, they have developed a brand-new weapon of awesome power.

As the Zargons plot another attempt on the planet Kestra, a group of friends must band together and rescue their only hope for survival – John Lovell!

Five Star Five: The Battle for Kestra

THE TIME: THE FUTURE
THE PLACE: THE UNIVERSE

As the Zargons prepare their last, desperate attempt to invade their enemy planet, John Lovell and his gang of misfits stand accused of acts of terror on Kestran soil.

With a new President in place, the 'Five Star Five' are forced underground before they can confront the enemy within and thwart the Zargons' plans.

STINGRAY

Stingray: Operation Icecap

The Stingray crew discover an ancient diving bell that leads them on an expeditionary voyage through the freezing waters of Antarctica to the land of a lost civilisation.

Close on the heels of Troy Tempest and the pride of the World Aquanaut Security Patrol is the evil undersea ruler Titan. Ahead of them are strange creatures who inhabit underground waterways and an otherworldly force with hidden powers strong enough to overwhelm even Stingray's defences.

Stingray: Monster from the Deep

Commander Shore's old enemy, Conrad Hagen, is out of prison and back on the loose with his beautiful but devious daughter, Helga. When they hijack a World Aquanaut Security Patrol vessel and kidnap Atlanta, it's up to Captain Troy Tempest and the crew of Stingray to save her.

But first they will have to uncover the mystery of the treasure of Sanito Cathedral and escape the fury of the monster from the deep.

A GERRY ANDERSON PRODUCTION

Thunderbirds: Terror from the Stars

Thunderbird Five is attacked by an unknown enemy with uncanny powers. An unidentified object is tracked landing in the Gobi desert, but what's the connection? Scott Tracy races to the scene in the incredible Thunderbird One, but he cannot begin to imagine the terrible danger he is about to encounter.

Alone in the barren wilderness, he is possessed by a malevolent intelligence and assigned a fiendish mission – one which, if successful, will have the most terrifying consequences for the entire world.

International Rescue are about to face their most astounding adventure yet!

Thunderbirds: Peril in Peru

An early warning of disaster brings International Rescue to Peru to assist in relief efforts following a series of earth tremors – and sends the Thunderbirds in search of an ancient Inca treasure trove hidden beneath a long-lost temple deep in the South American jungle!

When Lady Penelope is kidnapped by sinister treasure hunters, Scott Tracy and Parker are soon hot on their trail.

Along the way they'll have to solve a centuries-old mystery, brave the inhospitable wilderness of the jungle and even tangle with a lost tribe – with the evil Hood close behind them all the way…

Thunderbirds: Operation Asteroids

What starts out as a simple rescue mission to save a trapped miner on the Moon, soon turns out to be one of International Rescue's greatest catastrophes. After the Hood takes members of International Rescue hostage during the rescue, a chase across space and an altercation among the asteroids only worsens the situation.

With the Hood hijacking Thunderbird Three along with Brains, Lady Penelope and Tin-Tin, it is up to the Tracy brothers to stage a daring rescue in the mountain tops of his hidden lair.

But can they rescue Brains before his engineering genius is used for the destructive forces of evil?

Intergalactic Rescue 4: Stellar Patrol

It is the 22nd century. The League of Planets has tasked Jason Stone, Anne Warran and their two robots, Alpha and Zeta to explore the galaxy, bringing hope to those in need of rescue.

On board Intergalactic Rescue 4, they travel to ice moons and jungle planets in 10 exciting adventures that see them journey further across the stars than anyone before.

But what are the secret transmissions that Anne discovers?

And why do their rescues seem to be taking them on a predetermined course?

Soon, Anne discovers that her co-pilot, Jason, might be on a quest of his own...

SPACE: 1999 Maybe There –
The Lost Stories from SPACE: 1999

Strap into your Moon Ship and prepare for a trip to an alternate universe!

Gathered here for the first time are the original stories written in the early days of production on the internationally acclaimed television series SPACE: 1999. Uncover the differences between Gerry and Sylvia Anderson's original story Zero G, George Bellak's first draft of The Void Ahead and Christopher Penfold's uncredited shooting script Turning Point. Each of these tales shows the evolution of the pilot episode with scenes and characters that never made it to the screen.

Wonder at a tale that was NEVER filmed where the Alpha People, desperate to migrate to a new home, instigate a conflict between two alien races. Also included are Christopher Penfold's original storylines for Guardian of Piri and Dragon's Domain, an adaption of Keith Miles's early draft for All That Glisters and read how Art Wallace (Dark Shadows) originally envisioned the episode that became Matter of Life and Death.

Discover how SPACE: 1999 might have been had they gone 'Maybe There?'

available from
shop.gerryanderson.com